The Novel of the Future

D1477355

The Novel of the Future

by
Félix Bodin

Translated by
Brian Stableford

A Black Coat Press Book

ISBN 978-1-934543-44-3. First Printing. September 2008. Published by Black Coat Press, an imprint of Hollywood Comics.com, LLC, P.O. Box 17270, Encino, CA 91416. All rights reserved. Except for review purposes, no part of this book may be reproduced or transmitted in any form or by any means, electronic or mechanical, including photocopying, recording, or by any information storage and retrieval system, without permission in writing from the publisher. The stories and characters depicted in this novel are entirely fictional. Printed in the United States of America.

Introduction

Le roman de l'avenir, here translated as *The Novel of the Future*, was first published by Lecointe and Poucin in Paris 1834. Unlike the author's first novel, *Eveline* (1824), it was signed, both with his name and the subheading "*Membre de la Chambre des Deputés*"—the French equivalent of "Member of the House of Representatives." As his postscript explains, its publication was an attempt to claim credit for having come up with the idea of setting a novel in the future—credit that was not, in fact due to him, and to which his claim might have been deliberately disingenuous.

Although the book attracted little attention at the time and was not judged to be one of Bodin's more important works in the various capsule biographies that appeared in 19th century reference books, it was solidly established within the canon of landmark works in the prehistory of science fiction by a glowing report in Pierre Versins' *Encyclopédie de l'utopie et de la science-fiction* (1972). It subsequently became the climactic work considered in Paul Alkon's study of *The Origins of Futuristic Fiction* (1987), in which it is described and discussed in considerable detail, and it was also the subject of a descriptive essay by Nadia Minerva in *Vita Fortunati* and Raymond Trousson's *Dictionary of Literary Utopias* (2000).

Not unnaturally, all of these articles concentrate on the work's academic interest as a commentary on the possible viability of futuristic fiction and a hesitant example thereof. As critics of futuristic fiction, Versins and

5

Alkon are primarily interested in the non-fictional aspects of *Le roman de l'avenir*, and primarily interested in its fictional content as a hesitant exemplification of the argumentative points made in its preface, whereas Minerva's brief requires her to concentrate specifically on the book's utopian ideals. Although Alkon is happy to damn the fictional component of *Le roman de l'avenir* with faint praise in describing it as an "intriguing story," all three critics maintain a diplomatic silence as to the possibility of it being read for pleasure in modern times—a possibility somewhat undermined by the fact that it is brusquely fragmentary, introducing its characters and sketching out their initial situation and then stopping dead, in mid-scene. Despite its fragmentary nature, however, the relentlessly self-referential story told in the novel is often funny—deliberately as well as accidentally—in an oddly flirtatious fashion, and many of the ideas it deploys are still interesting, provided that the modern reader can set their particular manifestation in its biographical and historical context.

Bodin was elected as a *deputé* (at the second attempt) to the government that took power after the July Revolution of 1830, and most of the biographical sketches that appeared after his death concentrate on his significance as a politician and a political historian. His first love, however, had been literature, and he had already established a considerable reputation in the 1820s as a popular journalist. *Le roman de l'avenir* is part of a long and robust tradition of French satirical *contes philosophiques* that had descended from Voltaire and, more remotely, from François Rabelais—both of whom had written about deadly serious things in a flagrantly comic vein because it would not have been diplomatic, or nearly so effective, to conduct their assaults on received wisdom in earnest.

Le roman de l'avenir is, however, as much a *jeu d'esprit* as a *conte philosophique*; although Bodin admits to having written it in a hurry—in 20 days—in order to stake his claim to the invention of the putative genre to which it belongs, and obviously made it up as he went along, it also features a number of self-indulgently introspective passages in which Bodin revisits almost all of his previous preoccupations and either summarizes his conclusions in a blithe manner, or admits to his continuing confusion with ironic modesty and a certain degree of critical self-analysis. His postscript attributes his failure to get to grips with the task sooner to the deadly sin of *paresse* [sloth], but he was actually a busy man, and must have squeezed the book's composition into an interval between parliamentary sessions, when he undoubtedly had other things to do as well. It is not surprising, in view of the circumstances of its composition, that the attempted novel is unashamedly rambling, calculatedly unfocused, and cheerfully sarcastic—characteristics that are doubtless not suited to everyone's taste, but are appealing in their fashion.

Bodin borrows the English word "hoax" to describe the work, describing a hoax as something "*burlesquement sérieuse et sérieusement burlesque*" [farcically serious and seriously farcical]. Although he had written a great deal of non-fiction in earnest, almost all of his literary work had been satirical, and there is some evidence that he might have been something of a practical joker too. An article by Ilana Kurshan in *Victorian Literary Mesmerism* (Rodopi, 2006), edited by Martin Willis and Catherine Wynne, observes that Volume XVIII of the *Phrenological Journal* (1845) features a report that a

French parliamentary *député* named Félix Bodin had been treated by a mesmerist on one of his several trips to England, after falling victim to an attack of "brain fever." Once the fever had calmed, he began to compose poetry—which, the report solemnly claims, he had never done before—not only writing the words a piece entitled *"La langueur"* [Languor], but improvising a tune to which they might be sung. It is possible that this anecdote had been grossly exaggerated in the decade-long interval between the occurrence and the report, but it is also conceivable that Bodin—who was, in fact, an experienced and accomplished composer of comic songs—was stringing his audience along, or at least collaborating in their misapprehension. If so, that would exhibit his keen interest in "somniloquism"—the oral testimony of hypnotically-entranced subjects—in a slightly different light than the one in which it is represented within the novel and its postscript.

Although the book has not attracted any attention as an account of the psychology of somniloquism, it is arguable that its idiosyncratic depiction of that phenomenon, and the curious kind of multiple personality with which Bodin associates it, is the aspect of the novel most likely to be of interest to modern readers—a point that I shall expand in the afterword, so as not to give too much of the story away in advance. It must also be noted however, that the book's title is calculatedly and interestingly ambiguous; the text is also unusual and original in reflecting on the possible future development of the novel as well as the possibility of developing a genre of novels set in the future, and the inter-connectedness of the two issues. Although he is generally optimistic about the future in general and the future of the novel, Bodin does have some interesting and significant reservations

about the latter—reservations that proved all too justified, and still remain pertinent today (an eventuality that
would probably have saddened him as well as amusing
him).

As an image of life in the second half of 20th century—the era in which its action is set—*Le roman de
l'avenir* is understandably wide off the mark, although it
scores significantly higher in its anticipations of moral
progress than technological progress. Writing in 1834,
Bodin is easily able to anticipate the increasing importance of steam power in shipping, railways and all kinds
of manufacturing processes, but he has not the slightest
inkling of the internal combustion engine or electrical
technology. His anticipations of the future of aerial
travel are, inevitably, solely based on his experience of
balloons; he is able to imagine dirigible aerostats pro-
pelled by artificial wing-power, but the wings in question are explicitly based on those of birds. He is on safer
ground in anticipating the further decline of monarchical
power, a corresponding increase in democracy, the increasing importance of "associations"—including societies akin to the anti-slavery movement as well as joint-
stock companies—and the eventual globalization of
world politics, all of which are changes that seem to him
to be highly desirable; although he was on the left wing
of the parliament in which he served, it is on democracy
and capitalism that his hopes of future progress are
firmly pinned. His conviction that it will not be easy to
put an end to war, even after the last major global-
political issue has been apparently settled for good and
all, also proved sadly justified, although he would surely
have been horrified by the extent to which warfare remained a familiar and ever-present method of settling
disputes throughout the 20th century.

Bodin was also mistaken in anticipating a large-scale reform of Islam that would re-mold it in an image closer to that of Christianity, leaving advocates of polygamy and slavery in a desperate minority, but he can hardly be accused of irrelevance in taking the potential future role of Islam in world affairs so seriously. It is however, arguable, that the most original of the remarks he makes about and within his story have to do with the role of literature—particularly, but not exclusively the hypothetical novels of the future—in both reflecting and participating in patterns of sociopolitical change. He refused to take those remarks very seriously—partly because the one within the story supplied a running joke for him to develop in continual asides observing that his readers, especially female readers, will not like it, because it is so very different from the fashionable novels of 1834—but there is enough substance in them to warrant further discussion and comment in the afterword.

Had Bodin not confessed in his preface that his novel of the future was rushed into print while woefully incomplete, it might have been possible for a modern critic to claim that its incompleteness is deliberate, intended to make a point about the necessary inconclusiveness of anticipation. Given that the whole enterprise is clearly labeled as a hoax, one might even suspect that the confession in question ought to be taken with a pinch of salt, but that would probably be taking skepticism too far. In all likelihood, he really did stop the story where he did simply because he wanted to rush the book into print, and really might have continued it in a second volume if the book had been more successful, or if he had had more time to do it. Alas, he had not; as well as being a busy man he was a man in poor health, and he published little more before dying, at the age of 41, some three years after its publication.

Le roman de l'avenir was not, in fact, the first novel of the future, no matters how one elects to splits hairs in the matter of definition, and Bodin was certainly not the first man to have the idea of writing one, but—as he takes great pains to point out in his postscript—his own attempt does provide sufficient proof that he did have the idea, independently of the predecessors of whom he seems to have been unaware. More importantly, his method of developing that idea was not only original, but of an originality that was to prove enduring. Indeed, the novel contains a few elements that have never been replicated, and which still offer substantial food for thought. Although it has never been reprinted in France, it is fully deserving of this belated English translation.

Félix Bodin was born in Saumur in the Loire valley on December 29, 1795. He was the son of Jean-François Bodin (1776-1829), a noted local historian who published two volumes of historical researches on Saumur and Angers. Jean-François Bodin had done military service in the *Armée de l'Ouest*, and had then served a term in parliament during the Restoration, as *député* for Maine-et-Loire, between 1820 and 1823. It might be worth observing that a Pierre-Joseph-François Bodin (1748-1809) appears on lists of members of the National Convention, the Revolutionary assembly that governed France from 1792-1795; although the circumstances of the latter's career make it unlikely that he was closely related to the Bodins of the Loire valley, Félix Bodin must have been aware of his existence, and a mere coincidence of names might well have been enough to augment his particular fascination with the historical development of "representative assemblies."

Bodin's continual bouts of fever undoubtedly allowed him to become very familiar with various contemporary schools of medical treatment, and presumably provided both the scope and stimulus for him to overcome his initial skepticism in developing a particular fascination with "magnetism": the surviving remnant of the theories and therapeutic methods initially made famous by Anton Mesmer. The principal technique still in use in the early 19th century would later be renamed "hypnotism," but when Bodin encountered it was still generally known—misleadingly, as he was fond of pointing out—as "somnambulism." Exactly what the disease was from which Bodin suffered is not clear, but it may have been a recurrent tuberculosis, whose effects were presumably more severe while he was in Paris or London than they were in his native province.

The article on Félix Bodin in Francois-Xavier de Feller's *Biographie Universelle* (1848), on which the subsequent entry in the first edition of Larousse is obviously based, declares that he dedicated his youth to the study of literature and the fine arts, but also developed a passion for history while collaborating in his father's historical research—Jean-François Bodin had also studied architecture, so he would have been able to make a contribution to his son's education in that respect too. The brief (and entirely gratuitous) description given in *Le roman de l'avenir* of Politée's young son, Jules, is unlikely to be a straightforward reflection of the author's own youthful enthusiasms, but Jules' fascination with historical theorizing and the perception of odd but aesthetically-pleasing patterns of cause-and-effect probably says something about the particular nature of Bodin's interest in history. At any rate, Bodin's most enduring contribution to that field was his enthusiasm for historical *"résumés"* (single-volume synoptic histories); the only works of his that were extensively reprinted and translated were his short histories of France and England, initially published in 1821 and 1823 as the foundation-stones of a series whose prospectus he had drawn up.

Bodin was active as a writer before his father was first elected as a *député*, publishing *Economie et réformes dès cette annéee, ou Le cri général sur les dépenses publiques par un contribuable sans appointements* [Economics and this year's reforms, or The general outcry regarding public expenses by a taxpayer with no official position] in 1819, but it was in the early 1820s that he established his career as a journalist. He wrote for various republican newspapers, including the *Constitutionnel* and the *Globe*, and was on the editorial staff of the *Mercure du XIXème siècle* for some while. He published *De la France et du Mouvement Européen* [On France and the European Movement] in 1821 and *Etudes historiques et politiques sur les assemblées représentatives* [Historical and Political Studies of Representative Assemblies] in 1823, but many of his journalistic writings were considerably lighter in tone. The *Biographie Universelle* article states that they included several "fragments of historical novels"—presumably referring to the fragments of the "Roman novel" to which Bodin alludes in the postscript to *Le roman de l'avenir*—but adds the comment one such fragment describing the end of the world and one set in the year 10,000; if the latter pieces actually existed, Bodin would surely have mentioned them in his postscript, so it seems probable that they are garbled references to the article that he does reproduce there, and to *Le roman de l'avenir* itself.

Bodin published a substantial collection of his journalistic essays, *Diatribe contre l'art oratoire, suivi de Mélanges philosophique ou littéraires* [Diatribe Against the Art of Oratory, followed by Philosophical and Literary Pieces] (1824), whose title-piece had attracted considerable attention, but his greatest popular success appears to have been a series of "*complaintes*," three of which were separately reprinted in pamphlet form. A *complainte* is a popular song, usually on a pious or tragic subject; "authentic" ones were supposedly traditional, dating back centuries, but the stock had always been continually augmented, and there was a vogue in the early 19th century for fitting new words to traditional tunes, usually in a satirical fashion—these newly-fabricated *complaintes* became, in effect, the comic "protest songs" of their day. The three that made their way into bibliographies of Bodin's work, even though they were either anonymous or pseudonymous, were *Complainte sur la loi d'amour* [Lament on the Law of Love] (1825), *Complainte sur l'immortalité de M. Briffaut by "Cadet Roussel"* [Lament on the Immortality of Monsieur Briffaut—who actually spelled his name Brifaut—by Roussel junior; "Roussel" was undoubtedly intended to be reminiscent of "Rousseau"] (1826) and *Complainte sur la mort du haut et puissant seigneur le Droit d'aînesse, déconfit au Luxembourg, faubourg Saint-Germain, et enterré dans toute la France en l'an de grâce 1826* [Lament on the Death of the Noble and Powerful Right of Primogeniture, defeated at the Palais du Luxemburg in the Faubourg Saint-Germain and Buried in the Whole of France in the Year of Grace 1826] (1826). The last-named—also signed "Cadet Roussel"—

was supplemented in its book version by notes and justificatory essays; it was reprinted several times, the edition of 1832 being further augmented by "two famous couplets."

The subject-matter of all three of these works is extensively recapitulated in *Le roman de l'avenir*. I shall leave elaborate commentary on his thoughts on "the law of love" until the third part of this introduction and the afterword, but it is worth observing now that the second of the three must have been composed immediately after the elevation of Charles Brifaut (1781-1857) to the *Académie Française* in 1826. Brifaut was a poet, dramatist and journalist, founder of the Royalist *Gazette de France* who became notorious in the final years of the Restoration when he was appointed as a government censor and embarked upon a fierce ideological struggle with the rising stars of Romantic republicanism, most famously Alexandre Dumas and Victor Hugo. Bodin, who was on the left wing of his own party, let alone the government in which that party held a majority, was inevitably moved to take issue with Brifault, even though he had his reservations about literary Romanticism. The third also celebrates a recent event, reacting to the official abandonment of the principle by which the first-born son of an aristocratic family automatically inherited the entire estate—a measure which, as *Le roman de l'avenir* makes clear, Bodin believed to be highly significant as a likely influence on future social and political developments.

Bodin went on to publish more work in this vein, including *La bataille électorale, poème politi-comique* [The Electoral Battle: A Politicomical Poem] (1828), and had obviously established a considerable reputation by that time as a lively political commentator. A current catalogue of manuscripts advertises a letter written by him on June 6, 1828, addressed to a "Mr. Moore," which mentions that he had been invited to stay when next in London at Jeremy Bentham's house—still a highly important center of liberal discussion, although Bentham, the founder and popularizer of "utilitarianism," was then in his seventies. Bentham would not have seen anything incongruous in the use of satirical verse as a political instrument; it was routinely employed by both reactionaries and radicals in the English political periodicals of the era. Bodin's regard for Bentham's ideas is obvious in *Le roman de l'avenir*, where the meeting of the "Universal Congress" takes place in the republic of Benthamia, evolved from a hypothetical colony founded in Guatemala by disciples of Benthamite utilitarianism.

The precedent set by his father obviously influenced Félix Bodin's decision to stand for parliament after the July Revolution of 1830, which resulted in the overthrow of Charles X, the last representative of Bourbon dynasty—a dynasty that remained symbolic of absolute monarchy despite the relative curtailment of its power after its post-Imperial Restoration—in favor of the strictly constitutional monarchy of the Orléanist King Louis-Philippe. He was, however, also heavily influenced by one of the most important friendships he had formed, with Adolphe Thiers (1797-1877). Thiers had arrived in Paris in 1821 and had asked for Bodin's help in achieving publication for his ten-volume *Histoire de la révolution française* [History of the French Revolution] (1823-27)—a slightly risky enterprise under the Restoration. Bodin had persuaded his own publisher to take it on, and added his own name to the by-line of the first two volumes in order to reduce the risk of its commercial failure. Thiers went on to enjoy a much longer and more successful political career than Bodin; he not only became an important statesman in Louis-Philippe's government, but remained a *député* after the Revolution of 1848, kept his place after Napoleon III's *coup d'état,* and survived the Second Empire to become the first president of the Third Republic after putting down the Paris Commune in 1871.

Bodin's political career was not conspicuously successful even before it was cut short, mainly because he was regarded as a radical even by other Republicans, by virtue of his opposition to the prevailing governmental philosophy of *juste-milieu,* which sought to strike a balance between Royalism and Republicanism by negotiating a balanced compromise on every practical question. The capsule biographies do, however, give him credit for contributions to the establishment of several useful social institutions, most importantly *caisses d'épargnes* and *salles d'asile,* both of which are mentioned *en passant* in *Le roman de l'avenir* as small but significant elements of future civilization. A *caisse d'épargne* is a saving bank, akin to the modern building society; *salle d'asile* is normally translated in contemporary documents as "maternal school"—a usage I have conserved—but it was actually a new kind of foundling home, in which effective quasi-maternal care was provided for the children unlucky enough to end up there. Previously, foundling homes had been virtual deathtraps; Bodin was undoubtedly aware that Jean-Jacques Rousseau, of whose philosophy he disapproved—all the more so because there was still a strong Rousseauesque Romantic streak in republican politics—had taken all his children to the local foundling home in order to be able to work in peace, and that all of them had perished there.

It is unsurprising that the flow of Bodin's literary work petered out after 1830; indeed, the surprising thing is that he found time to write *Le roman de l'avenir*—an achievement made all the more surprising by his admitted tendency to "go to sleep on" his ideas, failing to complete all but one of the novels he had previously thought about writing, including those on which he had managed to make a start. The one exception is, however, particularly interesting, if not because of its intrinsic merits then because of the light it casts on his attitude to the contemporary novel, and his anticipation of its likely future development.

Contemporary readers of *Le roman de l'avenir* might be surprised by Bodin's less-than-enthusiastic attitude to the novel, especially to the contribution of Romanticism, given that we now look back upon the great French Romantic novels of the 19th century as peaks of literary achievement, at least some of which were steeped in Republican fervor. When Bodin wrote *Le roman de l'avenir*, however, the second wave of French Romanticism, to which Victor Hugo served as a key father-figure, had only just begun. Stendhal's *Le rouge et le noir* (1830) and Hugo's *Notre-Dame de Paris* (1831) had recently appeared, but Alexandre Dumas and Eugène Sue had only just launched their careers, while Théophile Gautier and Alfred de Musset were still effectively unknown. Honoré de Balzac had published *Les Chouans* in 1828, but was still most celebrated for the allegorical Faustian fantasy *La peau de chagrin* (1830); the quintessentially Balzacian *Le père Goriot* (1834) did not appear until *Le roman de l'avenir* was complete.

In Bodin's mind, therefore, the presiding genius of French Romanticism was still Jean-Jacques Rousseau, by virtue of the cult of *sensibilité* that Rousseau had launched, and its principle contemporary apostle was Charles Nodier—who, despite the careful praise that Bodin heaps upon him in his postscript, was ideologically antipathetic to Bodin by virtue of his political conservatism and frank disbelief in the idea of progress. He might well have continued to disapprove of the subsequent development of Romanticism even if he had witnessed the movement's swing to the left, but it would certainly have encouraged his willingness to make excuses for it, and it would have eroded his conviction that the movement was too deeply rooted in its "Gothic" affiliations to make the kind of contribution to reformist zeal that Hugo eventually made, while in exile from the Second Empire, with *Les misérables* (1862).

Like Jane Austen, Félix Bodin favored polite common sense over Rousseauesque sensibility, and like Jane Austen, he thought that the flood of Gothic novels (*romans noir* in French) that had been the most conspicuous literary phenomenon of the last decade of the 18th century and the fist decade of the 19th had been a flagrant absurdity, potentially injurious to young and impressionable minds. For Bodin, "Romantic" still implied "Gothic," and hence "absurdly over-melodramatic"— that is the reason his brief dismissal in his preface of the Romantic genre as one whose ideological anchorage was in the Middle Ages—so the whole Romantic philosophy thus seemed to him to be averse to and opposed to the further progress of democracy and capitalism, and hence to the summary concept and value that he held higher than any other: *civilization*.

Readers of this translation will need to bear in mind that the French word *civilization* implies rather more than its English equivalent; it was routinely used to refer to the process of educating children as well as the business of living in cities, and literature had long been regarded as a potentially useful instrument of civilization. Charles Perrault's fairy tales, published at the end of the 17th century and extremely popular in the 18th, had been equipped with formal morals specifically to enable them to play a useful role in the *civilization* of children. It is hardly surprising, given this emphatic double meaning, that French ethnographers inspired by the great exploratory voyages of the 18th century were in the forefront of a theoretical tendency to draw analogies between "the savage mind"—i.e., the thought-processes of preliterate tribesmen—and the unformed minds of children. Nor is it surprising that Jean-Jacques Rousseau, the champion of "noble savagery," should recommend in his treatise on education, *Emile* (1762), that children should not be given books to read at all—with the single exception of *Robinson Crusoe*—lest they be corrupted by *civilization*. Félix Bodin, on the other hand, was a great believer in *civilization* in both senses of the word; its progress was, in his view, the true goal of politics and literature alike—and he seems to have believed that, while politics often sustained or thrown up manifest obstacles to that progress, literature was, in the main, currently helping to undermine it.

Romantic literature, in Bodin's eyes, was a threat to *civilization* in two principal ways: firstly because of its nostalgic regard for the past, which embraced a fascination with Medieval codes of behavior and Medieval superstition; and secondly because of its glorification of *sensibilité*: the spontaneity of emotion conceived as an instinctive source of virtue. These two elements were not unconnected; Bodin knew that the Romantic mythology of love was a bastardized descendant of the myth of courtly love developed by the troubadours of old, providers of the raw material of the French Medieval "romance" whose name had been reclaimed by the contemporary literary movement.

By the time Bodin learned to read, the Gothic novel was already in decline, heading for temporary oblivion, but it left a marked legacy behind, especially in the form of sentimental melodramas. While his literary career was attaining its first flush of success, Claire Lechat de Kersaint, Duchesse de Duras, obtained a striking commercial and critical success with her first novel *Ourika* (1824). The book is only remembered today because it is claimed as the first novel to feature a black heroine, but that seemed incidental at the time. Ourika's color is only significant in the novel because it raises a barrier to conventional marriage for the heroine, who has been adopted and raised by French aristocrats; the point of the story is to demonstrate the tragic nature of the antipathy the convention has to the spontaneous and irresistible force of love. The Duchesse de Duras repeated the formula, less successfully, the following year in *Edouard*, in which the black heroine is replaced by a similarly-adopted working-class hero, whose problems are further compounded by the fact that the girl with whom he falls madly in love is his adoptive sister. In the meantime, though, dozens of other novels appeared bearing their heroines' first names as their titles. One of them was the anonymous *Eveline* (1824), which was Félix Bodin's first (and only completed) novel. It carries a preface explicitly linking it to *Ourika*, but claiming—unsurprisingly, given the predilection Bodin that reveals in the postscript to *Le roman de l'avenir*—that he had written *Eveline* before *Ourika* had been published.

The heroine of *Eveline* is the daughter of an Irish aristocratic family, whose parents intend her to marry within her own class, but who falls hopelessly in love with an impoverished painter. Like Ourika, who eventually dies in a convent, and many similar heroines, Eveline eventually finds it impossible to defy convention by any other means than death; she perishes in her lover's arms. The story is not advertised as a hoax, and does not seem to be a parody, but Bodin probably did not take it seriously. Although it is impossible to guess how the plot of *Le roman de l'avenir* would ultimately have worked out, the representations of romantic love contained within it seem too thoroughly jaundiced to be heading for any kind of ringing climactic endorsement.

I shall comment further on *Le roman de l'avenir*'s idiosyncratic representations of erotic attraction in the afterword, but there are a couple of minor observations that might better be made in advance of the main text. One is that none of the capsule biographies of Bodin make any reference to a marriage. This does not necessarily mean that he never married—none of the capsule biographies of his father make any reference to a wife, although he must have had one—but it seems likely that he did not, and if certain remarks made by Philirène in the novel can be construed as expressions of the author's own attitudes and feelings, he may well have been disappointed in love. (The *Bibliothèque Nationale* catalogue does list a book published by a Madame Emmeline Bodin in 1833, but that author is more likely to have been his mother than his wife, if she was related to him at all.)

The other point is a curious one, which might be completely irrelevant. A review of *Eveline* appeared, alongside reviews of two other French novels heavily influenced by *Ourika*, in the English *New Monthly Magazine*, where the novel was misattributed to the Duchesse de Broglie. The misattribution might conceivably have arisen simply because *Eveline* was forwarded to the magazine in the same parcel as the nonfictional treatise bracketed with it in the review column, *Invitation à des personnes pieuses pour former des sociétés bibliques de femmes* [Invitation to Pious Women to form Female Biblical Societies], which presumably was by the Duchesse; the reviewer might simply have jumped mistakenly to the conclusion that both works were by the same hand. On the other hand, it is not impossible that the confusion arise by virtue of a practical joke, and that Bodin had deliberately encouraged the misattribution.

Whether Bodin knew the Duchesse de Broglie in 1824 is unclear, although he certainly made the acquaintance of the Duc de Broglie at a later date, because the Duc served as a Minister in the parliament to which he was elected as a *député*. He must, however, have been familiar with the work and reputation of the Duchesse de Broglie's famous mother, the brilliant and ever-controversial Madame de Staël (1766-1817), a fierce defender of Rousseau and outspoken critic of Napoleon, who had established key exemplars for the fashion of writing novels titled for their heroines in *Delphine* (1802) and *Corinne* (1807). Among Madame de Staël's most significant contributions to scholarship was *De la literature considérée dans ses rapports avec les institutions sociales* (1800), which examined the relationships between the ideologies of literatures and the society that produces them: an examination with which Bodin was certainly familiar, and might well have had an important bearing on his notion of what the literature of the future might look like—and on the corollary judgment that the present-day audience would not like it.

Eveline proved not to be a crowd-pleaser, even with the assistance of a sly hint that it came from a more prestigious source than it did, but Bodin certainly knew when he wrote it that it was the kind of book that was likely to please the modern audience. When he makes sarcastic remarks about his female readers in the course of *Le roman de l'avenir*, the sin that he is attributing to them is that of liking books like *Eveline*, and of perpetuating the cult of *sensibilité* in an era when it should, in his opinion, have been laid to rest. It is highly significant that when Bodin itemizes the membership of the Poetic Association, which embraces all the internal enemies of European progress, democracy, capitalism and civilization, the list includes not merely the remnants of hereditary aristocracy, supposedly-redundant military men and conservative churchmen, but also literary men and artists whose stubborn commitment to obsolete values seems to have remained unreasonably tenacious.

When Philirène, who often seems to be serving as the author's mouthpiece, is actually called upon to pass retrospective judgment on Romanticism, he treats it gently, making an apology for it, but his apology is tempered by the fact that he regards it as something dead and buried, which has largely given way to a much calmer kind of literature—whose readers would, we must presume, have regarded *Eveline* as a thoroughly silly book. It is clear, however, that Philirène's own idea of love is neither generalized in his era, nor personally satisfactory, nor even coherent—which it is why it is one of the more interesting features of the story.

This translation is taken from a pdf file downloaded from gallica.fr, the *Bibliothèque Nationale*'s internet archive. The cover of the book photocopied to produce that version is dated 1835, but there is no other indication that it might be a second edition; it is probably a late binding of the first edition. As is usual with humorous texts, some of the wordplay did not translate very well, although I have done my best to duplicate the tone of the original. I have provided extensive footnotes to explain references that are nowadays arcane, and to provide a little more contextual background for the text; following Bodin's invariable practice, I apologize to the reader for any annoyance this might cause.

Brian Stableford

THE NOVEL OF THE FUTURE

Who shall live, shall see

TO THE PAST [1]

> "Do you know what a *hoax* is?"
> "No, I don't know what a *hoax* is."
> "A *hoax*, sir, is something farcically serious
> and seriously farcical."
> "I am indebted to you, sir."
> "It's no trouble."
> *Dialogue between an Englishman and a Frenchman*

It is you, respectable past, which have provided all the elements of this book, for, when you had the advantage of being the present, you were pregnant with the future (as Leibniz aptly put it). In dedicating this work to

---

[1] Louis-Sébastien Mercier's utopian account of *L'an deux mille quatre cent quarante* (1771), the only future-set novel with whom Bodin's readers could be assumed to be familiar, begins with a dedicatory epistle to the year 2440, which is extremely scathing about that year's past, especially the sector composing the 18th century's present. Bodin's blithe parody helps to distance his own work from Mercier's in both outlook and tone.

you, I am only making restitution of that which belongs to you (to make use of a phrase which is no less apt).

I am not, you see, one of those inconsiderate people who, incessantly turning their gaze towards the Eden or Eldorado of future centuries, heap blame and insults upon you, as if it were your fault that you were not better than you were, you poor immolated victim of the law of progress, of whom ill-fated generations have painfully made use as a stepping-stone for the elevation and improvement of those which followed them.

It is true that, in olden times, people made the mistake of lauding you as the apogee of perfection, but today even the old are beginning to give up singing the eulogy of the past,[2] as in the time of Horace, and may well tend excessively to the contrary in not giving due credit to your merits.

I am, therefore, careful not to be scornful of you because you marched modestly on foot with a walking-stick, or mounted on horses, camels or donkeys, or in galleys, vessels powered by oars or dependent on the wind, or even in carriages, cabs, and even, if you wished, in mail-coaches. Today, when we devour distance, when science and wealth are distributed more equally and to an even greater number of individuals, there are still a great many highly intelligent thinkers who doubt, even so, that we are really better and happier than you.

Personally, I gladly admit, at least, that you had grandeurs, whose seed is lost or no longer germinates nowadays, and glories, whose aureole has vanished: wellsprings of poetic emotion and religious enthusiasm

---

[2] Bodin inserts a footnote here: "A bizarre epoch, in which one sees optimistic old men and disenchanted young people."

that seem to have run dry; pictures of patriarchal simplicity or royal splendors that can no longer be reproduced! Should we call forth a Jeremiah to weep on the banks of that great river that carries with it into the abyss everything that is finished on the Earth?—or even a St. John the Evangelist to break the seals, empty the cups and sound the trumpets that herald the end of everything that has begun? Or should we, rather, raise towards the future, not a prideful gaze of confidence in human power, but a gaze of pious hopefulness in divine Providence?

For the moment, it is not appropriate for me to examine that great and serious question, so I shall come back to my dedication.

I admit, noble past, that the homage I am offering you here is good for absolutely nothing, but I can also boast of giving firm proof of my independence, by placing my work under the auspices of a fallen power like you (as is often done in other dedications). Nevertheless, I hope that the future will give me some credit for this politeness, which is due in every respect, to whatever extent—which I strongly doubt—it might have knowledge of this book and its author.

Preface [3]

The author, being keenly desirous of not inspiring unfavorable prejudices in persons who deigned to open this book because they fully expected to read a novel, has the honor of warning them that this preface is extremely boring. As it is quite unnecessary to the understanding of the narrative, he invites them simply to skip it, without any fear of offending him in the least.

In times dominated by belief in the progressive degeneration of humankind, imaginations only launched themselves into the future fearfully, painting it in the darkest colors. Under the empire of that belief, which I shall call *pejorativist*, the Golden Age was placed in the cradle of humanity and the Iron Age upon its deathbed; people dreamed about ends of the world and the last man.

When progress towards improvement, the striking result of the comparison of several phases in our history, had been accepted in its turn, as a belief that I shall call *ameliorist*—which seems to be gradually supplanting the former—the future offers itself to the imagination resplendent with light. Progress, conceived as a law of human life, became both a clear demonstration and a holy manifestation of Providence. It was impossible that such a noble and great idea, which has been gradually sinking into minds for half a century, providing particular illumination in the few years that it has been pro-

---

[3] Bodin adds a footnote: "A part of this preface was published in a literary miscellany at the beginning of 1831."

31

claimed with dogmatic assurance and poetic enthusiasm, should not give birth to religions and utopias. There have been no lack of them recently—but I do not believe that anyone, until now, has attempted anything with respect to the future but the application of utopian theories or the envisioning of apocalypses.

In some such works, the author only seeks to find a frame in which to exhibit a political, moral or religious system, without attaching any action to it, giving neither relief nor movement to things or persons—without, in sum, getting to grips with the living creation of an ordinary world to come. In others, geniuses endowed with exalted, and consequently poetic, inspiration have envisioned the future while preoccupied with the increasing degeneration of the world—a belief that dominated the greater part of antiquity,[4] and gave rise to

Damnosa quid non imminuit dies?
Aetas parentum, pejor avis, tulit
Nos nequiores, mox daturos
Progeniem vitiosiorem.
Horace. *Ode.*

---

[4] Bodin inserts a footnote: "Pliny (book vii) says that it is generally recognized that the human species cannot compare in numbers, stature or force with what it was before. That is only the physiological aspect of the question, but there is no lack of passages in which the moral aspect is judged by the pessimism of old men, as in the case of Horace." Bodin gives French translations of most of his Latin quotes, but evidently thinks this one too familiar to require that service; it translates as: "What do the ravages of time not injure? Our parents' age, worse than our grandparents', has brought forth us, [who are] less worthy, and we are destined soon to yield offspring more wicked still."

32

Christianity informs us of the same thing; such is the foundation of all prophecies, among which the mysterious and gigantic imagery of the famous visionary of Patmos stands out, and many other examples of which terminate in the last judgment.

The entirely oriental and ascetic idea of the progressive decadence of the world and of humankind is undoubtedly very respectable, since it is indirectly based on so widespread a dogma, but it must be admitted that it is not at all consoling. The idea of perfectibility founded on history at least has the merit of encouraging the human species to do better, since it embodies the hope of arriving at a better result, while the doctrine of progressive deterioration—or even that of permanent degradation, which some people prefer—can only result in the repression of all energy, thus engendering apathy, carelessness and worse among men.

The partisans of asceticism say that this doctrine conforms better to true religious ideas, in that it tends to detach human beings from a perishable and imperfectible world, in order that thy may turn all their hopes towards a world in which the last will become the first, but the doctrine of progress, applicable as much to moral as material progress, is not at all contradictory to spiritualist philosophy. It is undoubtedly a poor consolation to offer to the unfortunate to say: "Don't worry; the generations that will come after us will have much less to complain about." They will always greet the promise of the Kingdom of Heaven with greater interest and more joy—but that is not incompatible with progress on Earth.

The philosophical opinion that, according to the beautiful expression of an audacious innovator, has transported the Golden Age from the past to the future, ought therefore to give birth to inspirations that are more moral and more useful, if not more religious. If ever someone succeeds in writing the novel or the epic of the future, he will have a vast source of marvels to draw upon, and of marvels that are, so to speak, entirely plausible—which will makes reason proud, instead of shocking or depreciating it, as the machinery of all the marvelous epics it has so far been possible to create has done. In offering perfectibility in a picturesque, narrative and dramatic form, he will have found a means of gripping and stirring imaginations and hastening the progress of humanity that much more powerful than the finest displays of theoretical systems, even if they are presented with the highest eloquence.

The attention of elevated minds will, however, hit upon a difficulty. Great questions have divided intelligent society for centuries. Widely divergent opinions have always raised their banners over the Earth. Every system of thought claims to be good and true, and hopes one day to prevail—for without that, why would it be worth taking the trouble to defend a system? Who would dream of attaching himself to that which is perishable? In consequence of that, every human mind has a tendency to model the rest of the world on its own particular type. Every civilization that spreads has the pretension of reducing to uniformity the civilizations that it supplants.

This is not a particular characteristic of European civilization; when the Muslims expanded through the Old World, they subjected it to the domination of their civilization. Now that they are losing ground instead of gaining it, it is ours that is making progress—but where will it stop? Will ideas of the European type one day expand over the entire planet? And, since our European races are as diverse as our systems, our types and social forms, will it ever be given to any single philosophical, social and industrial system to prevail over all the others, and consequently to reign alone over all human races, apparently for their greatest improvement and their greatest happiness? Now that, I admit, is a question that we do not have the means to resolve.

It appears that the great diversity of races will long oppose itself to that unity in the mode of existence of societies—and is it yet proven these powerful races will ever be entirely mixed, whatever movements of populations take place from age to age? Does not Nature always reproduce the primitive seed-germs that numerous crossings have been able to modify, after a long succession of generations, without ever destroying them?[5] This good physiological question is still shrouded in obscurity. The science of ethnography is too little advanced, too few observations having been assembled for any opinion to be hazarded on this subject. In any case, I have no pretension to be able to solve in passing difficulties on which books will one day be written.

Even if one takes the human species at one sole point on the globe, moreover, in a country where it has had the time, over a series of centuries uninterrupted by invasion or colonization, to acquire every appearance of homogeneity, do we not observe many differences between individuals: various temperaments, and, in consequence, various characters, and various philosophical, political, and religious systems? The interminable quar-

---

[5] "Seed-germs" is an admittedly-clumsy rendering of *germes*, but may help to emphasize the observation that the idea of what are now called genes did not begin with Father Gregor [Mendel].

reling between spiritualists [6] and physiologists, dogmatists and empiricists, ascetics and utilitarians, etc., etc., is apparently founded in the variety of human organisms. There will also always be poetic minds and positivist minds, even though the tendency of our civilization towards uniformity of type and equality of existence is eventually to bring everything—so to speak—*into alignment*, and to level off by legislation all the inequalities of the former social state of affairs, as the invasion of positivism assures us.

So long as there are good and evil, sympathetic and hateful passions; so long as Nature displays her horrors and her richness, inflicting humans with her scourges or giving freely of her benefits; so long as women, love, the religious exaltation of tender hearts, sublime souls and the superstitious terror of feeble minds exist; in sum—forgive the physiological blasphemy—so long as the nervous system exists, there will be poetry on the Earth.

The progress that must be anticipated is that the different systems will increasingly adapt themselves to their own order of things. The positivist systems will gradually prevail with regard to material organization

---

[6] The word "spiritualism" had yet to acquire its modern meaning in the 1830s; "spiritualist" refers primarily to a belief in the existence of an imperishable human soul, but also, and importantly embraces various "idealist" philosophies that challenged all sorts of materialism, which were extremely popular in 18th century Germany and closely related to German Romanticism. By contrast, "physiologists" were committed to theories that regarded mental phenomena as a by-product of physical processes in the brain and the soul as a myth. The fact that Bodin lists the dichotomy between spiritualists and physiologists ahead of all the others reflects his own keen interest in it.

and the state of society; the poetic systems will be in possession of religion and the arts. Perhaps the separation of these systems will finally bring to an end the long discussions that have held them all back until now. People will no longer argue as much about matters of sentiment or inspiration; they will cede less authority to enthusiasm in matters that can be decided by experiment and reasoning. But can that separation ever be perfect? I scarcely dare to believe it.

All that we can hope is that each system will improve and develop for each branch of organization. They will subsist because they are in the nature of human being, whether they co-exist peacefully, mingled in the same country—which sometimes seems to me to be the true ideal of perfection—or whether they each try to isolate themselves in some corner of the globe, in order to cultivate themselves with greater liberty and apply themselves entirely to the modeling of a whole social order. As for the dogmas and political forms of today, who can guarantee their eternity? How many similar forms that have reigned among powerful populations have completely disappeared from the world? Can we identify those that are most deeply rooted in human nature? It is certain that one of them will extend progressively within the world wile others will become gradually rarer and more circumscribed.

This, therefore, is one of the difficulties of "futurist" literature (I, like everyone else, have been infected by the mania for inventing new words): that it will be unable to satisfy everyone. A similar inconvenience, however, is found everywhere else. We cannot agree about the past; how can we be in accord with regard to the future—which is, it seems to me, a little more airy-fairy?[7] Everyone prepares a future according to his fantasy; every sect and system has its own. One cannot satisfy them all, but one can give each its part, at the risk of disappointing them all equally. It might be as well that I have succeeded in obtaining this result. There is something rather odd about carrying the principle of the *juste-milieu* into the future, but even when the result is not perfect, the goal may none the less be good.

Given the way that European civilization appears to be going nowadays, I imagine that calm and prudent minds cannot look upon the rapid pace of progress without a certain anxiety, especially after having seen it interrupted by such terrible accidents. Perhaps one ought to treat utopias as Fontenelle treated verities.[8] Is there anything eternal in this world, though? Does not every century bring about some change—or, in other words, does it not have its revolution? Let us leave to speculation the privilege of always imagining the best, provided that the practice is carried out with the desire and the ability only to contrive the best that is actually possible. One can consider the tendency of things in the future without ceasing to be strongly attached to the laws of

---

[7] The phrase I have translated as "airy-fairy" is *dans le vague*, which is usually used in the phrase *regarder dans le vague*, meaning to stare into space; it would, of course, give a misleading impression to invoke the word "space" in the present context.

[8] Bernard le Bovier de Fontenelle (1657-1757) obtained a great popular success with his *Entretiens sur la pluralité des mondes* [Conversations on the Plurality of Worlds] (1686), which made the then-controversial theory of Copernicanism into the subject of a series of light and witty—but argumentatively cogent and cleverly inventive—didactic dialogues in an informal setting.

nature. This is a rational forbearance that is more valuable than certain blind enthusiasms, certain impetuous devotions which, in their impatience, extend their anticipations over a century or two. One may put the best into fiction as much as one likes, but in reality, one can simultaneously support the better against the premature best. I have little fear of the agitators who, tranquil in the present century, can only be implicated in the conspiracies of the future.

If it is necessary to pass on now to the purely literary considerations associated with this subject, only a few things remain to be said, although it is always tempting to set the poetics of a genre at the head of a work. But this is only an essay, so short, so incomplete and so utterly without pretension that, in truth, the conclusion would be rendered ridiculous by the premises. I shall merely reproduce a few words that I wrote elsewhere:

"Civilization tends to distance us from everything in the past that is poetic; but it also has its own poetry and sense of the marvelous."

This aphorism, extracted from *Un coup d'oeil sur l'histoire de civilization* [A Glance at the History of Civilization], encapsulates all the poetry of the *Roman dans l'avenir* [the Novel in the Future]. We desire new paths for literature, new fields for the imagination; it seems to me, if I am not much mistaken, that this is one of them. Those who complain that the past has been sufficiently exploited will not say the same, I hope, about the future. They will say the opposite: let us finally try to get away from that so-dismal past in which we live in literature, to hurl ourselves into a so-seductive unknown! Here can be found the revelations of somnambulists, flights through the air, voyages into the ocean depths, just as one finds sibyls, hippogriffs and the grottoes of nymphs in the poetry of the past—but the marvelous of the future, as I have said before, bears no resemblance to the other, in that it is entirely credible, entirely natural, entirely possible, and will therefore strike the imagination more vividly, and grip it firmly, by painting therein as in reality. We shall thus find a new world: a new milieu that is entirely fantastic, and yet not unbelievable, in which human beings may be deployed, with the mutability of their ideas and the immutability of their propensities.

One final question presents itself, and perhaps for many people will be the first. Literature seems to have been divided for some years into two genres; to which does this work belong? I am afraid that it does not belong to either, if all literature is merely the reflection of its era. It is not Classical, for it expresses neither former social conditions nor the order of ideas that has served our literature as a type for the last two centuries. It is not Romantic, if Romanticism is the expression of the Middle Ages. What is it, then? To tell the truth, I don't know! It is, if you wish, of the Future genre—let that be said without consequence, for I have a higher opinion of the literature of tomorrow. The essential things is that it should *not* be of a genre that has been cultivated throughout history, but which no one has yet taken the trouble to define: I mean the boring genre. It has at least a chance of avoiding boredom by means of *bizarrerie*. If it were very serious, it would need to be very long, but would run the risk of being much *too* long. If it is only a joke, at least it will not outlast its welcome.

In the meantime, the epic of the future remains to be written; I hope that someone other than me will undertake it. In that vast empire Literature, there is plenty of room for a Moses, a Homer, a Dante, an Ariosto, a Shakespeare and even a Rabelais. Great and fortunate will be the Moses or the Homer; he will be simultaneously the prophet, the poet, the moralist, the legislator and the artist of future generations. At our present point of spiritual development, we might be deemed to need a second Bible: one which will recount the future.

For the moment, the question is whether, after the grotesque and amusing fantasies of Rabelais, the amusing and satirical inventions of Cyrano and Swift and the sparkling philosophical romances of Voltaire, it is possible to find something new but nevertheless analogous: something that will be neither an excessively profligate fantasy, nor a purely critical exercise, nor a product of the philosophical spirit that is injurious to interest and illusion in perennially substituting ideas for individuals and in subordinating the action and the characters to the thesis that it sustains, and yet will be fantastic, romantic, philosophical and somewhat critical at the same time; a book in which a brilliant, rich and vagabond imagination can be deployed at its ease; and, finally, a book that is amusing without being futile. I believe a book of that sort to be possible, but I am quite convinced that it has not yet been written.

Someone else will attempt that; I hope with all my heart that he obtains a greater success than me.

Introduction

Prudens future temporis exitum, etc.
The divinity has acted prudently in plunging
the future into impenetrable darkness.

Audax omnia perpeti / Gens humana, etc.
Ever-ready to dare aught, the human race hurls
itself upon that which is forbidden to it.

Horace. *Odes*.

What! An introduction after a preface! Isn't that an unnecessary duplication? I beg your pardon. A preface is something imposed, straight-laced, serious and boring, which an authors sometimes feel obliged to address to an over-demanding portion of the public, for its edification, or to set their own minds at rest and assuage their modesty.

It is ordinarily in a preface that one says: Here is the subject that I am treating; I shall show it to you from the loftiest possible viewpoint; I shall envisage it in all its aspects; you will find that I understand it better than anyone else, and that no one has perceived anything similar therein until now. One sometimes also says there: It is obvious that it will require someone other than me to do better; I have not embraced the entire subject, but only because it was not convenient for me to do so; we shall see in due course whether the public will welcome this trial run as it deserves. Finally, one says many other equally impertinent things. I therefore understand perfectly why immense numbers of people never read prefaces.

As for introductions—I am only speaking of those to novels—that is another thing entirely. The introduction is virtually an integral part of the novel, just as a porter's lodge is part of a château. The author ordinarily displays himself there in an agreeable and engaging manner. He presents himself as the obliging cicerone whose job it is to guide you around the building and explain its marvels to you.

It is, therefore, in this introduction that I must explain how *The Novel of the Future* came to exist, in human terms. At the same time I shall accomplish the duty that every conscientious author has to the most amiable and most numerous class of novel-readers, whose principal desire is to find every appearance of reality therein.

To inspire a confidence here equal to that which very great ladies often accord to many an oracle drawn from cards or fashionable sibyls, one might imagine, as usual, some dusty manuscript found in the depths of a Greek monastery, or even suppose some old long-bearded astrologer living among the owls and the ospreys at the top of some ancient ruined tower. The detailed and extensively dialogue-laden account of the circumstances that brought this person to the acquaintance of the author or editor; the minute description of his appearance, mannerisms and costume, along with that of the antique castle, and even that of the surrounding woods, rocks, heaths, ravines and torrents, including all those that are out of sight, plus that of many other subsidiary characters; and, finally, interpolated glimpses of incidents, interruptions, parentheses and certain mysterious insinuations: all of that would easily extend to the point of forming an introduction that would fill at least half a volume, following the custom of illustrious predecessors.[9]

The respect the author—or, rather, the humble representative who is publishing the work—has for scrupulous readers, however, obliges him to admit that the source from which he has drawn this veridical future history is not nearly so romantic, although it is no less worthy of trust.

It is probable that not many people remember one of the Italian refugees of 1820, named Fabio Mummio, who was in London in 1823 and 1827, at which times I met him there. I hasten to say, in order to obtain more credit from readers on the other side of the channel—if this work should ever cross the straits of Dover—that this modest savant, who simply named himself Mummio, was none other than the *Marchese di Foscanotte*, of the illustrious house of Mommj.

---

[9] Bodin is poking fun at the standard method of Gothic novels/*romans noirs*, whose authors routinely tried to enhance the plausibility of their fantastic tales by attributing them to some imaginary ancient manuscript or mysteriously venerable teller—a method which cannot reasonably be adapted to romances of the future, although that did not prevent several subsequent scientific romancers from making the attempt. The particular attribution that he employs might suggest to a modern connoisseur that he was familiar with the most obvious contender to have beaten him to the punch in the production of a future-set novel, the anonymously-issued *The Mummy! A Tale of the 22nd Century* (1827)—actually by Jane Webb, later Mrs. Loudon—but he is actually referring to a notable Roman family whose most notable member was Lucius Mummius, a consul of the 2nd century B.C. who completed the Roman conquest of Greece

If he restricted himself to bearing none but his family name in the country where titles produce a more striking effect on the imagination than any other in the world, it is for a reason that people familiar with that country—where money is considered an indispensable accessory to aristocratic luster—will easily understand. Doubtless his landlady, Mrs. Wilson, a thoroughly respectable haberdasher of Bishopsgate Street, would have treated the Marquis of Foscanotte with much greater respect and deference, although a continental marquis is considered, in the vanity of that insular people, as the equivalent of an English squire, at the most. At the same time, though, it is quite likely that she would have thought it obligatory, by way of compensation, to double the weekly rent of two pounds sterling that the refugee paid for his lodgings, tea included—which would have left a big hole in poor Fabio's budget. He had, therefore, very wisely preferred to hide his peninsular nobility beneath the cloak of a strict *incognito*, in order not to suffer avoidable charges—which, I hasten to say, he would have found it impossible to pay, being completely ruined.

This immediately explains how it came about that he had taken up residence in a district so diametrically opposite to the fashionable West End of London, and will allow me to dispense with offering any apology for him to my readers, who might otherwise lose all respect for him in by virtue of his association with the vulgarly disreputable name of the street I mentioned just now—a street that is only inhabited by nobodies, veritable *cockneys* (begging everyone's pardon).

I perceive, though, that my style is tending a little too much towards exactly that verbosity that I am determined to avoid. I shall try to speed up. Fabio Mummio had, therefore run through funds of 100,000 pounds, either before or after the events that had banished him from his fatherland. How had he done it? You shall find out.

A native of Tuscany, his family claimed descent from the house of Mummia, which, he said, had furnished a large number of augurs to the eternal city. The fact is that he believed in all honesty in that genealogy, fabricated by some complaisant Florentine scholar; he talked about it with a seriousness that his illustrious ancestors undoubtedly did not maintain when they found themselves face-to-face with their colleagues from the augural college. Whether it was the Etruscan blood manifested in him, or whether he was dominated by this preoccupation, he had shown since infancy an invincible inclination to acquire knowledge of the future. Forensic astrology, chiromancy, necromancy and all the other occult sciences had featured in his studies, and he spared no effort to enter into communication with people in Europe, and even further afield, who were given to these singular speculations. Long voyages, immense correspondence and the most complete cabalistic library had only served to cost him dear. It is necessary to add that he devoted this laborious work to an end that was sufficiently noble to excuse his extravagance in the eyes of the world. Constantly occupied with the fate of his beautiful fatherland, so worthy to figure outstandingly among the nations, he had undertaken to find a means of divination in order to discover the highest possible future destiny for that famous land.

During his sojourn in Egypt, Marquis Mummio had made the acquaintance of a most extraordinary ecstatic who, establishing rapport with Egypt's entire past in a state of magnetic sleep, recovered the lost history of several Pharaonic dynasties and recounted that of the centuries-old monuments of the ancient land, in such a manner as to make us regret no longer having that brave fellow, in order that we might put him to sleep at the foot of our obelisk from Luxor. He passed on to a better world a long time ago—but not without having left us the heritage of his hallucinations, for they have been collected and printed at the expense of a rich Englishman in a stout quarto volume produced in an edition of 50 copies.[10] No more was needed to persuade the enthusiastic Fabio that he might find in magnetism and the study of somnambulism the fateful agent that he had been seeking for such a long time.

If this were the place to raise objections to the opinion of our worthy Italian refugee, I might be able to raise some serious ones. I could say, for instance, that although their medical prognoses, which somnambulists often give with so much precision, even for the distant future, contain nothing that embarrasses reason—because all the elements of that foresight can often be found in the present state of an invalid's organs—the same is not true of the prognosis of facts dependent on what we, in our ignorance, call chance. Nevertheless, if I were asked to prove the impossibility of this latter prog-

---

[10] Bodin inserts a footnote here: "This is true. I have held a copy of this curious book, which is printed in English and Italian, in my own hands. I frankly confess that it seems to me to be a rather tedious farrago of nonsense." Unfortunately, he does not include a specific reference. The author's suggestion that the *somnambule* in question might have been able to shed some light on the origins of the Paris obelisk reflects contemporary doubts—which were wholly justified—as to the historicity of the legendary Pharaoh Sesostris, in whose reign it was reputed to have been fabricated.

48

nostic process, I admit that I would have difficulty in doing so. It is probable that the old question of fatalism and free will remain unresolved for a long time. In the meantime, therefore, I believe that it would be as well not to quibble overmuch with the good Fabio, any more than with the English authors who have published numerous and surprising examples of the infallibility of predictions made by means of the "second sight" of the highlanders of Scotland and Ireland.

In the various countries he visited, therefore, the Marquis of Foscanette carefully applied himself to the magnetic interrogation of young women of very diverse types: pale Italian girls with beautiful shoulders and severe profiles, afflicted by aneurisms; bronze-complexioned Spanish girls with bright, black, almond-shaped eyes, suffering from liver disease; plump and rosy-cheeked German girls with chestnut-colored hair and pearl-grey eyes, who, without being ill, talked in their sleep with marvelous facility; pretty and piquant French girls with svelte figures, elegantly dressed, who complained of "nerves" and "vapors" in an era that had not yet invented the word *gastritis*—not to mention Greek girls, Asiatic girls and African girls of different races, whom I do not know how to characterize specifically. With the same end in view, the *would-be prophet* (as the English say) had magnetized the beauties of the three kingdoms, with large, moist blue eyes and long swan-like necks, whose naïve deportment was graceful in its timidity, and who were mostly suffering from consumption. He had gone into the Highlands, and as far as the Isle of Skye in the west of Scotland—an island renowned for the quantity of its resident "seers"—which is to say, people endowed with "second sight."

It is true that this part of his task was not easy to fulfill. Bizarre religious scruples and the severity of reverend clergymen, who condemned even spontaneous second sight as a temptation and a sort of possession by the evil spirit, often put serious obstacles in his way, in spite of the chaste—I might even say pious—restraint with which he conducted his experiments. He was not put off by that, though, and the numerous and striking cures that were manifest almost everywhere he went served to dispel prejudice and bias.

In the belief of the eccentric Fabio, these women must have had foreknowledge of the fate awaiting the posterity of their entire families, which produced future information about all parts of the globe. The more the human species travels, the more marriages between distant populations multiply! At other times, adopting the Egyptian idea of metempsychosis, he attributed to every individual the presentiment of conditions in store for his soul, in the various bodies through which it would pass. A famous Brahmin ecstatic in Calcutta, with whom he linked up, imparted that opinion to him, along with numerous secrets.

Fabio was nevertheless convinced that this prescience could only be obtained by means of a powerful intuition exercised by fasting, prayer, the respiration of certain gases and aromatic vapors, and the use of certain opiate and other potions known for their powerful effect on the nervous system. In this way, he reproduced within himself, completely, that state of ecstasy in which the exalted of all religious persuasions, and even a few philosophical sects, employ as a means of rising above terrestrial things in order to float in etheric regions and to enter into contemplation of the supreme intelligence, the source of all good—whereas the physiologists, experimenters, thoroughgoing positivists on their guard against hallucinations, think that the best means of arriving at any result in the quest for truth is quite simply to maintain one's brain in its normal state, one's organs in good health, and to fortify one's reason on that solid terrain instead of throwing oneself into a sea in which one runs tremendous risks, and, finally, not to select sleep, intoxication and madness as good guides to understanding. You see that I never neglect the objection—but the subtle and savant Fabio had no lack of specious responses to this point; he presented them with calm and patient conviction, when he did not allow himself to be carried away by eloquence and enthusiasm. In brief, this honest illuminate was what the world benevolently calls a poetic mind—or, less politely, a madman.

I shall not devote much space to his appearance, of which I could, however, paint a rather curious portrait. I shall limit myself to saying that he had a thin face and features that were pronounced and remarkable: a very long nose, a very pale complexion, sunken brown eyes, and a jutting chin. He only shaved a tiny part of his beard, formerly of the finest black hue, and that singularity gave him a rather *gentlemanly* air, in an epoch when the world did not leave the growth of facial hair the latitude that it enjoys today. I will even add that he allowed his extremely long hair to descend to his shoulders, which doubtless gives a man a very interesting appearance—although, I must say, at the inconvenient expense of maintaining the collars of one's clothing in a state of permanent dirtiness. I shall spare you further accessories, and will not describe his costume, his various expressions or the manner in which he took his tobacco. It is sufficient that you know that he quit this life on May 26, 1828, and that before his death he bequeathed his manuscripts to me. That was the sole and unique legacy contained in his will.

This testimony of supreme confidence was scarcely less surprising to me than it was flattering. It was on receiving the several enormous boxes that contained my unexpected inheritance, which were conveyed to me by the Spread Eagle Office, that I learned of passage of the poor Italian visionary into a world in which he probably has more exact notions of the future that those he procured in this one. His legacy was, however, some consolation. Indeed, the testator authorized me to make whatever use seemed fitting of his papers, for the good of humanity.

I confess, however, that I found myself rather embarrassed at first on looking through the immense repertoire of visions, anticipations and prophecies thus delivered to my discretion. The 333 thick folio notebooks comprising this sibylline treasure offered me, in the greatest possible disorder and without precise dates, the future of every country in the world. Apparently, no magnetic means had been able to allow the interrogator even to establish any sort of chronology. All the somnambulists contradicted one another in this regard, to the extent that I have been able to understand it by means of the marginal notes. All that I have gleaned is that the greatest prophetic efforts do not reach beyond the 21st century of our era. Everything else contained in leaps of visionary thought into that era appears to be covered in clouds of obscurity. That is easily understandable, given the prodigious changes that a century brings about on the face of the world.

What political brain among the ancients could have imagined the possibility of a state without slaves? The vast mind of Aristotle and the great inspiration of Plato would not been unable not only to foresee, but even to comprehend, that a single Italian city would end up conquering and civilizing a world twice as great as the one they knew. What genius, in the 17th century, would have been able to conceive an idea of what would happen within 50 years in the two hemispheres? The honest and sometimes amusing declaimer Mercier, who aspired, 50 years ago, to dream of the year 2440, did not even push so far as representative government, underwear and close-cropped hair. He went no further than the ideas of a few French philosophers and economists in vogue in his time, and his philanthropic monarchy, which is merely a modification of absolute power, appears scarcely more advanced than the minds of his future citizens, with respect to whom he thought it audaciously innovative to limit himself to whitening them with a "hint of powder" and putting up their hair in chignons.

My old friend Fabio Mummio attributed this limitation of his investigations of the future to some cataclysm that will upset our planet in a not-very-distant era. He sometimes explained the obscurity of the inner sight of his somnambulists as they reached that era by means of the tail of a comet that is due to envelop our atmosphere and plunge our posterity into hibernation, drown it or roast it, sometimes by means of the increasing augmentation of a crust interposed between the solar rays and our globe, and sometimes by an avalanche of austral ice that will result in the continual deviation of the ecliptic towards the boreal pole. For myself, I attach less importance to these astronomical anxieties; I believe that the boundary proves that thought, even aided by magnetic interrogation, can go no further. There are things so very extraordinary even in prophecies falling towards the end of the 21st century that I abstain from mentioning them, for fear of putting the credulity of readers to an excessively harsh proof. I am therefore publishing, at present, only a very small part of what I could have extracted from this abundant literary mine. I ought perhaps to be anxious for another reason, though, for the worst that can happen to me is that I shall not be thought a sufficiently powerful sorcerer.

As it has been impossible for me to give precise dates for the events that form the substance of this story, I ought at least to indicate the epoch in which the principal action occurs. As far as I can conjecture, it is somewhere in the 20th century of our Christian era. I have made immense efforts to arrive at this result; I have assembled a host of passages extracted from various somnambulistic verbal reports and from handwritten revelations made during sleep by the somnambulists themselves, who brought the tributes of their own nervous systems to enrich the precious collection. Is it the middle or the end of the 20th century? I don't know. As to that, the imagination of readers will have plenty of space to roam, and many of them may hope that their grandchildren will find out what it is worth. After all, if this book is to survive until then, and the novel becomes a history, I think that it will be infinitely more fortunate than it deserves.

As for the form of the narrative, it is necessary, for the sake of clarity and flow, to recount all these future things as present or past, as if the novel itself had been written and published 200 years hence, and as if it were addressed to the public that will exist at that time.

There is only one more thing to say. For everything bad that might be found herein I boldly disclaim all the responsibility, which must weigh entirely upon the manuscripts that I have consulted. My Italian visionary will be, for me, a kind of Trithemius.[11] If the reader does not wish to accept him as an oracle, it is still necessary that he takes him for a responsible editor.

---

[11] Johannes Heidenberg (1462-1516), commonly known as Trithemius, became abbot of the Benedictine monastery in Sponheim in 1483, where he began a distinguished scholarly career—which led (almost inevitably, in those days) to a reputation as a magician being retrospectively foisted upon him; the same fate befell his two most famous pupils, Cornelius Agrippa and Paracelsus. His most famous work, *Steganographia*, a partly-encrypted account of methods of secret communication, became a key text in the development of practical and theoretical cryptography, but Bodin was presumably more familiar with his *Annales Hirsaugiensis* (1509-1514), reputedly the first humanist history, and might well have claimed, with his tongue in his cheek, that this reference was intended to draw a comparison with the reputable historian rather than the disreputable occultist.

I. Carthage. The Pavilion. The Dream

Multa renascentur, etc.

Many things that have fallen into decadence
will be reborn, and others that are standing today
will fall in their turn.
Ovid.

Dreams contain infinitely less mystery
than ordinary people believe, and a little more
than powerful minds think.
Bayle.[12]

Of all the new cities built upon ancient and glorious ruins in order to revive the immense shore of the Mediterranean, Carthage is, in everyone's opinion, the most exciting and the most picturesque. If you are familiar with the delightful pleasure-houses with which its environs are ornamented, mainly in the direction of Utica, you have doubtless noticed the one that dominates all the others by its elevation, surpassing them with a magnificence at least equal to the finest palaces in Constantinople. I shall offer no description of it, because it is necessary, in general, to avoid describing ordinary things, especially at the beginning of a book. There would be no end to it: colonnades of marble, breccia and roseate granite, vast alabaster bowls, gushing springs and foun-

---

[12] Pierre Bayle (1647-1706), a Protestant moral philosopher who frequently attacked the follies of superstition.

tains in the African style; arbors of laurels and myrtles, porticos of vegetation such as one sees in all cities, but with a character of their own.

Everyone knows that this sumptuous habitation is the favorite residence of the beautiful Politée, the founder of re-established Carthage. Politée is sitting in a porcelain pavilion with her pretty sister Mirzala, breathing in the evening breeze.[13]

To the right the sea is visible, like a horizon in flames, and a less distant plain with a few rounded hills, uncultivated as yet, covered with fig trees and aloes in flower, scattered with pleasant plantations of palms, lemon-trees, orange-trees, arbutuses, terebinths and other decorative or productive trees of two hemispheres. In a distant blue haze, a gap allows a glimpse of the Moorish city of Tunis, and, on another plain, a part of the vast aqueduct of the ancient city of Hannibal.

To the left, as if at the edge of a precipice, the eye looks down upon the new city, its terraces, its domes, its minarets and its vast and monumental buildings, some completed, others bristling with scaffolding, cranes and machines operated by thousands of men. Further away, there is the port, so ingeniously excavated with the aid of a new machine, and already covered with buildings of every size and shape.

Those who have enjoyed the spectacle of a city seen thus, from a bird's eye view, will also remember the

---

[13] Politée, like many of the names in the novel, is symbolic. The Old French *politie* is equivalent to the Latin *politia* and the English "polity," but the modern *politesse* signifies politeness and good breeding. Mirzala—which Bodin defines later on—might have been borrowed from Alaric Alexander Watts' prose-poem "Mirzala" in Poems and Sketches (1823).

confused noise that rises up from these human formi-
caries, which reaches the ears as the vain and vague
summation of so much movement. That movement is in
large part work: industry, the material aspect of civilization. There are other noises too, including those of suffering and joy, but the great voice of labor drowns them
out, and that is undoubtedly a good thing.

This is what offers itself to the senses and thoughts
of the two friends as they take tea in the beautiful pavilion decorated with the most delicate paintings of the new
Greek school.

This tall woman with the majestic bearing and noble visage, whose features are so handsome that she
seems scarcely 30 years old, is—as has already been established—the famous woman popularly known as the
Modern Dido, the grand-daughter of the skillful engineer
who made six millions [14] from his machine for excavating ports and river-beds, which opened up the most direct route from Europe to India via Antioch and the Euphrates, and reunited the two oceans formerly separated
by the isthmus of Panama, and, finally, the daughter of
the richest shareholder in the European Africa Company.

I have already said that the charming maiden with
the slightly Asiatic appearance, large black almond-
shaped eyes, gracefully-arched eyebrows, and long
silken hair that falls in thick tresses over her pale broad
shoulders, is called Mirzala, but what is she? At first
glance one can see that she is probably not Politée's
natural sister, so different are they in their manner and

---

[14] Bodin inserts a footnote: "Given the progressive deprecia-
tion of money by the increase in its circulation, these six millions only represent three and a half in the French valuation of
the beginning of the 19th century."

complexion. For the moment, the secret of her birth is only imperfectly revealed in her.

About 15 years before the era in which this narrative begins, at the end of the last war against slavery and polygamy, all the newspapers in the world, in reporting the capture of Babylon, mentioned a pretty little girl, still at the breast, found in the harem of the last of that empire's sultans. Politée's father, the rich Pontarque—one of three powerful associates who had contributed their talents and financial resources to the completion of that long and terrible war—took her, it is said, under his protection and soon adopted her. The greatest mystery surrounded the orphan's cradle, and if Pontarque knew better than anyone else what was contained therein, unknown motives led him to exercise the utmost discretion, to the extent that the charming infant was quite uncertain as to whether or not nature had give her the same father as Politée.

A woman who lived perpetually behind the veil, according to ancient Oriental custom, devoted herself with an entirely maternal tenderness to the education of little Mirzala, whose charming face would never again be exposed to the eyes of a man, save only for the one she was on the point of marrying. This woman, whose influence on Pontarque's mind was remarkable and to whom he even showed respect, finding herself on the point of death, made him promise that her pupil, his adopted daughter, would continue being raised according to Asiatic mores and ideas and in the reformed Islamic faith— which, as everyone knows, is very similar to Christianity.

When Mirzala lost this devoted instructress, who was thought by many people to be her real mother, Pontarque entrusted her to his daughter Politée, who, being much older and endowed with a precocious intelligence, was fully capable of serving instead of a mother for the little sister she cherished so tenderly. Pontarque's death left the two sisters completely orphaned a short time afterwards, when Mirzala was still a child and Politée only 15—but virtually free despite her youth—under the relatively unburdensome surveillance of an aged aunt. It was not until five or six years after that, however, that Politée had her adventure with the famous warrior Philomaque.

The marriage created quite a stir at the time, and the striking abandonment that followed a few months later furnished all the newspapers in the world with material for rather long commentaries, in order that the facts could be placed among the facts of history. Everyone remembers the parallels which gave birth to that sad similarity between the destiny of the new Dido and that of her poetic predecessor. The fine minds of two hemispheres—white, black, light and dark brown—struggled with the subject in prose and verse and in all languages, but the reputation for virtue that the founder of modern Carthage enjoyed was so solidly established that it did not receive the slightest injury in that mêlée of poems, dramas and novels.

Politée's situation being familiar, therefore, it is not difficult to explain the melancholy expression spread upon her handsome features, the poignant pallor of her complexion, pure and diaphanous nevertheless, and the slight bluish tint in the corners of her eyes, which add to their beautiful expression as turquoises serve to heighten the brightness of diamonds. Her carriage is still majestic, her stance still noble, because that is the way she is made: because her frame is both tall and elegant; because her mind is elevated and her heart proud; and because she is playing the role of an ancient queen, and is also a queen of sorts in reality. From time to time, though, when memories or reflections assail her, and her gestures seem nonchalant and casual, she seems to have fallen from her throne and to have become a mere woman again.

It is in this exact disposition that she finds herself now, leaning negligently on Mirzala's shoulder, with a tear ready to escape her eye, gazing at the shining mosaic floor with that fixed stare which sees nothing.

Mirzala, who is seated on the same divan, with her legs crossed in the Turkish fashion, lifts up one of her long jade tresses to wipe her friend's eyes. Putting her arms gracefully around Politée's neck, she lavishes a young girl's chaste kisses upon her: caresses so naïve that no chagrin can resist them; the sweet perfume of hope and happiness, with no admixture of regret and anxiety.

"Dear sister," murmurs Mirzala, "I have not dared to tell you about the dream I had last night, because I feared that it might be indiscreet to raise the subject, and that it might not give you pleasure."

"Oh! Why is that?" says Politée, excitedly. "On the contrary, you know how your dreams interest and amuse me. Tell me about this one, my dear Mirzala."

"Well, lovely sister, I saw *him*. He was in the sky, and I have a feeling that he is coming here."

"Oh, no, no!" Politée replies, blushing slightly. "I can't believe that for a moment, dear Mirzala, although I know from experience how lucid your dreams are—often as certain as the best magnetic visions. This time, I strongly doubt…"

"I swear to you, Politée, that I saw him quite distinctly, as I see you, with that clarity and force of vision that immediately distinguishes from my ordinary dreams those which apprise me of distant and present facts."

"It's rather a long time since you've seen him, though, Mirzala. Are you perfectly sure of being able to recognize him?"

"Oh, my dear! How could anyone forget that masculine bearing, so proud—especially someone who has only seen a dozen men's faces, at the most, having spent her life, as I have, hidden behind a veil?"

Politée assumes an expression of indifference. "Yes," she says, "I admit that his physiognomy was rather remarkable, although too warlike for our peaceful century. He would have made a fine model for the battle scenes of the old painters of the French Empire. But what a sad advantage! You, Mirzala, who knows my heart, know that his image was erased therefrom a long time ago; it is the pride of outraged womanhood that suffers in me, and would almost make me desire vengeance if I were not a Christian. In eight years I have not been able to accustom myself to so public a humiliation of my self-respect."

Mizala, who is as delicate as she was good, does not insist; fully of the same opinion as her sister, she approves wholeheartedly of the complete obliteration of the infidel's memory, and undertakes to show how few qualities he has that might render him worthy of a profound attachment. Then she passes on, a trifle maliciously, to another subject of conversation.

"Are you saying, then," Politée says, harking back, "that you have really seen him? How was he?"

"Oh, but he was always handsome," Mirzala replies, smiling. "His features delicately outlined, albeit with grandiosity, his fiery gaze, his elevated stature…"

"I know all that," says Politée, a slight impatience hidden within her exceedingly soft tone. "What I'm asking you, dear Mirzala, is...is..."

"How can I tell you that?"

"Oh, you irritate me with your mysteries!" Immediately giving the charming Babylonian girl a little kiss, as if to beg pardon for that outburst, she adds: "Tell me if he appeared at all changed to you."

"Not much...no, a little...I think."

"Ah!" says Politée, with a slight muted sigh. Then she falls silent. After a brief pause, she goes on: "You aren't saying anything more. I'll have to get the rest one question at a time. What was he wearing?"

"Oh, that's what struck me: he was wearing a turban, a large and handsome white turban, truly, with an expensive diamond spray that sparkled in the sunlight like a group of stars. He also had a very long black moustache, which gave his mouth an even greater severity. Finally, I saw an Arab yataghan in his belt, the hilt of which was similarly covered with those enormous diamonds that chemists cannot make as yet."

"There!" Politée says to herself, letting her head fall upon her breast. "A vision of him, clearer and more detailed than I have been able to obtain for a long time from any magnetically-entranced Pythoness.[15] There's something strange about that." Turning to Mirzala, she says: "This dream, dear child, must relate directly to you."

"I'm tempted to believe so, because..."

---

[15] Bodin inserts a footnote: "The somnambulists, or rather the magnetic somniloquists [*somniloques*] of the 18th century were sometimes called by the name by which they were known in antiquity."

"Ah! You haven't told me everything, then?"

"You didn't give me time, dear sister. Well, it seemed to me that Philomaque looked at me very hard—with a step-brother's tenderness, as before, but nevertheless with an air of authority that intimidated me. I still shiver even in recalling it."

"Did you think that he was talking to you?"

"His lips quivered, and I thought that he was going to open his mouth, but his aerostat—doubtless a warbird of the first rank, manned by a powerful crew—cleaved the air in swift flight and, assisted by the wind, passed in a flash. It was as if my breathing were suppressed by the rapidity of his progress and the atmospheric disturbance; that woke me up with a start. Since that moment I've had a sad presentiment that something is going to happen to me, but I said nothing to you, dear sister, for that very reason. I am seriously anxious about not having seen *him* arrive during the three days that we have been waiting for him—you know full well, you, too, dear child, already have your own anxieties and dreads; you will no longer belong to yourself, and you imagine that another will belong to you. You're going to be married…are you afraid that he might kidnap your fiancé?"

"I don't know, but I have everything to fear; there is such antipathy between them—or, to put it more accurately, Philomaque has such a strong detestation for my poor Philirène,[16] who, I believe, is incapable of hating anyone himself."

"That's why you love him so much, sweet dove."

"Truly, I can't say that. I don't know if I love as you say that you yourself have loved, as people love in

_____

[16] Philirène translates as "peace-lover."

the poems and plays I've read. I love calmly and safely, with a delicate happiness, like this light breeze that brings us the perfumes of the countryside. I love with the certainty of being loved uniquely, because it seems impossible to me that he loves anyone else, inasmuch as he has told me so. He told me that in front of you, dear sister, and you seemed to believe him. Is it true, though, that he once loved you? I've heard vague mention of that—you've become pensive; is that because it's true? Tell me, tell me quickly."

"You'll know all that when you're married."

"No, I want to know now."

"Come on, Mirzala, are you getting jealous? May God preserve you from that. Continue to love Philirène tranquilly, and beware of loving him too much. I promise to tell you some day what there was between us. Oh, it's already very old, and you, with your 15 years and your charming face, have nothing to fear from memories."

Mirzala darts a rapid glance at a mirror, as women never fail to do in any circumstances where their beauty is involved in an issue. Then, sufficiently reassured by that furtive inspection, she says: "Why not, dear Politée? But you love me too much to be capable of trying to please him—and then again, it seems to me that a man like him would never be able to satisfy you."

"Who knows? Poor child, you've scarcely clapped eyes on anyone else but him."

It is in our nature not always to accept the disadvantages of our situation. A recluse, who has only seen the world through the barred window of her visiting-room, can at least claim to know exactly what she has seen, and even to have seen that which is to be seen more clearly. The naïve Mirzala, therefore, her self-respect somewhat wounded by the reminder that she had only ever seen one man, finds herself drawn to forge common cause between the merit of that man and her own self-respect, rendering them interdependent. She wants him to be the first among men, in order that she should not be the most inexperienced of women.

"Oh, yes, I'm well aware of that; he's the only one to whom I've appeared unveiled; he's the only one that I've been able to observe since I ceased to be a child. How well I've studied him, my Philirène, how I know him by heart! How good he his, how amiable he is, how witty he is! How great and generous his ideas are, always directed towards the happiness and moral dignity of the human species! How much religious elevation he has, what tender sentiments beneath his skepticism— which I do not share, but which seems to me, personally, to be pious and almost devout. Then again, if anyone says that he is not handsome in Philomaque's fashion, like the fine warriors of your art gallery, I shall say that he is handsome as the busts of savants, thinkers, poets and artists that I often admire in our collections are handsome. I love him in that way, my Philirène...but I'm annoyed with you, because he's beginning to pay too much attention to you."

"Bravo, bravo!" cries Politée, planting a kiss on her sister's round and shapely neck. "What fire! What richness of words! I'm delighted that you love him thus, for he certainly deserves it; I'm glad that you're both happy!"

"Oh, if I could give you a part of that happiness, in exchange for your sorrow, I would do it with the greatest pleasure!"

"I believe you would, but I would not dream of consenting to it."

"And yet, beautiful sister, how many advantages you have over me, how many elements of happiness that I have not! You do great things; you have fame; you, who, being your own mistress and mistress of an immense fortune at the age of 15, had he idea—so novel for a young woman—of founding an empire, almost a civilization. You're a superior woman; you're more than a woman, for you've gone as far as men in their sciences, their useful arts, and their philosophical speculations; you're what they call a *thinking woman*—while I will never be more than a mere woman of sentiment."

"All these distinctions, my dear, that you wish to apply to me in flattering terms, are never very real. Personally, I don't think of myself exclusively as what they call a thinking woman, entirely exempt from the passions of our sex. I am not so lucky, or unlucky—you know that very well, you naughty girl. And you, who are so profoundly poetic, so gracefully artistic, are you pretending that you do not think a little?"

As the two young women continue this conversation, sometimes sad and sometimes cheerful, often mingled with soft smiles and interrupted by tender caresses, a drawing-room door begins to open.

II. A Child

There are no longer any children.
Old proverb.

I told you that this is a hoax.
Anonymous.

A young and handsome child, about eight years old,
enters excitedly and runs to throw himself into Politée's
arms. A large woman, who appears to be over 50, but
whose face is well-preserved, comes after him, wearing
a serious and dignified expression. From her somewhat
proud bearing, and her handsome features—whose expression is almost haughty, although she seems to be
trying to render it modest—one would be more likely to
take her for a princess than a governess. She is indeed of
royal blood, descended from one of Europe's illustrious
ruling houses.

People in the polite society of the African shore often ask why the restorer of Carthage, in the high intellectual and industrial position that she occupies, has
taken it into her head to place her son in the care of a
woman whose principles are so notoriously opposed to
the social order of this part of the world; the point is thus
worthy of an explanation.

When Philomaque married Politée, he introduced
his wife to this respectable governess, who had raised
him with the sort of care that one only finds in an old
mother. He had introduced her under that title, and as his
oldest and best friend. She called herself Madame

Charlotte; no one knew whether she had ever been married. She gave evidence of the most ardent desire to raise Philomaque's children, not as an instructress—for outside of music, painting and the three modern languages that she spoke, her knowledge was rather limited—but in a more intimate capacity; the profound attachment that she had conserved for the father would guarantee the tenderness that she would bring to the education of the son. It was obvious that she was not inspired by any interested motive; it was well-known that her fortune was quite considerable, and although she consented to receive a salary from Politée in order not to offend her vanity, she passed it on directly to a number of unfortunate families without even touching it.

What had convinced Politée to accept was, on the one hand, the warm recommendation of her husband, and the certainty of a boundless devotion and round-the-clock surveillance, while on the other, there was a consideration that would not have surprised those who were familiar with the new Dido's elevated mind. The ancient feudal vanity has been succeeded by the new vanity of the grandees of our day, our manufacturers and engineers, and founders of cities, colonies and even empires in Asia and Africa. Politée, who wanted her son to be perfect, was desirous first and foremost of shielding him from those ideas of glory which so easily seduce youth and often release all of its moral energy and desire to learn. She dreaded that he might acquire the habit of availing himself of the science and industry of his parents, contenting himself with the consideration that it would one day be his, and live in apathy.

"It is not necessary," she said, "that my son should take pride in the origin that God has seen fit to give him, any more than one should take pride in wealth, beauty, talent and intelligence—other gifts from God, which He takes back from us when it pleases Him. My Jules does not need governesses who will say to him perennially: 'How glorious it is for you to have for your great-grandfather the celebrated engineer who, born a simple working man and without overmuch education, has aided maritime commerce so greatly with his canals, who invented such a simpler and powerful instrument for excavating ports and clearing river-beds, and, by virtue of his achievements, has change the face of oceanic navigation! How glorious it is to have for your grandfather the wealthy capitalist who undertook the commercial conquest of Timbuktu and began its civilization, and whose illustrious daughter created such a stir in the world!' "

Politée preferred to place her son in the charge of a woman as little disposed as Madame Charlotte to spoil him in that regard. She could rely on the fact that he would not lack protection against the pride that Roman triumphs had been designed to gratify. Lofty industrial, financial and even intellectual affiliations, far from obtaining the least sign of admiration from the royal governess, or even deference, were only acknowledged with smiles whose disdainful intent was only concealed by good breeding. There was no fear that she would not see her way to insinuating to her pupil that he was the grandson and great-grandson of honest and ingenious artisans, who would not have played any part in the social order of the European monarchies, who would merely have been entitled to claim a patent accorded by the administrative authority and a few benevolent words from some gracious regal lips. Moreover, one could be quite sure that she would not let any opportunity escape to make him hear that there is nothing noble in this mundane world but the exercise of civil and military power united in the same hands, as in feudal times; to the pitiless exclusion of all judiciary, administrative and other nobilities whose introduction had been attempted within these monarchies.

The young pupil often raises rather awkward objections to the prejudices of his respectable governess, and Politée, who takes a keen interest in them, occasionally amuses herself by listening to their discussions, but without ever intervening. She even pretends to know nothing at all about them. No one can deny that the conduct of his excellent mother is very wise, given that such a great illustriousness surrounds her family, in which two generations of men have been solemnly decorated by the Universal Congress with the name of Pontarque. The uninterrupted succession of extraordinary talents in the Wilson family—that being their former surname—is so easily capable of exalting the vanity of their sole descendant that it is extremely important to take precautions against that fault. But there is also a risk in another inconvenience, for Madame Charlotte, in telling her pupil about his father Philomaque, usually lets it slip that she knows the genealogy of that famous warrior better than anyone, and that there runs in his veins not merely a little of the blood of the great Tartar conquerors, but also royal European blood. Politée is by no means ignorant of this circumstance; she even knows something more, and it is noticeable that it has not made her discontented— such are the contradictions and bizarreries within the minds of superior women! But that would require too long an explanation.

"Well, Jules," says Politée, "have you been hard at work? Have you been doing repetitions with your tutor? Are you doing honor to my Lycée de Carthage?"

"Yes, Mama," the child replies, with a cheerful vivacity. "Ask me anything."

Politée did not want her son to be given an excessively premature education, in order not to hinder his physical development. He has been allowed to learn what he wished, whatever pleased him; faith has been placed in his curiosity, his natural aptitude and his competitiveness.

He has not yet made a start on the exact sciences; of natural science he knows only what it has amused him to learn; he only speaks the three principal languages of Europe because he acquired the habit in his cradle; he has not yet studied the conventional language, called universal and primitive, which the Polyglot Academy, sitting in the place where the Tower of Babel was supposedly erected, has succeeded in composing from the roots of all mother-tongues.

It was a truly bold enterprise to revisit the work of the separation of languages and the division of populations in order to bring the human race back to a chimerical unity. It is not probable however, that it will succeed. French jokers have called it a "root salad," and that pun has delivered a fatal blow to the work of the anti-Babelists, which might nevertheless be useful as a scientific language. Our friend Jules has devoted himself, much more judiciously, to logical and symbolic inscription, whose signs—which represent ideas rather than syllables and words—can be read and, by the same token, written in all languages without the necessity of translation. This idea, which was first proposed, I believe, in the 18th century by Condorcet,[17] has had a great deal of success in recent times.

The young schoolboy, interrogated by his mother on various rather delicate points of religion and morality, writes the answers for her in logical signs, which he then translates with equal ease into the three languages. It is, however, principally towards history that his inclinations have directed him. He is apprised on the facts, and then works independently to find the connections between them and to systematize them.

This marvelous child carries out historical synthesis with almost the same dedication as certain authors at the beginning of the 19th century, with a quasi-monastic mysticism. It is by this method that he has discovered quite independently, for instance, that the pig and the potato have vanquished the English aristocracy, regenerated Spain and saved the papacy. In effect, he says, it was the imposing alliance of Irish Catholics with English radicals that led to the ruin of the Anglican clergy and the suppression of heredity in the ancient House of Lords; it was the immense colonies of Irishmen in Spain that helped the representative government to sustain itself in that country against the power of the traditional and temporal clergy, and subsequently doubled the productivity of the soil and tripled that of national industry; it was the numerous Irish recruits that Pope Leo XVI formed into an army which enabled the Romans to repel the Austrian invasion and found a federal Italian gov-

---

[17] Antoine-Nicolas, Marquis de Condorcet (1743-1794) was the foremost propagandist for and popularizer of the philosophy of progress. He was permanent secretary of the Académie des Sciences and served in the Convention, but was imprisoned during the Terror and took poison to avoid the guillotine.

ernment, which has made the peninsula glorious and prosperous. Now, the pig and the potato were, in combination, the sole cause of the excessive increase in the population of Ireland, which was, it is said, no larger than ten millions in 1850—hence, etc.

Jules has made many other curious discoveries in history. He has been trying for several days to classify the human race historically according to its dietary habits, attaching the most dominant ideas to that sort of division. Thus, rice represents faith and dogma, wheat reason and experiment, potatoes material interests. It is true that the rules that he has tried to deduce in consequence are absorbed by the exceptions, but the prodigious little fellow in not at all embarrassed by the difficulties; before long, he will have produced a system entirely satisfactory to the imagination.

In response to his mother's question, Jules runs through the principal epochs of modern history: the spontaneous fragmentation of the Russian empire and the rise of the Slavic Federation under the auspices of Poland, causing the fall of the Ottoman Empire in Europe, so that Constantinople has been declared a free city and the Bosphorus has been opened, like the Sund connecting the North Sea to the Baltic, to all the ships of the world under European guarantee; the Turks, having been driven back into Asia, becoming more powerful, conquering Persia and founding the new Babylonian Empire in Baghdad that has flourished so spectacularly in the last 100 years; the conquest of Palestine and the re-establishment of the Kingdom of the Jews by a company of Israelite bankers under the protection of the sultans of the Euphrates and the modern Pharaohs.

I shall not go on any longer because the enumeration of such well-known facts cannot be interesting to the reader, even though their relation by the infantile mouth of a cherished son inevitably sounds delightful in the ears of a loving mother. I shall stop, therefore, and ask a thousand pardons of the amiable subscribers to "circulating libraries" and "reading rooms"[18] for the boredom this tedious chapter must be causing them. I shall make every effort to compensate them in the next.

---

[18] "Reading rooms" is a slightly awkward translation of "*cabinets de lecture*;" when books were still so expensive as to be beyond the budget of the average household and literacy was not yet universal, poor people could still obtain access to their contents by subscribing to such institutions, from which books could be borrowed, or to which they could go to read them. Bodin would naturally assume, in 1834, that many of his readers would have gained access to his text in this way, so the narrative voice appears to be speaking for the author at this point. It is not impossible, however, that Bodin had failed to anticipate that books would be much cheaper in the late 20th century.

III. A Surprise

Expertus vacuum Daedalus aera, etc.
Nil mortalibus arduum est, etc.

Daedalus has traveled the empty skies
with the wings that nature refused to man.
Nothing is impossible to mortals;
in their folly they are scaling the sky...
Horace, *Odes*.

When I am grown up I shall write a novel
of the future and I shall travel the skies
in machines in the form of birds;
there is no poetry in the future without that.
A schoolboy's sketch-book.

No other part of the Barbary Coast offers view more picturesque than that to which I have transported the reader. I am, however, astonished that, since the time when the wealth of Europe was first dedicated to the fashion of spending the spring in country houses on the African shore, such a vast number have been constructed in the environs of Carthage, rivaling those of Algiers, Hippo, Oran and Tripoli.

However little descriptive talent I have received by nature, I would rather like to paint the night extending its veils—as one still says—over the young city of Carthage, whose belfries and minarets stand out as black and pointed shadows against the remote plains of the horizon, and depict the Mediterranean still retaining a residue of light, as if the Sun could not quite resolve to abandon it. The greater number of readers, however, will like it just as much if I simply say that night is falling, and—as I am used to being the humble servant of majorities, given that that is often the only way of deciding many grave questions—I willingly concede to that desire, while begging pardon for making a joke as old as the metaphor itself.

The amiable Jules, led away by his noble governess, has gone to bed, as is appropriate for every well-brought up child at such an hour, and the two charming sisters have left the beautiful pavilion, and the grounds of the house, in order to savor the cool air of the night more fully. Each delivered to her own thoughts, they are only exchanging sporadically a few of those brief remarks that are sufficient signs of sympathy and intelligence between two souls that are thoroughly accustomed to one another.

When Politée raises her eyes to the firmament, whose astronomical study has made it, for her, into an interesting book to skim in the evening, a luminous dot catches her gaze. Eyes less expert than hers might take it for a planet, whose light, though closer at hand and more striking than those of the stars, is nevertheless less scintillating, but Politée soon makes a different judgment.

A short time afterwards, a rather bright fire is lit on one of the uncultivated expanses that border the sea. Curiosity and a certain adventurous disposition draws the two young women in that direction. By the light of the flames, they perceive a party of Berbers or Bedouins disembarking on the shore. These barbarians, armed and equipped in the old French fashion, religiously conserving military tactics forgotten in the civilized nations, are allies of Carthage and do not inspire any mistrust in

Politée, whose name has a good deal of authority among them, and who relies with reason on their sworn fidelity. Even so, this demonstration surprises her; she wants to know the reason for it.

A tearful young woman runs towards the two sisters; in the half-light of the beautiful starry night, and by the quasi-divine bearing described on the same beach by a verse in Virgil, she immediately recognizes the city's founder. She throws herself to her knees, pouring out tears, and a voice punctuated by sobs implores Politée to accompany her to the shore, to employ her powerful intervention in a pressing matter of honor, life and death.

Politée grips Mirzala's arm excitedly; the latter lowers her veil, and they move rather precipitately in the direction in which the unknown woman takes them, while telling them an exceedingly touching story in a naïve tone. This is imprudent, but one cannot reproach her too severely, since she is acting from a generous motive.

Meanwhile, the light that had almost been mistaken for a planet had increased in size—which is to say, drawn nearer—without Politée paying attention to it, because the new scene that was attracting her attention absorbed it completely. Besides, there was nothing surprising about presence of an aerostat in the atmosphere of this region.

The Berbers' horns and trumpets, however, are sounding a harmonious fanfare, in which the two sisters recognize a favorite tune from the Atlas mountains. At the same moment the traveling light emits a smaller light, which falls to Earth like one of those fast-moving meteors that used to be taken for falling stars in the eras of ignorance.

Neither Politée nor her friend, their attention absorbed by the military music and their guide's story—doubtless prolonged by design—is giving any thought to what might be happening in the air; they have not noticed this last circumstance. They cannot help starting with fright, therefore, when the dark shadow of a *crow*—a launch from a war-balloon—parachutes down to settle close by, fixing itself to the ground by means of three long supports armed with steel points.

Mirzala releases a little cry of joy. Her first thought is that her dear Philirène has finally arrived—for we know that he has been expected for several days, with an impatience turning to anxiety. It would be such a nice surprise to see him alight [19] one night and set foot to ground before his beloved, like an angel descended from Heaven! But she soon realizes her error as she recognizes, on the extended wings of the detached aerostat, the dark color of a war-bird's herald instead of the dove-colored fabric used in descents from Philirène's peaceful aerial vessels.

Scarcely have the two sisters had time to make this observation when half a dozen silken ladders are thrown out of the crow, weighted to hold them to the ground, and ten or twelve lithe and slim individuals, who can hardly be identified as men by their clothing or their voices, clamber down with a marvelous agility. Their dazzling white muslin tunics are easily distinguishable,

---

[19] The rather anodyne "alight" is a poor substitute for Bodin's invented *désaérer*; unfortunately, that French word was subsequently re-coined to mean de-aerate—i.e. to removed the air from a liquid, rather than to descend from an airship—and the decline of airships in our 20th century removed the necessity for any parallel coinage.

terminating in trousers narrowed below the ankles in the Indian style. Vast sky-blue turbans and wide enameled belts of the same color, fringed with silver, cling to their slender figures; turquoise necklets and little blue satin slippers ornamented with sapphires complete costumes as elegant as they are simple, to which Mirzala and Politée never dream of giving the attention they deserve, because they are momentarily occupied with something else entirely.

The members of the crow's female crew have approached Mirzala, folding their arms across their chests in the Asiatic manner and have knelt in front of her. She does not know what to think about this; she would be inclined to revert to her first supposition if it were possible to explain such a strange sending on Philirène's part.

One of the women, who appears to be in command, takes her hands with a show of great respect and attempt to draw her towards one of the rope-ladders. Mirzala resists, and Politée comes to her aid. But the leader of the airwomen,[20] drawing close to Mirzala's ear, whispers a few words to her that cause her to release a scream and to faint. The airwomen, who have caught her in their arms, drag her away from Politée's, taking possession of her in spite of the latter's efforts, pleas and tears, briskly climbing the silken ladders with their burden. Mirzala is set down gently within the crow, on a bed of fresh roses gathered in Sicily, and every possible care is lavished upon her as the black wings unfurl, beat and propel the machine upwards. Drawn by a long cord towards the aerostat, it does not take long to rejoin it.

---

[20] These are obviously the Amazons to whom Bodin makes later reference, but he does not appear to have thought of appropriating that term at this point stage in the story.

One can easily imagine the profound chagrin in which Politée returns alone to her residence, the Villa of Hannibal, while the unknown girl flees at top speed in the direction of the sea. It is clear now that she has been duped by a trick and that her sister is a victim of treason.

She deplores, too late, the negligence of the Carthage observatory, which combines security and astronomical functions, and should have noticed a warship passing over the city. She also prepares a sharp reprimand for the chief of police, who should have been warned by intelligence and signals exchanged with the aerostat that there by a landing. Finally, she reproached herself for not having consulted her Pythoness for several days to find out whether any plots were being hatched against her or her relatives.

This proves that, under the most advanced civilization as in the ages of barbarism, in spite of the numerous precautions of governmental power, the evildoers who are always on watch, ready to seize the opportunity to commit a crime, will always succeed in catching the good unawares.

As for the company of Berber infantry, it will not be easy to get hold of them because they have re-embarked with their arms and baggage to return to one of their ports, which are, as everyone knows, well-fortified, and no one would consider attacking only unless it were absolutely necessary. Even less could one think of giving chase to a war-eagle, whose flight is fearfully rapid and which has the advantage, given that Carthage only possesses aerostats for commercial and leisure usage.

IV. A Modern Pythoness

The grotto of the goddess, etc.
Télémaque.[21]

Ingenii commenta delet dies;
naturae judicia confirmat.
Systems fall every day,
and nature ends up being in the right.
Cicero.[22]

Politée is obliged to pass a very sad and restless night. The following day, when dawn has scarcely begun to break, she hastily dons one of the simple garments she uses when she wanted to pass through her city incognito. She tells her son to get up for a morning excursion, such

---

[21] *Télémaque* [Telemachus], by the Abbé de la Mothe-Fénelon (1651-1715)—usually known simply by the latter part of his surname—was a didactic prose sequel to the *Odyssey*, whose action begins with Telemachus being shipwrecked on Calypso's isle. It was the most frequently-reprinted French novel of the 18th century; Bodin's decription of Poonah's cave is obviously derived from the description of Calypso's cave given in its opening pages.

[22] I have translated Bodin's rather free French translation of this misquotation, which originates from the report of a committee appointed to investigate animal magnetism in 1833. The actual quote from *De Natura Deorum* is "*Opinium enim commenta delet dies, naturae judicia confirmat,*" which is usually translated as "Time destroys the groundless conceits of men; it confirms decisions founded in reality."

as people often take for pleasure in the hot climate, and gives orders for her young lions to be hitched to and uncovered carriage, modest and undecorated.

Everyone knows how gentle and docile these animals are when properly domesticated; they offer not the slightest danger and have no inconvenience other than being dearer than the most beautiful Arab horses, which puts them slightly beyond the range of ordinary incomes.

The Ethiopian charmer who tamed the founder's four lion cubs, and is the only one who can supervise them in total security, leads them calmly from the stables, their muzzles in place. When they show signs of excessive excitement, he makes them hear his powerful voice and gives them a terrible stare, which makes them tremble, and settles them in harness as easily as a coachman's whip settles a pair of Norman horses in front of the carriage of a Parisian bourgeois.

Politée climbs into the cart with her son, whom she wraps in a cloak of ostrich-down because of the morning chill. The black driver emits a soft whistle, and the lions, impatient to make headway, set off at the gallop.

Meanwhile, Madame Charlotte, who has brought little Jules to his mother, watches the departure—not without anxiety—from the top of the antique green steps and releases a resentful sigh, thinking somewhat ill-humoredly that the granddaughter of a mechanical engineer and daughter of a businessman travels in a carriage whose like her august ancestors never saw: a carriage superior even to that of the mythical goddess Ceres (whose own carriage, I believe, only had two lions).

After a quarter of an hour's traveling, the carriage stops not far from the sea shore, in front of a cave hollowed out in the rock, directed towards the north. I ought to give a brief description of this cave because, after all, it bears scant resemblance to the many others that we find in the epic poems of antiquity and modern times.

The plants surrounding it comprise a singular vegetation; they are amphibious plants, half-marine and half-terrestrial—transitional, so to speak—zoophytes, which dwell in the margins of the vegetable and animals kingdoms; plant-animals that contract when they are touched, agitating their strange plump leaves or quasi-enchanted stems as if they were arms, hands and jaws about to grab you, grip you, wind around you and bite you without knowing why, with the malevolence of a turkey and the stupidity of a cabbage. It is necessary however, to leave these things to be described by naturalists. Botany, conchology, ornithology, mineralogy and even entomology would have had an enormous amount to say about the surroundings of that picturesque and romantic dwelling. A great variety of flowering lianas, aromatic plants and spiny bushes, of whose names I am absolutely ignorant, hang from the rocks or sprout from their verdant fissures, along with the prettiest shells and the rarest pebbles, which might have enriched a curiosity-seller's shop. To cap it all, a host of birds and insects of every form and color are fluttering about, humming and chirping. The latter are more likely to interest savants than the ordinary people of the neighborhood.

Would I not be ill-advised to attempt such a description without consulting the dictionary in order to insert little-known names thereinto? I am too honest, and I candidly admit my insufficiency. I shall limit myself to pointing out the palms and the tamarinds that crown the heights of the rock, and the trees imported from the Indian Ocean and the American continent—bamboo, coconut-palms, rubber-trees, breadfruit trees and so on—which border the little garden set at its base.

Now we shall follow Politée into the cave, where she has already been for five minutes. The neatness and artistry of it is worthy of note: skillfully-woven reed mats laid out on the marble; a simply-upholstered plush silk divan, perfectly imitative of the moss that grows on the trunks of old trees; modest curtains made of fine tree-bark, which bear representations, to the extent of illusion, of the clumped foliage of an arbor of shrubs; mirrors made up of prismatic facets in rough-hewn alcoves, framed in ivy-leaves made of bronze; the ceiling encrusted with enamel-work variously imitating pendant stalactites and various wild animals and plants; such is the whole of its decoration. As for furniture, the only item that would fetch a high price is a sort of rock crystal stump, so artistically attached that one would think it integral. There are a few books bound in zebra-skin, and a fly-swatter made of the feathers of birds of paradise is set overhead. There are also a cedar-wood organ and a citrus-wood harp. I forgot two beautiful paintings representing landscapes of Hindustan.

At the moment when the founder, accompanied by her son, enters this modest but comfortable abode, inaccessible to the heat of day, a woman is strumming the harp-strings with distracted, almost careless, fingers, which stroke them gently and hardly make them vibrate. She is murmuring a sad lullaby whose words translate as:

"Travel the Earth, plough the ocean, fly swiftly through the skies; see everything, enjoy everything, grasp everything; that is your role. Ours is to remain clinging to the rock, waiting, often in vain, for you to deign to return to us, to pay with a smile for a year's sighs, to wipe our moist and blinking eyes with a kiss, to reap in an instant all the treasures of our love, those treasures that you combine with so many others, amassed for you everywhere."

The person who has sung this song—in which many women would find too much humility and tender resignation—is a woman whose cheeks seem hollowed out, and whose figure seems to have become thinner than slender, by virtue of sorrow. The white linen robe that is her only garment gives even greater prominence to the dark tint of her skin, by which she is easily recognizable as a daughter of the Ganges. Her black eyes, deeply-sunk in their orbits, seem lifeless, and their vitreous immobility would seem almost frightful were it not for an occasional rapid thought crossing her mind, reanimating them as a gust of wind sometimes brightens a spark within the cinders. Her long black hair, gently separated by a headband over her forehead and cheeks, is plaited behind her head. Her gestures are graceful, her manner distinguished, her voice delightfully soft although a trifle vibrant. In sum, this woman, who must once have been ravishing, is still very handsome.

It is said that she is the widow of an artillery-mechanic in a steam-battery in the Tartar-Mongolian army, who died in Philomaque's service in the famous campaign that the great captain undertook to conquer part of Hindustan. She presented herself to the founder of Carthage a little while after the latter's abandonment by the infidel. Although every memory connected with Philomaque wounded Politée's feminine pride, she welcomed the widow generously and made her a gift of the habitation she now occupies, instructing that she should lack nothing needful. Poonah had a daughter a little older than Jules; that was almost a bond, or at least a pretext for two young women to see one another—I almost said the two widows, for Politée has all the inconveniences of that status, without any of the advantages. It did not take Politée long to acquire a genuine affection for Poonah, and another motive often drew her to the cave, for visits that were rather mysterious.

After polite compliments and a few sincere apologies for being slightly negligent in the past month, Politée instructs the Moorish serving-woman who looks after Poonah to take the children into the garden, and the two friends remain alone, sitting on the divan and chatting about trivial things.

Politée, who takes Poonah's hands tightly in her own during an interval of silence, looks at her in a manner whose softness scarcely disguises a singular, almost imperative, fixity.

Poonah, scarcely conscious of the pressure exerted upon her, immediately lowers her eyelids, releases a slight sigh, places one arm behind her heads, which is supported by a cushion, and goes to sleep.

Politée, seemingly self-absorbed, continues her work of fascination, and the pretty fingers of her plump white hand pour opiate force into the forehead and breast of her friend.

If I might lend Greek mythology an image whose significance is purely magnetic, Poonah is, as it is easy to see, an excellent *Oneirophant*, or somniloquist. After a few moments of profound sleep, more calming and more fortifying than natural sleep, she raises herself into a lighter sleep, similar in some respects to the waking state, which must equip her with the use of a new sense of perception that we cannot understand. She gently rubs her eyelids, still completely lowered, places one hand on her forehead and another on her breast, which soon swells effortfully under a weighty oppression.

"Ah!" she says. "Why haven't you come to see me for nearly a month? It's too late now."

"Do you now where they've gone, then, dear Poonah?"

"I think so. As for him, I see him clearly—as usual, for you know full well that it's him I always see first when you put me to sleep, so often do you and I think of him and so many things do I have upon me that have touched or were part of him: his hair, for example."

"And Mirzala—do you see her too?"

"Yes, but less distinctly. She is weeping and sobbing. She does not want to see her abductor, with whom she is extremely irritated."

"Tell me, though—where are they going?"

"I think they're heading for the Indies; at least, Philomaque is headed for the equator in search of useful currents that will carry him eastwards. I can't be certain."

"Have you any inkling of what his plan is—do you know what his motives and objectives are?"

"Oh, my God, how could I know that? The last time you put me to sleep I saw nothing, nothing at all, whether because my vision was obscured or because he had no such idea. As for his objective, perhaps it's to keep your sister from Philirène, whom he detests, and to whom he would be embarrassed to be related."

"I agree with you," says Politée, with more chagrin than indignation. "What a passionate soul! What a narrow mind!"

"Ah!" says Poonah, excitedly. "Don't talk like that; at present, it makes me feel ill. I don't know whether it's my fault—I think it's more likely your doing—but when I'm in this state, I'm weaker and more irritable on the point of awakening…" After a pause, she lifts her handkerchief to her forehead, which is streaming with large beads of sweat. "My head's aching, and my nerves too. Calm me down; I don't want to direct my sight in this fashion and longer. It tires and exhausts me. I hope to see better to another occasion."

Politée calms her by moving her hand over her at a distance.

"Oh, that does me good! How I feel your love! It seems to me that your friendship is palpable, touching me like a caress. I sense, too, that we both feel the same grief, and are thinking the same thing; that consoles me. I would like to reveal that; I want to now, although I dreaded it once. How can I, though? How shall I be able to accept that you know my secret, who I am? Oh no, the mere idea that when I wake up, I shall know that you have discovered that he once loved me, and that I loved him too, that my Noémi is sister to your Jules, scares me, because I am too fearful of the grief it would cause you! Then again, do you know that, when I am awake, I am far from seeing you in the same manner as I do now? In truth, I'm afraid of you; you intimidate me with your status and the superiority of your mind. Try to inspire me to distance myself less from your intimacy."

"Very well! I shall direct my will in that direction; I strongly desire that you will entrust me with this confidence without dread or shame; I shall extract it gently..."

"No, no!" Poonah puts in, interrupting excitedly. "Please wait; it's not yet time. Especially since I never know how you've learned all that. It's necessary to treat my poor mind tenderly; it has so little to hold on to. It seems to me that my brain is in your hands, and that you might throw it on the ground, like something useless. Oh, dear Politée, I'm very calm, I know that you care for me as for yourself. Let me, therefore, remain for you, in my normal state, the pretended widow of the artillery-mechanic, until it is time for me to appear to your eyes as an Anglo-Indian princess, the daughter of the Rajah of Nepal."

"Yes, yes, have no fear—I promise you that."

"Wake me now, because I mustn't sleep any longer, without perceiving...."

Politée carefully dispels as many traces of that agitated sleep as she could; she takes up exactly the same position relative to her friend as they had before—and Poonah, rubbing her eyes, opens them in a half-astonished manner.

"I think I fell asleep," she says.

"And how are you, Poonah? Your headache and your nerves."

"My nerves are settled and calm, as they always become when you put me to sleep, but my head is a little weak."

"Dear Poonah," says Politée, putting a hand on the other's forehead for a moment.

"Ah, yes, that does my head good. Thank you, thank you. Where are the children?"

And then the conversation resumes its previous course.

Such a mundane manifestation of magnetism has no need to be explained to anyone. Everyone knows that all somniloquists, without exception, conserve no memory of what they have seen and experienced during their sleep; that many of them are extremely reluctant to hear any mention of it when they are awakened; and that some, to whom one cannot speak of it without dire consequences, can never be convinced that they have been asleep. As for the fairly general reluctance to enter into that extraordinary state or to submit to any influence, the epic poets and other writers of antiquity have represented it perfectly in scenes in which they have shown us Delphic priestesses and other inspired individuals.

It is easily divinable that Poonah must have complained one day about her nerves or her head in Politée's presence, and that the latter calmed her and put her to sleep. Then, having communicated a total confidence to her, in that state in which the soul of the fascinator displayed itself uncovered to that of the inspired, she received from Poonah all the confidences that she would never have betrayed outside ecstatic sleep. Moreover, Politée has never let her become aware of that in a waking state, and they have continued to treat one another in a normal manner.

The young lions, however, which have apparently not had a sufficient breakfast, are beginning to make noises a little less reassuring than those of a horse that scents the stable. That is the sole inconvenience of this kind of rig. The warning reminds Politée that it is time to return to the Villa of Hannibal. She and her son climb into the carriage again, and bid a further farewell to Poonah, who is sad to see them go. A young Moor closes the carriage door and leaps up to the driver's seat with the agility of a monkey—and the lions bound forward gracefully to resume their gallop.

V. Travels and Meetings

Paulo majora
Virgil.[23]

More and more powerful
Nicollet
(famous dramatic author of the 19th century).[24]

Movement is the condition of life. Since that is the case, people have never lived as much as they do in our time. It is now a question of finding out whether that is too much life. Did we not live better when we lived less?

The marvelous improvements that have, in the last two centuries, given the locomotive faculty of human-kind the greatest extension that it is capable of attaining, to all appearances, have produced singular effects on the physical constitution and moral condition of the human species.

On the one hand, the interbreeding of races and the mixing of nations have been effected more and more profoundly; the original types of the different varieties of

---

[23] This quotation is slightly truncated; it is usually rendered as *paulo majora canamus* [Let us sing of greater things].

[24] This attribution is misrepresented in almost every respect; Jean-Baptiste Nicolet (1728-1796) was a theatre-director of the 18th century famed for putting on spectacular shows, and the saying with which his name is associated is *"de plus en plus fort comme chez Nicolet"* [more and more powerful, as at Nicolet's].

he species have been gradually erased; languages have grown more similar and a few have almost disappeared; the passions, beliefs and individualities of populations are scarcely observable outside history, and the word "nationality" is beginning to lose any but a vague significance.

On the other hand, European mobility and anxiety have been given ample scope to exploit and perhaps even to torment the poor globe. Sedentary, internal and tranquil life, family affections, the love of the domestic hearth—which old England calls "home"—the simultaneously gentle and sad habituation to seeing the same trees, the same rocks, the same belfry, not to mention the same tombs, the tombs of our fathers, our kin, our friends, would all seem to near to being lost if the most stubborn sentiments of human nature were not indestructible.

Fortunately, too, one of the universal laws, which applies to the social life of human beings as well as their bodily movements, does not permit any reaction without reaction. A stopping-point has been reached, and not only has the locomotive fury abated, but the spirit of fixity has regained considerable favor in the most distinguished sector of society. The voyages of Europe's idlers to Africa or Asia are scarcely undertaken nowadays more than once a year, and we no longer live in an era in which a young man scarcely days show himself in a drawing-room, and finds difficulty is getting married, before having made his tour of the world.

To cap it all, the classification of different types of traveler that was made 50 years ago still holds good. Commerce still travels by sea, by canal, by river and by rail; the rich travel by air; the poor travel by carriage.

Philirène has been traveling thus while his bride-to-be awaited him, but this is not an age in which people go globe-trotting with no other objective but education or amusement. A highly important duty demanded his presence in Centropolis on the isthmus of Guatemala. Indeed, it was in this city, in the republic of Benthamia, that the Universal Congress met this year. He could hardly dispense with the accomplishment of the useful mission and the noble duty that gave him the honor, immense at his age, of presiding over that august gathering of the greatest and most illustrious intellectuals, industrialists and politicians in the world. He was the one who, in that capacity, had to open the session with a speech.

Those who have been present at a Universal Congress in one of the Earth's capitals have no need for anyone to describe the movement and life that its solemnities bring with them, and it was certainly impossible, without injustice or exciting keen jealousies, to avoid calling all the metropolises successively to that honor, accompanied by a circulation of several 100 millions.[25]

A prodigious number of aerostats of every size and shape—storks, pigeons or swallows, according to the status and wealth of the travelers—has come from every inhabited part of the world to set down on the vast plain that is Centropolis' landing-ground. Several delegates notably those from Australia, have come by sea. Some of those from the American continent have arrived overland.

---

[25] Bodin inserts a footnote: "It is unnecessary to make further observations regarding rates of exchange. There is no longer any question of translating sums in dollars or pounds sterling, since the French monetary system was adopted by the Universal Congress."

What can I say about them right away? How various—in their faces, their color, their form and their costumes, if not in their character—are the people of the highest class and the numerous individuals which comprise their followings! How many different languages one hears in the streets: sibilant languages and guttural languages, some tangled up in the consonants, others fattened in the vowels, as if filleted! In the reception-rooms, however, French—once the diplomatic language of Europe, now the intellectual and industrial language of the world—is predominant.

It is also to the reception-rooms that curiosity ranges to see and hear the individual celebrities of the epoch: the physicists, chemists, engineers, naturalists, technologists and philosophers of Europe and America; Oriental theosophs and poets; Indian or African moralists; Chinese agriculturalists and tradesmen. Then there are kings, more or less limited in their power, leaders of republics, and pontiffs of various religions, who have been sent quite simply as delegates to the Universal Congress by the states they govern or on which they exercise their spiritual influence. For the most part, they deem it a great honor to come here in person, whoever they have the privilege of representing here, assuming that their mandate is not exclusively attached to their abilities, but due in some small extent to their status.

Finally, women are not the least interesting fraction of the deliberative assembly, in which they have played a glorious role on more than one occasion. Frankly, that beautiful half of the human race has been unjustly treated for far too long, in being subject to an exclusion from business matters that did scant honor to masculine presumption and domination. When it was first decided to admit women to councils, precautions were still taken in that regard that were scarcely merited, in only giving them the right to vote without a consultative voice. Since they have been allowed to speak, it must be admitted— to the displeasure of vulgar and malicious jokers—that they have not abused it al all, and that discussions have not been extended by orators more loquacious than those who, at all times, take it upon themselves to temper by tedium that which might be irritating in deliberative struggles.

In sum, on examining what Centropolis brings together of science, virtue and talent, one cannot help thinking that those philosophical political or religious sects which have prohibited the elective method, as a poor instrument for bringing abilities into the light, are mistaken, in spite of the numerous examples that support their theory. It is more than doubtful that the hierarchical way, the election from high to low, can produce results as satisfactory. Doubtless there are capabilities in the world superior to those of this assembly; but that is in the nature of things. A body that must direct and moderate the movement of society should not represent the highest intelligences in society but the median level of the intelligence with which the society is provided.

I beg pardon for the little aphorism of political and social science that has just raised itself up in the middle of a modest story, with a rather pedantic self-assurance. I shall get back to the point.

There had been an initial suggestion that the assembly might be held in mid-air, as had been done a few years before in Calcutta, gathering 50 aerostats under an immense white taffeta tent, stacked on top of another.

This kind of *local*,[26] if I might be forgiven a vulgar expression, offers great advantages in the torrid zone. In going up to a higher altitude we find a temperature that is much more bearable and air that is more rarefied, purified and free of vapors, we clarify our ideas, almost lightening our minds and inclined to become detached from earthly things. In addition, the particular associations of spiritualists that flourish principally in Germany, and the academies of men and women instituted for the respectable aim of encouraging, honoring and propagating platonic love, and who are devoted to *excessive refinement*,[27] rarely fail to hold their sessions in aerial salons; there they have the advantage of being completely separated from the profane. One condition is indispensable for the success of this kind of meeting, however, which is that a perfect calm reigns in the upper regions of the air; without that, the deliberative assemblies run the risk of traveling long distances against their will.

---

[26] The French word *local* (literally, premises; in argot, a bedroom) does not have the same slang implications as the English term "local," which is narrowly applied to public houses, but there is enough similarity of implication to sustain the direct transcription, and it would be pushing vulgarity too far to substitute "knocking shop."

[27] The italicized word I have translated as "excessive refinement," *quintessencier,* means "to extract the essence [from something]" and does not always carry the implication that such a practice is injurious. The German idealist philosophers who are mischievously bracketed with enthusiasts for chaste and platonic love might be regarded as *quintessenciers* in a non-pejorative sense, but Bodin evidently means to insult them, so it seems appropriate to reproduce the implication, albeit a little more brutally than he does.

Aquatic halls also have their merits with regard to holding assemblies in warm countries, or in others during heat-waves. They have done marvelous service in Holland, China and Japan. Lake Geneva, a few years ago, was host to what was certainly the most ingenious application of a simple hydraulic process in which a jet of water was caused to fall back in the form of a hemisphere, like one of those glass bell-jars in which clocks or other objects are sometimes placed. It was said to be a truly curious sight: an assembly of 400 or 500 people separated by a great circular raft from the tranquil and diaphanous surface of the lake, set beneath a vast cupola that might have been taken for crystal, so uniform, homogeneous and polished was the immense sheet of water formed by the uninterrupted flow. Unfortunately, that kind of moist roof has even less protection against accidents than other human constructions; everyone knows that at the moment when the discussion in the erudite assembly suddenly becomes heated, the apparatus will break down and the beautiful sheet of water will fall like an unexpected downpour on to their heads, which will be sharply cooled again. That said, a hall of this type offers great advantages in terms of acoustics. It is an idea that I recommend to the attention of architects who have to build concert halls.

As for the ascensional method, it has been renounced, quite independently of the troublesome conditions in the atmosphere, in respect of the opening session, in order not to abuse a means of rendering the solemnities imposing, which strikes the popular imagination very forcibly. If I might be permitted one last digression, I recall, with respect to this subject, that it is for the proclamation and promulgation of resolutions of the Universal Congress, above all else, that aerial sessions produce the most powerful effects. No one will ever forget that it was in this way that the memorable Congress of Constantinople terminated its long and glorious session, of which the result has been the establishment of a new human right, centralizing the power of human reason and changing the destiny of hundreds of millions of individuals. On a serene and gentle night whose fame will last forever, as beautiful as any night on the Hellespont, the august assembly, floating over the former site of the seraglio, voted its great law in two articles:

War is Prohibited.
Slavery and Polygamy are Abolished on Earth.

That law appeared immediately to an innumerable audience that had crowded the shores of Asia and Europe in order to be witness to such an innovative spectacle. It appeared and was promulgated in letters of flame in all languages, in the midst of the lightning-flashes and thunderbolts of the 6000 cannon protecting the neutrality of Constantinople, and all the fiery prodigies with which the pyrotechnics dazzled and delighted the eyes. Spiteful individuals did not hesitate to say that civilization, in that huge consumption of gunpowder, was making a sacrilegious parody of Mount Sinai, and that it was unnecessary, in proclaiming a law of peace, to break every window in Constantinople—but the fact is that a racket like that must have been very impressive, and in order to be finished with the business of warfare, civilization could not have designed a more worthy funeral. It is also true that warfare has not completely disappeared, and that, in place of slavery and polygamy, there are other miseries and other abuses, but that does not make the gesture worthless. After all, there has been,

as everyone knows, manifest amelioration and real progress; that is certainly something. I mean that seriously.

VI. A Rural Amphitheater

The voice of the human race is the voice of God.
Free translation of the Bible.

This is another chapter in regard to which I am not without anxiety relative to the gracious subscribers to reading rooms. I imagine their pretty fingers turning with disdainful rapidity and crumpling bad-temperedly the pages of a book that threatens to do them the gravest of wrongs: that of boring them. I even thought I saw, just now, their charming mouths contracting slightly in an entirely genteel *moue*, the usual symptom—discreetly suppressed, it is true—of a disjunction of the maxillary system that physicians employing vapor treatments, in the days when they existed, called by the technical term "pandiculation"[28] but which is more generally known as a yawn. To complete this description of a fairly common phenomenon of the nervous system, and to demonstrate the extent to which I am here sacrificing all authorial self-respect, I have already imagined several of my amiable female readers, no longer able to resist the sadly magnetic effect of these pages, abandoning them without ever taking them up again, extending their delicate arms and finally shedding a few of those tears which, alas, are not tears of compassion. It is a singular jest of nature that

---

[28] "Pandiculation"—the word is identical in French and English—means stretching, and is more usually applied to stretching one's limbs on awakening than to flexing one's jaw, although it will serve in either case.

has permitted boredom to adorn itself ridiculously with one of the symptoms of our noble emotions and our poignant sorrows, which has often allowed me— scarcely tearful in appearance— to pass, during the performance of some play or other, for an individual endowed with an unexpected sensibility.

Having excused myself with such good grace relative to the fraction of my not-very-numerous audience whose approval I hold most dear, I beg them to have a little patience, to skim rapidly thorough the boring chapters, and, above all, not to give evidence before witnesses of a displeasure that disfigures the prettiest of faces, and which, in addition, can do a great deal of damage to the success of a work.

The place in Centropolis ordinarily devoted to conferences or to the assemblies, 100 times more numerous, which come to hear some great musical performance or some famous orator, has all the picturesque and majestic simplicity of the rustic arenas that have been increasing in number for more than a century in various parts of the world. Everyone knows that sites of this sort—the customary choices of Methodist preachers in Great Britain and North America, deep valleys hollowed out by nature in the form of a funnel between hills that join together in circular fashion, such as the one not far from Hampstead rendered famous by enormous popular assemblies—are marvelously favorable both acoustically and visually, giving the impression of open-air halls. Considerable use was made of them in antiquity, and the Germanic nations knew no other, but the tradition was lost in the Middle Ages, when political assemblies had fallen gradually into disuse; nevertheless, modern history has produced numerous examples in the southern countries of Europe, whether for assizes, plenary courts or the courts of love instituted by chivalric gallantry.

Nature has contributed a great deal to the rustic hall of Centropolis, but art has not spared its efforts. On one side there is a sheer rock-face composed of superimposed prismatic layers of basalt, rising like a big wall to a height of about 50 feet. On the other, there is an almost semicircular hill, whose gentle slope extends almost to the base of the rock, closely approximating the customary form of an amphitheater—and it was not necessary to import a considerable mass of earth to attain an exact resemblance. The site is occupied by those immense trees of the virgin American forests whose elevation leaves 30 or 40 feet of freely-circulating air beneath their foliage. This roof of verdure is entirely impenetrable to the Sun's rays. Canvas sheets coated with rubber are disposed at intervals, extendable in the blink of an eye thanks to a very simple mechanism to provide shelter from the rain. Steps or banks of grass are set all around the semi-circular slope. This is the amphitheater that accommodates the assembly, in which some people are provided with armchairs, others with divans or cushions, according to taste or their national fashion of sitting or lying. Others, preferring patriarchal simplicity, extend themselves on the scented grass, dappled with flowers.

The President's armchair and the seats of the conference-table are situated at the foot of the rock, on a bizarre basaltic promontory, in the lowest part of the quasi-natural hall, ornamented by a curtain of olive-trees. One climbs up there by a stairway, which it was scarcely necessary to hollow out in the rock. A podium of turf has been fabricated slightly below that level, according to the acoustic principle that sounds always tend to rise up. A limpid stream whose spring is nearby runs silently in a straight line in front of the podium, as if to remind the orators of the principles of moderation, brevity and clarity of language. But the most remarkable peculiarity of this conference amphitheater is the procedure by means of which the shabby and prosaic hand-bell used by former presidents has been replaced. When the assembly becomes too noisy and tumultuous, the president only has to press a button and two large waterfalls suddenly cascade down either side of the rock into two deep ravines, in which the water is noisily engulfed.

One might think that the small voice of human passion would fall silent before the more imposing voice of nature, but one can get used to anything, as birds do to scarecrows, and you may be sure that, in spite of the warning of the stream, there are still orators who are verbose, obscure and intemperate.

Finally, to conclude this description—for which I have been obliged to pause, as with any object unfamiliar to most of my readers—the external perimeter of the amphitheater is overlooked by an elegant portico in marble from the isthmus, designed for spectators of the session and surmounted at intervals by statues of benefactors of humankind and great legislators who have influenced its destiny.

Although the population of Centropolis only amounts, as yet, to 350,000 souls—which is nevertheless quite impressive for a city that is scarcely 150 years old—the crowd summoned by the solemnity of the opening ceremony of the Congress is immense; all the bells are ringing and the streets through which the crowds must pass in procession on their way to the meeting-place are decorated with sumptuous hangings, superb paintings and bunches of flowers.

No solemn celebration can be commenced with dignity without a religious ceremony—religion has to be involved in every important circumstance of the life of nations, as in that of individuals—but the diversity of beliefs, each with its own prescribed rites and prohibitions, according to the preferences of some particular cult, has led to a simplification of religious ritual, generalizing it into a form acceptable to everyone.

When the entire assembly has gathered, the president gives the signal by prostrating himself on the ground. A hundred cannon—whose explosive clamor, in these peaceful times, only serves as a manifestation of public sentiment—are fired simultaneously, not only bringing the entire assembly to its knees, but also 100,000 people thronging a neighboring valley, singing a universal hymn in chorus.

The Benthamian population is so skilled in music that the four-part choral performance leaves nothing to be desired. In order that the powerful rhythm should be marked at the same time by a mass of performers distribute over such a vast space, a large flag, set at the top of a pole not far from the colossal statue of Bentham and moved by means of levers by the president of the republic's musical institutions, communicates the beat by means of its precise and regular movement to the most distant eyes. The harmony of the piece is complete, everyone having long ago chosen the part that best suits his or her voice and the entire chorus having been memorized by everyone. The complete freedom of the performers results, it is true, in some of the intermediate parts being somewhat neglected, but, by way of compensation—and this is what is essential—the melody and the bass are marked with a very ample vigor. Besides, all the voices are supported by an orchestra of 10,000 artistes and amateurs, which sets and maintains the tone. What is more, without denying the power of harmony, it must be admitted that the stanza that produces the most powerful effect is the one that is executed entirely in unison. For myself, I know of nothing beneath the surface of the heavens more capable of moving me, swelling my breast, making me tremble on the brink of tears and causing my brain to vibrate to the point of vertigo, than 100,000 voices singing in chorus.

I thought that I ought to emphasize these details, because it seems to me that they will interest those musicians who have only heard assemblies of a few thousand voices and have not had the opportunity to witness a *festival* or a *musical meeting* [29] planned on such a scale. But I ought to make the observation here that it is not on ground level that an audience ought to be placed in order fully to appreciate such musical effects; its members ought to be positioned at a height of about 800 feet. More than 500 aerostats, which accommodate every elegant lady in the upper echelons of Centropolis society, are also floating above that vast and magnificent scene, and the 1000 colors in which they are decked out form a rainbow of an entirely new sort. At that height, the sound of 100,000 voices and instruments reaches the ears in delightful fusion, as a single sound of an indefinable character, like an immense mist of harmony, of the most ineffable sweetness.

---

[29] Bodin gives both italicized expressions in English, although it is not obvious why he should choose to do so. (There were, after all, both French and English choirs present on the Field of the Cloth of Gold, which seems to be the kind of assembly he has in mind in this flight of fancy.)

When the hymn is finished, the assembly rises to its feet *en masse*, and everyone simultaneously extends a hand towards the rock-wall, where the formula of the oath is traced in garlands of foliage, swearing everyone to work for MORAL AMELIORATION AND THE HAPPINESS OF HUMANKIND.

Then the assembly sits down again, and the President, who has remained standing, expresses himself in these terms:

VII. A Solemn Discourse

My intention is to propose means of bringing
perpetual peace to all Christian nations.
Should anyone ask me what qualifications
I have to treat such an elevated and important
question, I have nothing to say in response.
Preface to the Abbé Saint-Pierre's
Projet de paix perpétuelle.[30]

I pray the Lord to bless His design.
Advertisement of Antoine Schouten,
bookseller of Utrecht, 1715.

The question at issue before you, gentlemen,
involves the destiny of the world.
Discours sur la pêche de la morue
dans une chambre du 19ème siècle.[31]

---

[30] Charles Irénée Castel, Abbé de Saint-Pierre (1658-1743), not to be confused with the more famous writer Bernardin de Saint-Pierre, was a pioneer of economic and social science and a would-be political reformer who was expelled from the Académie Française for holding subversive opinions. He is credited with introducing the word *bienfaisance* [benevolence] into the French language, but his reputation was unjustly harmed when Jean-Jacques Rousseau took the trouble to condemn him as an impractical Utopian. The quoted work sets out an ambitious prospectus for a federal Europe.

[31] The title of this presumably-pornographic text, which might or might not be fictitious, translates as "A Discourse on Codfishing in the 19th century Bedroom."

"Noble intellectual capabilities, illustrious industrial powers, I bow before you.

"The satisfactory state of the terrestrial globe invites our hearts to rise up in gratitude towards the Divinity, invoking the continuation of His benefits.

"Humanity is happier than at any previous time; it enjoys the fruits of the memorable treaty of Constantinople and the wise laws with the aid of which the Universal Congress has continued to interpret and fortify it, in ensuring its execution.

"Save for a few disorders in the other hemisphere, principally in Asia—disorders of which I shall have the honor of acquainting you—the peace of the world has not been significantly troubled.

"Not only has strife between various political systems been completely abandoned, as if by exhaustion, but the rivalry of peoples and territorial ambitions are almost extinct, now that individual and commercial liberty is written into universal law. The most heterogeneous governments co-exist on good terms. The extreme facility with which families may move around, and the tendency to emigration that has been noticeable in populations for more than a century, has rendered governments so careful of people's welfare, in order to retain them on native ground, that they have not neglected any means to improve and render more economical the administration that is now the sole purpose of government.

"Religious, philosophical and political beliefs too exclusive to support the proximity of different beliefs have, in the course of the last century, been subject to triage and classification, each one isolating itself in some part of the world in order to develop at its ease. Some people feared that such isolation would only increase their fanaticism and intolerance; fortunately, the opposite has been the case. Finding themselves devoid of contradiction, resistance and the stimulus of an ever-present rivalry, alone in the face of their rigorous consequences, they seem to have wearied of their own contemplation, to have become bored with themselves, and are tending to resume their place in the hurly-burly of civilization."

(There is a stir of approval.)

"The easy relationships manifest among this august assembly are the most striking proof of this disposition to understanding and tolerance. Some people even dread that harmony might be extended to the point of lethargy, but, to consider only religious beliefs, frequent reliable reports on the recent correspondence that has taken place between the sovereign pontiff of Christianity, the great mufti of reformed Islam and he high priest of Buddhism have assured us that people have not been led by examples set on high to too great an indifference to matters of dogma and ritual."

(Gazes are directed towards the Pope's bench, occupied by his legate, who is sitting next to the Great Mufti's emissary, wearing a slight smile.)

"Nevertheless, I shall not attempt to hide from you the gravity of the symptoms presented in Asia by the exploits of the warriors of polygamists, despots and slave-masters, the audacity of aerial brigands—who infest all regions of the atmosphere alike, even extending their depredations to Europe—and the no less culpable and immoral actions of modern Amazons. I shall also pause to consider the exorbitant extension to which the right of association appears to aspire."

("Hear hear!")

"You have understood that I am alluding to the projects, nowadays scarcely disguised, of the Association which has, for a long time, hidden beneath the title *Poetic* or *Universal Anti-Prosaic* its evident *anti-civilization* tendency."

("Hear hear!")

"The almost encouraging reception that it has given to requests for help addressed to it by agitators threatening terrestrial peace is sufficient indication of its real purpose. This subject demands your serious attention. Without wishing to prejudice your discussions, I might remind you of the established principles and the social jurisprudence of the Congress is such matters.

"Every portion of the human race, where it calls itself an association or a nation, certainly has the right to regulate itself by laws that render it as unhappy as it likes, but it does not have the right to make individuals unhappy against their will. The supreme social power ought only to intervene with the greatest circumspection for the suppression of violence exercised in contempt of its laws, but there are cases in which such intervention is its duty.

"Since governments no longer maintain permanent armies, the exercise of social force has passed into the hands of auxiliary associations which, to uphold the principles of the Congress, deploy considerable forces in the field, with the aid of subscriptions open to everyone on Earth. It is by that means that the recent wars against slavery and polygamy have been sustained.

"Opposing associations, however, believe that they have an equal right to compete with and triumph over the resistance of rival principles. This is a source of disorder, and it is important to declare that this claim has never been recognized by the Universal Congress.

"When the Association for Commercial Liberty asked the Congress for authorization to raise an army of 200,000 men, 100 steam-batteries, etc., and to equip 80 ships of the line to force the Chinese to abolish their import duties, the request to be denied, because it was not proven that the Chinese were dissatisfied by the privation of foreign products, but that was not the end of the matter. If the prohibitive society had still existed, no doubt it would have been perfectly in order to offer subsidies or aid to the Chinese government, but when unequivocal manifestations of the determination of the Chinese nation to enter into commercial and intellectual relations with other nations burst forth from all points of that empire, then the Congress could not help but make an exception by which China was removed from the law of commercial liberty and permission was given to employ force to constrain the Chinese government in its execution. By the same token, if ancient prohibitive opinion had clung to the determination to be ready to support Chinese import duties against the nation itself, it is improbable that the Congress would have tolerated it. Well, that procedure applies even more strictly to present circumstances, in which it is no longer a matter of commercial interests but the life and liberty of millions of people."

(Numerous lively expressions of approval.)

"If, therefore, it is necessary to allocate strong support to the zeal of the Association for Civilization, which keeps watch with a numerous army, and sometimes repels enemy incursions, you will doubtless make that allocation, in spite of the insufficiency of our annual income, and you may take that sum from the communal social security funds included in the budget of humankind, which reserves for the most difficult circumstances the sale of a few million square leagues of desert territory in Africa and Australia."

(Obvious agreement.)

"One matter, fortunately not urgent, and to which you have devoted the attention of a permanent committee, may be postponed without inconvenience to another session. I am referring to the petition of more than ten million Israelites ("Hear hear!"), in Judea and various countries of the world, to obtain the withdrawal of your opposition to the proposition that the 580 millions raised by their subscription be applied to the rebuilding of the Temple in Jerusalem. Considering that this request touches a delicate question of religious faith, and interests the peace of mind of a significant fraction of humankind, the Jewish government itself, in agreement with its parliament, more enlightened than that part of the nation, is not much disposed to support a project whose utility and ease of achievement are not obvious. It prefers that the ancient rites, such as animal sacrifices, should continue to be carried out in remote places, as in Samaria, in order not to injure the relations of commerce and friendship that exist between Jews and Christians."

(The high priest of the Jews rises to his feet and asks to speak in person. The papal legate does likewise. The observation is made to these honorable members that the moment for consideration of the question has not yet arrived.)

"All in all, the Jewish government and the enlightened part of the nation think that the sum would be better employed in the drainage work that might return the Dead Sea to health and redirect the water into the river Jordan. At any rate, the file on this serious business has been sent on several camels to the committee whose sessions are held in Babylon; it had notified me that its report is not yet ready.

"Summoned, at the close of your last session, to the honor of presiding over this Congress during the session that is commencing, I have, in the interval between the two meetings, with the enlightened agreement of your permanent officials, given all my attention to the questions of humanitarian interest that you have reserved for subsequent consideration. We shall have the honor of submitting to you a proposition for legislation on the means of guaranteeing property rights in important inventions and works of art in all the nations of the world. This difficult matter will require long discussions and, without taking into account the proposals that individual initiative might bring forth or international matters that demand prompt solution, the present session will be sufficiently full.

"I shall conclude by remarking that the introduction of the triennial interval between the meetings of this august Congress has had good results. The effervescent activity of minds, which presses them, often unreflectively, towards novelties whose failed trials only serve to compromise the real progress of the human race, has been visibly calmed by this measure. Questions now have time to ripen, thanks to discussion in the press and local assemblies; and the free concourse of all human intelligences and interests thus prepares for your deliberation the elements of solutions that conform most closely to experience and reason."

This discourse is welcomed by excited exclamations repeated in all languages: *Glory to God, Peace on Earth!* The assembly is suspended for a quarter of an hour, and animated conversations break out in all parts of the hall.

After the official announcement that the session is open, it proceeds with the nominal appeal to all the members to take note of absentees, to take brief account of the apologies presented, and to admit their substitutes. When the name of the beautiful Politée, the delegate of the estates of Carthage, is pronounced—not without some emotion—by Philirène, all eyes go with lively curiosity to the place where she usually sits. Her apology, based on her sister's marriage, whose imminent celebration retains her in Carthage, is admitted without discussion. The gazes turn towards Philirène, who blushes slightly, and a good deal of whispering is manifest in the assembly.

It is not my intention to say anything more about this session of the Universal Congress, interesting though some of its remarkable discussions might be to a small section of my audience. It is only important, for the understanding of this true history, to say that the assembly has voted an annual sum of 750 millions to the Association for Civilization until the conclusion of the war that it is sustaining in Asia against polygamists, despots and their associates. Not included in this aid is a special allocation of 150 millions for the useful institution of *storks*, great aerial battleships equipped to undertake crusades against birds of prey and to occupy surveillance-posts in various mountain ranges close to those pirates' lairs.

As for the truly anti-humanitarian activities of the Poetic or Anti-Prosaic Association, the assembly has delayed any pronouncement until that society, opposed to the resolutions of the Congress, has made its intentions manifest by patent and decidedly hostile actions.

A part of the public, far from approving of the conduct of the Congress on this last point, has judged it too circumspect and hesitant. It is thought that the association in question would take this moderation for timidity, and will redouble its arrogance. I will have occasion later on to inform the reader as to the extent to which that anticipation was justified.

VIII. An Intellectual Hero

No man is a hero to his valet.
Old French saying.

Although it would be well worth the reader's trouble to pause for some time in Centropolis and the Republic of Benthamia, so that he or she might observe the rather curious customs of the inhabitants of that country, I shall reserve what I have to say about the Benthamians for another time. I therefore invite the reader to come with me into ethereal space, where a numerous aerial convoy is sailing northwards over the Columbian hemisphere. This flying caravan is on patrol, ready to engage birds of prey—aerial pirates better known by the vulgar name of *fly-swatters*—who attack travelers with a truly incredible audacity.

Philirène's aerostat is mixed in with all the rest, for Philirène is no longer the leader here; he has returned to private life and, as a modest individual, in spite of his vast fortune, he only has some 30 followers, including the crew maneuvering his swallow,[32] a 50-ton vessel.

The minority of readers who have taken the trouble to follow this story attentively will have understood that in recounting the principal circumstances of the session

---

[32] Bodin italicizes and capitalizes the French word *hirondelle* [swallow] here, as if it were the name of the vessel, but he subsequently reverts to uncapitalized roman type; as he has previously used the term generically, I have unified its usage in that manner.

of the Universal Congress, we have gone backwards in time and placed ourselves in a period anterior to the events that have just occurred in Carthage, and which we entered *mediis rebus*,[33] as the ancient critics used to say. Now that the session has ended—having lasted far too long for the liking of the impatient Mirzala—Philirène has to travel to Carthage via France, in order to do the final shopping for his wedding in Paris, which is still the metropolis of luxury and good taste.

Philirène, therefore, has no suspicion as yet of the act of perfidy and violence so successfully perpetrated against his bride to be, nor the cruel disappointment that awaits him on his return. Even so, he is sad and preoccupied; one might think that he is agitated by some presentiment. Having no need to oversee the maneuvering of the rudder, in view of the propitious atmospheric conditions, he is in the bow of the swallow, in the little triangular gallery built into the very beak of the bird, in front of the room that occupies part of its head. This space, specially reserved by the captains of aerial vessels as their observatory, their office or their boudoir, is the place where Philirène usually goes when the members of his staff are busy playing games, reading, making music or painting. He has had it decorated with an elegance and good taste that would once have passed for magnificence.

After pausing momentarily at the telescope that is always aimed at the space into which the ship is heading, and having darted a glance at the compass fixed in the ceiling, he slumps down upon a sofa, putting his hand to

---

[33] "In the middle of things."

his painful forehead. His faithful Eupistos,[34] who is not so much a secretary as a friend, is sitting in front of him, looking at him with an expression of sorrow and commiseration, without breaking the silence that has briefly suspended their conversation.

We can take advantage of this moment to observe the two of them.

I have never read a novel without experiencing sentiments of veritable compassion for characters who are fat, plump-cheeked and ruddy-faced, who enjoy the perfect equilibrium of the humors and that abundant circulation of the blood that advertise an inalterable tranquility of the soul, complete self-satisfaction and excellent health: fortunate symptoms of a constitution over which the passions cannot exact long empire, and which is often beyond their reach. It seems to me that these men ought to be seriously mortified by never finding heroes in novels who resemble them in the slightest. As things stand, they are condemned to the dissatisfaction of encountering in books none but tall men with pale faces and bilious temperaments dominated by their nervous systems—passionate men, in short!

I myself shall have the annoyance of augmenting what I ascribe quite gratuitously to fat, plump-cheeked and ruddy-faced men. In fact, I too have an exceedingly pale hero to show them, but I will console them a little by telling them that is not the kind of noble pallor that creates passions by collecting, as it were, all the blood in some burning interior hearth. It is a pallor that is almost puny and painful. It is not the pallor of bilious heroes but

---

[34] *Eupistos* is presumably intended to be decoded as "good [and] faithful," but it might be worth noting that the Greek *pistos* can also signify "easily convinced."

that of a constitution that is both nervous to the highest degree and phlegmatic—or lymphatic, if you prefer; in sum, it is that of a skeptical philanthrope.

Such therefore is, at first glance, Philirène's appearance. I fear that he will scarcely appeal to my beautiful female readers, but that does not discourage me overmuch; they have Philomaque by way of compensation.

Philirène's delicate constitution, entirely incompatible with heroic proportions, is not, however, incompatible with slimness and elegance. His spiritually expressive physiognomy is ordinarily imprinted with a melancholy that is not unfamiliar in noble and fine features. Even so, his smile sometimes lacks charm, because it does not seem to reflect a soul at ease with any conviction. There is more benevolence to be found in it than sympathy, and one searches it in vain for any indication of a contended heart subject to lively bounds, whose beating is profound and relaxed. His eyes, which first call attention to themselves by their singular clear-sightedness, sometimes have that insouciant fixity that does not really see, and which chills because it is thought to be disdainful. As a matter of habit, he avoids meeting gazes that are too direct, not because he has the least dread of letting them look into him, but as if reluctant to squander unnecessarily his own capacity to look into others. When he wants to exercise it, though, his gaze acts promptly, with a dissolving power; like a chemist's reagent, it renders evil thoughts as visible as a precipitate.

His friend, by contrast, is a handsome young man with sparkling eyes, a mystical expression and long black hair.

"Have you fallen back into your vague mental state of disgust for everything, dear Philrène? You are, however, not far distant now from the moment when strong and intoxicating emotions ought to renew your self-respect—and your faith in yourself, for even that is lacking in you. I thought that you would carry a more excitement away from Centropolis, where you occupied the foremost chair in the world, than you would need to arrive in Carthage without suffering any moral subsidence."

"My dear friend, it's entirely a matter of self-respect. A long time ago, I formed a very exact idea of the position that I occupy, that a thousand others could occupy as well as me, and which proves absolutely nothing in my favor. Doubtless there is a moment of intoxication when one take it upon oneself to think that one is dealing with immense questions, affecting the interests of hundreds of millions of people, but when one is unsure of the final outcome of it all, it's difficult not to feel disappointed."

"How could anyone believe, if they heard you thinking aloud like that, that it is Philirène who is speaking?—the man who, in facing the world, as it were, seemed so convinced of the importance and sanctity of his mission, who always found a language so elevated, in spite of its simplicity, and such apt imagery to inspire a spirit of moral order and love of humanity!"

"My God! Don't you start flattering me as well."

"You know full well that I don't usually flatter you, but as to what you say and what you do—for your actions are in accord with your words—well, even though you aren't convinced, I certainly am. I believe, with all my heart and soul in…I won't say in your work, because you're no more than one of its instruments…in the work of humankind."

"Much good may it do you," says Philirène, with a smile that is humorous but not sarcastic. Resuming his sober and affectionate tone, he goes on: "Yes, much good may it do you, dear Eupistos; you have the benefit of a strong and sincere faith, a good fortune that I never cease to envy. I've sought that faith everywhere. I've been to Kantopolis to live among the spiritualists, the doctors of pure reason. I've visited Organopolis, the city of physiologists, whose entire society and politics is based on the study of the physical constitution of individuals, where all questions are subordinate to the observations of skulls, physiognomies and temperaments—where, ultimately, they expect to rectify our evil tendencies physiologically, modifying our temperaments by smoothing out the vexatious protuberances of our heads. Nowhere have I seen the image of a moral and happy society, as I hoped. I have been afflicted by the prodigious quantity of cheerful rogues and prosperous rascals that abound everywhere—and, it must be said, at least as much among the spiritualists and the dogmatists as among these Benthamian sybarites among whom we have lived most recently.

"Who knows how some achieve the accommodation of their conscience, or how to explain the inconsequentiality of interest in others? But I'm equally frightened when I think that, wherever people affiliate themselves to individual duty or the law of universal order, evildoers necessarily commit their infamous sacrileges, and that, wherever one strives for an accord between individual interest and universal happiness, the good can only be sublime idiots.

"I want to believe in the absolute—in the model of the best, the true ideal—with all the passion of my heart, not as I actually do, tamely, also admitting the real: the material world that presses upon me on all sides whether I like it or not, and which seems to be there to give the lie to the abstract, incessantly and ironically, making it seem an impossible illusion. I want to arrive at the exalted faith of the pure psychologist who, pursuing the absolute from argument to argument, gradually disembarrasses himself of matter like a burdensome garment, and finishes up denying everything. However comfortable that position might be, though, it's not up to me to take it. I don't have the good fortune of being able to deny matter, although I have the ill fortune of not being able to reckon it a source of well-being."

"Matter is doubtless imperfect," said Eupistos, "but I, personally, have the good fortune to believe that it the sole principle of evil is therein. Don't you believe, though, as I do, that the sum of evil has continually diminished, and that it will continue to diminish on Earth, in accordance with the law of progress, until the era when it will have completely disappeared?"

"Ah! There, my friend, is the door by which I have always sought to escape discouragement—but I doubt that men will ever be better and happier than in the past. I see many new miseries replacing the old, many new needs born of the multiplicity of pleasures. Even supposing that physical evil has diminished, has not moral evil—that which is produced by the actions of human will—perhaps increased? Doubtless evil is no longer done as violently, as brutally as it was in the times of ignorance and barbarity, but as enlightenment spread among peoples, it has had to clothe itself in other forms: polite and elegant forms. It is evil nonetheless, and, as the morality of an act is appreciable less in its material result than its correspondence with the intelligence of the actor, I would go so far as to say that in doing less evil, but with more reflection, enlightened humankind is more malevolent than barbaric and passionate humankind. The latter had excuses for its evil, and more merit in its good."

"Personally, I think it's an abuse of reason to take away humankind's credit for its amelioration in that fashion."

"Well then, I agree that evil has diminished—but I have the greatest difficulty believing that it was disappear. That supposition is contrary to the operation of the analogy that only admits similar terms. Between two terms in a progression there is analogy, but between a sum of evil, however small it might be, and its total disappearance, there is not. That is the abyss that separates the relative from the absolute. I admit that it's a little subtle, but when subtleties answer hypotheses, I don't see that anyone has the right to complain.

"If we can only diminish the sum of evil, the difference between the past and the future can only be a matter of more or less—and the more I think about it, the more I see how unimportant the size of the dose is to the fundamental question. What does it matter to me, who wants to have found, like you and many other brave men, that port in which my storm-tossed and exhausted mind might drop anchor, the absolute good—be it religious or philosophical—that we come down to rendering certain accidents and disorders rarer or less grave, certain pains less excruciating? The accursed question of evil, which the philosophers and fathers of the Church have circled around so often without finding a satisfactory solution, is still there to bring despair.

"In order to be finished with the problem of evil, the ancient and almost universal dogmatic tradition that Christianity continues, for the greater moral good of a considerable fraction of humanity, has informed us of the end of the world. I have no opinion on the eternal or temporary nature of universal matter, but I can easily believe that this terrestrial world will end somehow. Well, that only reduces the question to the proportions of a mere planetary affair, without resolving it at all. I would infinitely prefer to agree with your annihilation of evil, but, in either case, the multitude of human generations whose misery has been profoundly felt, albeit decreasing and necessary to progressive order, seems to me as an immense victim sacrificed to a pitiless divinity.

"I mourn the entire unhappy human past, as I lament the many wretches endowed by nature with inclinations to every kind of crime, and the many poor devils born without bread and without any aptitude for work. Is there, then, a law of the physical world: a law that is fatal and absolute, superior even to the very divinity that is all justice, all generosity, but which cannot be all-powerful? Does that law, then, by which evil is the condition and the necessary correlative of physical and moral wellbeing, embody the principle of its progressive mitigation—or, if you wish, a providential intelligence charged with its mitigation? These are only hypotheses, to which reason does not know how to attach itself. Even supposing that they offer an explanation, though, they cannot give satisfaction. When relative evil has disappeared, relative good, by a rigorous consequence, will also have disappeared. Then, you tell me, there will be absolute good: that good that our intelligence cannot conceive. So much the better, I reply, for those who will be there—but what of the past, the unhappy past!"

"Oh, my friend, are you trying to put your discouragement into my soul too? No, happily, my faith sustains me."

"God forbid, dear Eupistos, that I would want to deprive others of a benefit that I desire for myself. On the contrary, after having exposed my doubts, as a sick man reveals his infirmities, I shall show you, not heroic remedies, for I cannot, but the palliatives that I apply to them. Do you think that if I did not have some idea of being good for something, of fulfilling a ministry agreeable of God, that I would consent to live the active, often painful life that I do, bearing thus the cross of civilization?—me, who would like it 100 times better to dwell quietly in some remote corner of the Earth, living the pastoral life whose image in the Bible and the antique poets enchants me: that monotonous and often solitary life, in which human industry would leave me in peace, in which I would no longer be deafened by the noise and importuned by the sight of machines; in which I would be in the presence of simple nature, dreading nothing but its rigors, enjoying nothing but its benefits?"

"There's that bucolic exaltation that kings always have on their thrones, citizens in their cities and generals on their battlefields."

"All right, I see the joke. But it's still the case that, in view of the trouble in my mind, I've interrogated my conscience. Although it might perhaps be no more than the reflection of customs and moral beliefs in the midst of which we live, I think that it ought to be consulted in preference to reason—because all of us ought, whatever the circumstances, to accept the judgment of the tribunal of humankind, while humankind will never consent to each individual accepting no judge but himself. I have therefore made my conscience the conscience of the human species, and it is with the aid of that guide that I grope my way along all the paths of life, leaving it the responsibility of my actions.

"I sincerely desire the good; I seek it in the midst of clouds that sometimes make it difficult to make it out, and which render the means of doing it confidently—of doing it with the least quantity of evil, when an evil is indispensable to brig about a greater good—even more obscure. In that research, pressed by the necessity of playing a part and taking action, I sometimes experience frightful perplexities, but I set out to ascertain the majority opinion and to follow it, and I dedicate myself to carry out, without entire conviction, the will of the human species."

"If virtue and heroism consist in self-sacrifice, you're certainly a virtuous man, a hero—and as you go as far as sacrificing your thoughts, I would call you an intellectual hero."

"Many thanks," says Philirène, smiling. "But I admit to you that, in total, I have sacrificed very little as yet."

"I'm well aware of that," says Eupistos.

The conversation taking a more lively turn, more in conformity with the extreme flexibility of Philirène's ideas, the two friends talk successively about science, art and literature, and then set about improvising the music that my female readers would have greatly preferred to the boring conversation with which this chapter has been filled. I forgot to warn them, and probably should have made up for it somehow—but I swear to them that this chapter is the last in which there will be any philosophical drivel.

IX. An Aerial Combat

The empire belongs to science.
Anonymous.

Having as little time to pause in Paris as Philirène—who only stayed there for one day, which was just sufficient for him do his shopping for the wedding and visit three or four savants of the first order—I promise my readers to show them the French capital on another occasion. I invite them to climb back with that impatient lover into his pretty swallow, so sprightly, joyful and shiny as it spreads its large wings—which are not darkly colored, like those of the bird whose name it bears, but almost white, for the light does not have too deleterious an effect on its light rigging.

The cargo is augmented by the richest collection of diaphanous, silky and velvety fabrics of every sort, every color and every pattern, in which gold, silver, diamonds, pearls and precious stones are mingled with discreet and elegant taste. There are also jewels, plumes for feathers, flowers, and a host of those pretty trifles whose names exist only in the language of the moment. Finally, there are two Parisian chambermaids, exceedingly clever and skilled in putting on and taking off the most ingenious costumes without allowing themselves to be disturbed in the important exercise of their duty by impatience or by unduly animated chatter and occasional gestures.

Filled with this brilliant cargo, which occupies more space than is devoted to ballast, and moved by the well-known force of compressed air, liquefied and then vaporized, the vessel takes off and flies away towards the Mediterranean, seeming to devour the distance. After an hour, having traveled some 70,000 or 80,000 meters, the pilot, positioned at the tiller, signals the presence of a bird of prey, which is holding the red flag of war in its hooked beak and giving chase to the swallow.

Philirène goes aft with his telescope; then, having recognized the enemy, he gives the order to turn to face it. The way that the swallow is flying at present, this maneuver requires an enormous circuit, which gives the bird of prey time to catch up. Philirène would have preferred to approach its flank in order to launch certain projectiles that would prove to it that the swallow is not without means of defense, but the buzzard, veering in his direction, also heads straight towards him, with a slight upward movement, launching several volleys from its beak. It is already extending its immense steel claws, ready to seize its prey.

"They're no novices, these rogues," says Philirène calmly to Eupistos—who, in spite of his philosophical faith, is beginning to experience a serious anxiety. Then, addressing himself to the crew, Philirène says: "Gentlemen, we shall soon apprise these bandits of the fact that they are attacking a member of the European Scientific Institute."

At the same time, he gives orders for a maneuver and a doubling of the motive force which, with less precision in its execution, would have been extremely dangerous, but which gives the swallow a prodigious almost-vertical upward movement. The buzzard comes near enough at that moment to permit a glimpse of the astounded faces of its crew, who were far from expecting such a bold and skillful maneuver, and who clap their hands with the sincere and profound enthusiasm of well-brought-up brigands, ever-ready to render homage to the coolness and superior knowledge of their adversary.

Either by virtue of their astonishment or, more likely, out of a determination not to damage their expected prize or the rich cargo of which they have doubtless received reports from their informants in Paris, the pirates have not fired many projectiles, aiming directly for seizure. Now the situation has changed; it is no longer the buzzard that is on the offensive but the swallow.

"I've played leap-frog with these rogues," Philirène says to Eupistos, "when it would have been easy for me to fire a dozen rounds of Greek fire, which would have roasted the buzzard like a mere wild duck on a spit."

Meanwhile, Philirène, who has turned his head to follow the buzzard, on which he is looking down from a height of 20 to 30 meters, sends down a shower of fire upon its wings, sufficient to damage it and ensure that it will soon be out of action. He does not want anything more, satisfied with showing the pirate that he can do much more than that. Convinced that the buzzard is incapable of going very far in its present condition without descending to Earth, he limits himself to following its course and letting off a few fireworks as the pirates repair the damage to their wings. At the same time, though, he is forced to weather occasional volleys of incendiary projectiles launched with a precision to which he is equally obliged to render justice, and which might cause him considerable damage if he were not able to avoid them skillfully by making abrupt movements as soon as he sees them depart.

"I admire your generosity with regard to these rascals, who are enemies of civilization, odious obstacles to the complete triumph of our principle of *the greatest good of the most worthy*,"[35] Eupistos says to Philirène, who has not yet begun to feel secure from a peril as clear as daylight.

"What do you expect, my dear chap! I don't have that inflexible conviction with which anyone but me would have finished off these poor devils, whose principal fault is to be endowed with a bellicose constitution that cannot bear the flat calm of the peaceful state that we have imposed on humankind. All those heads down there must have a protuberance of destructiveness in the region neighboring the ear, and that of a highly-developed acquisitiveness. It's not their fault that it gives them an absolute scorn for the right of property, which would be cruelly punished by a bilious or sanguine dogmatic individual, but which only awakes pity in a phlegmatic and nervous doubter like me."

"A singularly sophistical forbearance!" says Eupistos, impatiently. "Even so, you're risking your life and ours. At least you're brave, bizarre skeptic as you are."

"On the contrary," says Philirène, laughing, "I'm what is universally known, according to received ideas, as a coward. The mere thought of the slightest scratch makes me tremble, and irritates my nerves horribly. I know full well that if I let myself be captured by these brigands, they would treat me with the urbanity in which pirates are no more lacking than we are in these times of

---

[35] This manifestly deliberate variation of the Benthamite utilitarian principle that one should always aim to secure "the greatest good of the greatest number" serves to make the point that Eupistos' diehard optimism, though not unlike Bentham's, is not identical to it.

advanced civilization; they would be so proud of their prize that they would have every consideration for my intellectual and industrial status in the world, not to mention the hope of a nice ransom. But I have a little self-respect, and with the means of defense that are at my disposal, it would have been painful for me to give these ignorant folk the right to boast of their superiority to a physician and technologist of my rank. It would have been unbearable for me to think of the news being broadcast all over the world that the president of the Universal Congress had let himself be gobbled up like a fly by vulgar brigands. I therefore took the very simple course that you have witnessed. If the maneuver had failed, we would have been blasted into 1000 pieces, and dropped 800 feet without our having the slightest awareness of it—painlessly, as dentists put it. If, on the other hand, I were to receive an excessively hurtful wound, you know that I have several vials of gas here which can relieve us of all suffering and all the cares of life. One of them is at your service."

"Much obliged," says Eupistos. "I would be able to suffer, because I believe in something."

"So much the better for you," says Philirène.

It is evidently Eupistos who is the brave one; Philirène is the coward, which suits him very well, and his precautions for suicide ought to be stigmatized with energetic disapproval.

Meanwhile, the buzzard is fleeing in a western direction, following the course of the Loire, doubtless in order to reach the Ocean, where it would be able to set its hull and its nacelles afloat, and where its crew, beyond the reach of national law, would be safer than on French territory. The obstinacy of the swallow in following it and harassing it, however, makes this difficult to accomplish, and the buzzard is soon forced to set down on the Loire, about 10,000 meters upstream of Saumur, near to a town named Chenehutte-les-Tuffeaux. It is just in time, for, despite the incombustibility of its cladding and the promptitude with which the crew use every available means to extinguish the flames, the buzzard has caught fire.

Philirène sets down on the shore nearby, in a place named Sainte-Radegonde. Two men in his crew have been killed, one of whom fell to the ground, and four or five wounded, two of them completely blinded by gunfire. We soon shall find out about the buzzard's losses.

X. A Cottage

Hoc erat, etc.

That was what I intended.
Horace.

The priest must become the teacher,
or the teacher must become the priest
of advanced civilizations.
Anonymous (19th century).

Whatever the present development of aeronautics might be in any country advanced in civilization, the descent of flying machines of such dimensions is too uncommon an event not to cause a sensation wherever it takes place. For the inhabitant of the surrounding countryside, the close-range sight of such birds, which they usually only see high up in the air, is a spectacle that cannot fail to excite curiosity. It was entirely expectable, therefore, especially on banks as populous as those of the Loire, that a considerable crowd should have gathered when the enormous buzzard came to rest on the wide and smooth surface of the river. Bold adventurers are already hastily unloading the buzzard's hull, and its auxiliary nacelles—fully deployed, in case of need, for navigation—are beginning to float downstream, the debris of their wings serving as sails and their motors converted into paddle-wheels.

If, contrary to all likelihood, no one were to ask them as they pass by to display official papers sanctioning an evidently warlike crew that cannot possibly belong to the Association for Civilization, they would pass through Nantes and attain the open sea—but Philirène restores order by means of a signal alerting the local guard, which is soon assembled. They are taken prisoner, inventory is taken of their vessel, and they are dispatched provisionally to the prisons of Saumur, where a special jury will sit in judgment on them. A phrenological commission will then examine them, to consider questions of leniency. Those who have the symptoms of entirely vicious natural tendencies will be placed in the penitentiary prison at Fontevrault, where attempts will be made—a trifle late in the day, to be sure—to neutralize these tendencies. Those, on the other hand, in whom indications of good tendencies are found, which bad education and the vicissitudes of life have succeeded in thwarting and perverting, will be placed in a house of correction and superior improvement, from which several will emerge with a useful trade and make their way in society honestly.

Philirène, thinking about that, says to Eupistos: "Our admirable philanthropy renders the situation of certain rogues preferable to that of honest men; but is it always their fault that they were rogues, and are those who are honest men always deserving?"

He says more about the judgment of the crew: "Here phrenologists are responsible for the application and mitigation of punishment. In Organopolis they judge for themselves the rascals whose actions have been in conformity with their constitution, limiting their punishment to sedative treatment, and ordering the most severe punishments for the least culpable, whose constitutions should have inclined them to good. Here are two systems of justice—how many others are there in the world, and which is the best?"

He deeply regrets the honest and intelligent men of his crew, dead or disabled for life. "Of the 50 men who manned the buzzard," he says, "seven were killed or lost during the maneuver, and a dozen crippled. I mourn their fate, for they have been punished much more severely than their comrades, without having deserved it, and it does not give me back mine!"

Thus Philirène finds in almost every circumstance a way to distress himself, and to drown his soul in the troubled and nauseating waters of doubt. However, in speaking about what would become of the crew of the bird of prey, I have neglected to follow Philirène into the house close to which he had set down.

His hosts are good people who live in a former hermitage—founded, I believe, in the 15th century. The ruins of the chapel are still visible along with the cavity containing the vestiges of the cell of the good hermits nourished by the charity of the nearby hamlet, which was situated at the foot of a hill on the edge of the river. It was a hamlet then, but now that France has a population of 54 millions, Minerolle can certainly be called a village.

Around the pretty cottage, admirably situated on the summit of a steep slope overlooking the Loire, three or four hectares of land are enclosed, the greater part of which is planted with vines whose produce is highly esteemed in the vicinity. In the remainder, there is an orchard, a little vegetable garden behind the house, carpets of Lucerne, a few patches of flowering sainfoin. There are carefully-trimmed and well-groomed hawthorn hedges here and there, and, near thick blocks of stones abandoned there centuries before, a few evergreen holly-bushes with red berries, decked with sweet-scented honeysuckle and clematis—which seem to display their flowers on their host bushes like flecks of white foam—and also eglantines, privets, and fusains with angular stems and coralline berries. In the highest place of all, tall green trees—a yew, a Norway spruce, an Italian pine—launch their ancient trunks and funereal foliage into the air, visible for 40,000 meters around in all seasons, like immobile telegraphs expressing but one sole idea. I fear that it would be boring to name the many other trees or bushes, indigenous or exotic, with odorant flowers or gleaming foliage, making up the copse on the north bank of the river, on the near-vertical slope of the hill, where the paths are so steep that it is often necessary to hang on to branches or the mossy roots of oaks and ebonies.

Let us go into the house by way of a terrace decorated with Italianate pillars surmounted with vases of geraniums. We are in a drawing-room whose modest furnishings would be far from advertising wealth without the extreme propriety that is manifest therein. The wallpaper is one of those old cotton velvets with arabesque designs, like those made 100 years ago; as for the large and heavy oak armchairs, upholstered with tapestries embroidered with landscapes representing the seasons and figures costumed in the style of the time of Louis XIV, it is easy to assign a date to them. On a rather beautiful false-marble fireplace, which might date from he early years of the parliamentary government of 1830, is a bronze pendulum clock whose mythological and martial decorations evidently recall the tastes dominant in the time of the French Empire. I shall not pursue this kind of inventory of the trivial furnishings any further. Better to look eastwards through the large glazed door: there is revealed a view worth more than the most sumptuous furniture. To the right, wooded hills, with green lawns and crags in clearings, landslides and sandy paths, grottoes hollowed out in the bedrock; in sum, a harsh rural landscape in the manner of Ruysdaël,[36] in the season when the leaves seem to be preparing for their fall, taking on, as if by way of bizarre disguise, so many different colors: some yellowing, others ruddy or amaranthine, according to the species of the tree. To the left, the beautiful valley of Anjou, so rich, so fertile, and so full of houses, villages, towns, cities and factories, bordered by hills that extend into the distance, melting into a pale violet horizon.

Directly ahead, though, there is something even better: there is the Loire, the beautiful Loire, with its sands the color of wheat ripe for the harvest, its pretty islets covered with clumps of willows, whose soft greenery, with hints of silver, gives the impression of thick, silky pieces of carpet; then the vast meadowland bordered with long curtains of poplars. Then, in the distance, there is the "pleasant and well-situated city of Saumur," as the old chronicle puts it, with its beautiful bridges, its bell-towers, its tall windmills and its former castle, now converted into a noisy factory, as is its ancient cavalry-barracks, where steam-powered engines of war were constructed in the last century. Then the eye returns again to the Loire, always the Loire, which runs so close to the hill that one imagines seeing it at one's feet: the Loire, once the most capricious and deceptive of the rivers of France, which has now become tractable

---

[36] Jacob Isaac Ruysdaël (c1628-1682) was a Dutch landscape painter famed for his fidelity to nature and his rich colors.

and docile, without losing its beauty, permitting navigation all the year round, thanks to the patient and immense works that have directed its course and dredged
out its bed. One can still contemplate the majestic sweep
of large sails, which, expanding to the breath of the "sea
wind," advance resplendently in the sunlight like the
white dresses of young girls in a Corpus Christi procession—more than in the past, though, one also sees the
benevolent flow furrowed by bold floating machines,
which churn the waters noisily while vomiting black
plumes of smoke like the dragons of fable.

Somewhat preoccupied as Philirène is by the inconvenience of the forced delay to his journey—in fact, the
significant damage sustained by the swallow requires the
crew to remain grounded for a day in order to repair it—
he cannot help abandoning himself completely to the
admiration to which so luxuriant a spectacle is bound to
give birth. After having thanked his hosts in enthusiastic
terms for their hospitality he says to Eupistos: "This is a
hermitage like the one I would like to live in some day."

"Me too," his fried replies, laughing. "I could easily
get used to such a solitude, in which the presence of man
is manifest everywhere."

"I admit that a hermit from civilization could not be
lodged here today, but it seems to me that I would have
been no less pleased to be here, even in the days when
the hill had fewer inhabitants."

"Although there are numerous habitations within a
short distance, we enjoy all the advantages of solitude
here," says their host, a respectable old man whom the
two travelers have begun to observe with interest and
discretion.

They soon learn that he is the former village
schoolmaster, who lives in this pretty retreat with his

wife—who was similarly formerly employed in elementary education—his daughter, his son-in-law and two little children, who are already old enough to take part in field-work. The family finds sufficient resources in the various produce of its grounds, and a few 100 square meters attached thereto, for an existence which, if not brilliant, is at least honest, and the modest sum that the good patriarchs of pedagogy have thriftily accumulated in the savings bank adds to the stock of their happiness. They have a son and a daughter-in-law, who have replaced them in their instructive functions in the village and whose only child, a young woman of 20 afflicted with pallor, is presently staying with her grandparents in order to receive the constant care that they can give her, whose efficacy will be assisted by the fresh and pure air of Sainte-Radegonde.

I mentioned that there are there our four hectares of land attracted to the house. The land has been parceled out to the point at which this is the largest property in the commune. It is true that it is a communal domain, entailed to the teachers and their family, of which the local pastor ordinarily has a share.

After having refreshments served to their guests, the venerable schoolmaster begs them to excuse him while he leaves them briefly; his beloved grand-daughter is asleep in a neighboring room, and he must go to see how she is.

XI. The Schoolmaster's Daughter

There is a double existence within us.
Psychology and Physiology.

A husband, a husband, a husband.
Molière.[37]

Since magnetism has become principally a medicine of the family,[38] its inconveniences have become less obvious and its advantages better appreciated. A husband who is caring for his better half, or a father for his cherished daughter, obtains surer results than strangers, and without the perils of that so-delicate curative method brings. What touching scenes this produces! How many family ties are more tightly bound thereby! Perhaps I should not say much about ties of marriage, for it sometimes happens that husbands discover, by the somniloquism of their beloved spouses, secrets that are not at all helpful to their peace of mind; the obstinate resistance of many wives to submit to such conjugal therapy is easily understandable.

---

[37] The quotation is from *L'amour médécin* (1665).

[38] Bodin inserts a note here—the only one that he explicitly signs as an "Author's Note," thus tacitly attributing all the rest to the narrative voice: "It appears that such is the future of magnetism; the future of homeopathy—which ought to be no less bright, according to every appearance—has not yet become manifest."

A young woman is asleep in an antique high-backed armchair; her pose is graceful, her figure slender, and her exceedingly dainty feet are protruding winsomely from a red velvet foot-warmer. Two rows of long black eyelashes, for which a crow's wings do eternal service as a comparison, extend above slightly hollowed cheeks, which an Asian poet would describe as "jonquil," worry have supplanted the lilies and the roses—but the young invalid's delicate and graceful features give sufficient indication of the fact that she must still be charming, especially when her physiognomy is animated by her eyes, which seem to be slightly open.

"Well, Eudoxie,"[39] says the old man, as he comes in, "have you thought about the infusion that you want to prescribe for yourself? Do you know now which plants we should put into it?"

"Oh, my God, no, dear grandpapa, I haven't been thinking about myself at all. For a quarter of an hour, while sleeping a calm and restorative slumber, I've been thinking of nothing but the strangers who have just arrived. Do you know that you have a great and illustrious person in your house?"

"Certainly! I suspected as much from his language and manner. What have you seen?"

"I've seen that he's come from the other hemisphere, from Benthamia, where he sat on an armchair placed on the summit of a rock; he was there among people who had come from every part of the world, and I've seen that he presided over them. He must be the famous Philirène."

"I think so too, according to these indications. Do you want me to bring him in here?"

---

[39] Eudoxie is translatable as "good opinion."

"No, no!" says Eudoxie, vigorously. "I don't want him to see me for the first time like this."

"Eh? What does it matter, my poor child?

"Oh, my God, I can't say. I see nothing of his visible self, but I find myself astonishingly in rapport with his moral self—I don't know why. How easily I can read his thoughts!"

She begins to weep.

"What's wrong with you, dear Eudoxie? Don't hide anything from your grandfather, from one of your best friends."

"How it pleases me to hear that! But my soul is a little short of heat, and it seems to me that I will give it to him." Her cheeks color slightly.

"What makes you think that, my child?"

"I don't know what to say. There are foolish and rapid ideas passing through my head. I see that he is loved a little by a very pretty girl—yes, a little, but not enough; not as I...oh! She doesn't understand him, he's above her. Oh! She's being carried away very rapidly— where is she going? I see her greatly disturbed." She rubs her eyes, then places her hand on her forehead. After a moment of profound attention, she says: "Dear grandpapa, don't neglect to warn him that the leader of the pirates can give him important information. It will hurt him a great deal, but it's necessary that he knows it. Unfortunate Philirène! He interests me a great deal."

"It's necessary not to tire yourself out in this fashion, dear child. About that tisane—how do you want it made up?"

Eudoxie makes a slight gesture of impatience. "Oh, my God, grandfather, the tisane. I know that it will do me good, but...oh! I shall never tell what I have revealed; I dare not even think it!"

The old man, with tender anxiety, says: "I have my suspicions, my poor Eudoxie."

"I know that. You understand that all my sickness is in my heart, this vacant, desolate heart. Oh, if I were loved, loved as I am capable of loving! But it's my fault; I've wanted to elevate myself too far above my station. I've cultivated my intelligence too much; I've pushed my talents too far, too far for a simple village girl—for that is all I know, dear grandfather. I have disdained the young men who would have been able to think of me, distancing myself from them by a certain arrogance. I was wrong; I shall be punished. Oh, please—don't talk to me about all this when I wake up!"

The worthy grandfather lets his granddaughter sleep again for a little while, then wakes her up again when he returns from a walk in the grounds. The travelers, who have accompanied him, come back in for dinner. Their host, with the discretion of a well-brought-up man, has not troubled their *incognito*, which no longer exists for him; even so, evidences of more marked respect might have allowed them to deduce that it has been penetrated. The old man has limited himself to giving the advice that was mentioned a little while ago to Philirène—who, quite naturally suspecting the oneirophantic origin of that information, is not at all astonished by it, and is disposed to take advantage of it.

The entire family of the instructor emeritus, half-literate and half-rustic, comes together for dinner. They sit down at table and he pronounces a prayer in a loud voice, to which everyone replies: "Amen." The patriarch does not make any lengthy apology for the extreme frugality of the repast that he offers with an excellent heart. It is obvious that the good people do not have the resources for such occasions in their larder, their garden or their cellar. The food is what they ordinarily eat, save for a sweet dessert course, to which the two cows in the shed have added the tribute of fresh milk. The *pièce de résistance* is a fat turkey-hen, simply stuffed with truffles, which have multiplied considerably in sandy regions since a means has been discovered of reproducing that tuber, so precious for the fattening of pigs.

In brief, these poor folk have done what they can, and Philirène—who is the most sober man in the world—feels infinitely more comfortable at that rustic dinner than at any of the galas to which he has been obliged to submit among the Benthamians.

Eudoxie, who has been introduced to him and whose modest grace he has noticed, pays him a little less attention that she pays to his secretary. A singular thing! Although she was preoccupied in her recent dream with none but Philirène, it is with Eupistos that she might have more *exterior sympathy*. Is there, then, also an interior sympathy? That is a world which still remains to be discovered, in spite of the labors of the German physiologists. Which of the two, Philirène or Eupistos, is the one that nature might have specifically destined for Eudoxie? Which might make her more completely happy, and for a longer time? And which might suit her better? That is something that neither you nor I know as yet, and perhaps never will. And while Philirène runs from one hemisphere to the other after a quasi-princess bride-to-be who has been abducted, here, perhaps, is the village schoolmaster's daughter who might be the wife made to understand and love him! And will the sad Eudoxie ever find herself with either of these two men, or will she remain on her hill by the Loire: a poor languishing flower, which will soon wither away and fall, without having

been, I do not say "picked," but scarcely even seen and
scented!

XII. A Rustic Dinner

They felt obliged to treat the century harshly.
Apparently, it is necessary that literature too
should pass through a Revolutionary regime
in order to be regenerated.
Extract from
The Literary History of the 19th Century,
1940 edition.

During dinner, the conversation is generally animated without being noisy, because no one behaves indiscreetly on such an occasion. It is to the stranger that honor is done, and it is from his questions that everyone takes the cue, more or less, as to what should be discussed. The exclusively agricultural part of the family is composed of simple but sensible people, who only talk about things they know about—an excellent means of avoiding saying anything stupid.

Philirène files the patriarch's son-in-law under the heading of "local agricultural industry." He does not find him ignorant in physics or chemistry, nor in natural history, and the women have the smattering of these sciences necessary for domestic economy. It is, however, the conversation of the retired schoolmaster that charms Philirène by its variety, its good taste and a solidity of education that makes itself manifest without any appearance of pedantry. After having shown that he is up to date with social questions and the great issues that are discussed nowadays in the world, he speaks with no less pertinence and common sense about the principal literatures of Europe, and that of France. He says quite reasonable things, notably about the literature that predominated in the first half of the 19th century.

"I neither praise nor blame," he says, "that unhealthy, neurotic and almost epileptic literature; I seek only to explain it. It is obvious that those people were making prodigious efforts to retain the poetry of the intermediary times that seemed to be under threat from the positivism of civilization. In order to save it, they were attempting to outdo it, to magnify it beyond all measure, making an Adamastor [40] before which the prosaicism of civilization would be forced to turn its vessels around— or, to put it another way, in a milieu of relaxation in religious belief and a thirst for material pleasures, they gave in to the corruption of the time and prostituted poetry in order to save it again. The intention was good, and I admit that great talents were devoted to its accomplishment."

"I should certainly like to know," says Eudoxie, timidly, "whether the need for terrible emotions that is supposed by the books of that era was entirely invented by the authors. Did real people act like their characters?"

"Oh, Mademoiselle," says Eupistos, "if that had been the case, the men of that time would have been insane, alternating between ennui and fury, and the women exceedingly bizarre creatures. Like you, I believe that the mores of that epoch were better than its literature tends to suggest. As for the young people who put on

---

[40] Adamastor is the phantom of the Cape of Storms (nowadays known as the Cape of Good Hope) in Luiz de Camoëns' *Lusiad* (1572), which appears to the epic's hero, Vasco da Gama, and foretells the dire fates that will befall less fortunate expeditions to the Indies.

airs of being blasé without having even made a tour of the world, and risked their lives 100 times over in the atmosphere, I find them very amusing."

"I should also like to know," Eudoxie continues, "if the jargon that succeeded the emphatic sensibility of the school of Rousseau and the Romantic mysticism in vogue under the Restoration was the language of society. Did they talk like that in drawing-rooms?"

"Let's not be too severe," said Philirène. "That literature was necessary; I share the opinion of our venerable host on that point. It was necessary to strike hard to obtain the attention of distracted and indifferent minds, and to lead the French to poetry violently, as Sulla[41] claimed to be leading the Romans to liberty. It is by that means that the way was prepared for out great poets of the 20th century: our poets of the future, who justify the title of VATES,[42] attributed to poets as to prophets."

The conversation is prolonged into part of the evening, running through various subjects. The Euxodie sits down at the melodion and improvises, on themes suggested to her by the travelers, poetic and melodic compositions in French, Italian and modern Greek. Eventually, when it is time to retire, the family unites its voices in a religious chorus, whose execution is obviously very

---

[41] Lucius Cornelius Sulla (c138BC-78BC) was a general who became dictator of Rome in 82BC after capturing the city in a civil war against his former commander Marius; after arranging the murders of all his enemies he then instituted various liberalizing constitutional reforms before abdicating in 79BC.

[42] The Latin term *vates*, attributed to prophets and soothsayers in general, had fallen into disuse before Virgil revived it; it subsequently became associated with Druidism, although the nature of the connection between the Latin word and its Gaulish equivalent is unclear.

satisfactory, given that it pleases a connoisseur as discerning as Philirène, a former regular at the Constantinople Opera.

Before separating from his hosts, Philirène obtains information as to the most convenient means of getting to Saumur, in order to make his deposition to the court and hear the pirates' revelations.

"The produce of civilization is spreading through our countryside very slowly," says the old man. "The buildings that serve as our elementary school, maternal school and concert hall, and the streets of our village, are only lighted by resin-based gas lamps, and the omnibus from Nantes to Saumur via Genes only passes through at hourly intervals—but the railway on the left bank is very efficient, and you'll arrive in the town in ten minutes.[43]

I shall not describe the cordial farewells of the travelers and their hosts. The reader must fill in things like that. The schoolmaster emeritus presents them with his modest visits' book, excusing his indiscretion. With the utmost grace, Philirène writes his name therein, and his motto: *Glory to God, and peace to men of good will.*

---

[43] Bodin adds a note: "This is gratifying, when one recalls that the route had not even been built in the year of grace 1834."

XIII. A Resolution

Minima de malis.
Between two evils one must choose the lesser.[44]

Civilization extends itself by example,
and defends itself by force.
Anonymous.

The leader of the pirates, in the hope of being treated leniently, has made no bones about confessing that he had been part of the immense aerial band commanded by the famous Aëtos,[45] whose main base is in the Caucasus. The hope that he and his friends might be considered as exchangeable prisoners of war also had something to do with this confession. He has spoken, perhaps with some exaggeration, of the vast armaments as the disposal of his leader, who has proclaimed himself Emperor of the Skies and is disposed to take the offensive. Finally, he has declared that he was on a special mission to capture Philirène, and that, at the same time, an eagle of the first rank made the crossing from Sicily to Carthage with orders to abduct the sultana Mirzala. He did not know whether this delicate operation had succeeded, but he knew that the supreme leader attached

---

[44] This maxim is from one of the fables of the Roman fabulist Phaedrus, active in the 1st century A.D.
[45] Aëtos means "eagle;" it is significant that Napoleon was also frequently compared to an eagle.

so much importance to it that he probably went in person to supervise it.

This sudden flood of information could only cause Philirène considerable distress. As soon as the swallow was in a fit condition to take off, he flew to Marseilles, assisted by the north-east wind that frequently blows in France. He hoped to find an aerial convoy in the port, ready to depart for Sardinia or Africa, or, if no such opportunity offered itself, to reach his destination quickly, without exposing himself awkwardly to the risks of an audacious crossing, to embark on the Carthage ferry. It was the latter course that he was obliged to take. When the ship called at Cagliari, he learned that a bold raid on Carthage had been attempted by a bird of prey, and he re-embarked with dread in his heart. A few hours later he is in front of Politée, who confirms that his anxiety was fully justified.

When shall we finally explain what love is? It is often a modification of egotism or vanity; in other instances it is a bizarre spirit of contradiction, the desire to triumph over an obstacle. She does not love me? Well, I want her to love me; I shall do everything to make her love me. They are opposed to her being mine; they have taken her away from me. Well, she *will* be mine, I shall get her back. That is how people reason who are often calm in their amours, and do not even give them much thought until they are thwarted.

"So, my poor Philirène, you are finally amorous! This was what it needed!"

"The expression is a trifle harsh, beautiful Dido," is the reply she gets from Philirène—who, given the degree of intimacy they have enjoyed for a long time, is able to permit himself this familiar allusion, and sometimes to season their conversations with a small measure of irony, which might well be born of resentment.

"Yes, *finally*," says Politée, blushing slightly. "Admit, my friend, that you have been exceedingly tranquil regarding your marriage, and that you have lent an all-too-exact confirmation to my aphorism that it is impossible for a skeptic to be amorous, in the true sense of the word."

"Oh, I admit it and I accuse myself of it; I'm a wretch, unworthy of her. Oh my dear Mirzala! My little sultana! My pretty *flower of the rose-bush*!"[46]

And he strikes his forehead violently with his hands, and his tears...no, it's necessary to tell the truth; he is not choked by sobs; his eyes are only a trifle moist—and perhaps the tears he is suppressing are more of indignation than of love.

All the women will say: "Is this a hero? Ah, the handsome heroes we have known! And he thinks that we can be interested in a man of this sort? Oh, truly, he does not know us at all."

Eh? My God, what do you want me to tell you? That's how it is. I can't do anything about it. Let's put it this way: that he isn't a hero, that he's simply a man like many others, and you don't have to be interested in him if you find it impossible. But I beg you please to have some indulgence for him, and to consent to tolerate him. After all, you've seen that he is good—and besides, I promise you a hero more to your own taste.

Politée examines Philirène with the penetrating eyes of women of her age who know the way the world

---

[46] Bodin adds a footnote to explain that the italicized phrase—*fleur de rosier* in French—"is the meaning of Mirzala's pretty name."

works, and continues: "Well, my dear Philirène, I maintain my axiom: a skeptic, especially one with a constitution like yours, cannot be authentically amorous."

"For myself, I swear that I am—you'll end up exasperating me, dear Politée."

"Too bad—or, rather, so much the better, for I'll be delighted to see you genuinely angry about this. But I say that, to be amorous, it's necessary to believe in something very strongly, even if only for a short time. It's necessary to believe that one is loved or that one will love forever—illusions, no doubt, but, in the final analysis, there's no point in love without them."

"I admit to you, Politée, that such illusions, as you so aptly call them, which are destroyed by everyone's experience on a daily basis, could never enter my head. I have always had trouble believing in the duration of a sentiment that the first breach of trust, often the first disagreeable sensation, is sufficient to enfeeble—and which, from one discovery to the next, often ends up vanishing entirely. I do not experience as much as others that stimulus which blinds us to the object of our love and to ourselves, inspiring complete faith in us and moving us to illimitable sacrifice. I see myself too clearly as I am to delude myself; I cannot persuade myself that an inconstant, indecisive and almost inaccessible creature like me could ever be the object of a serious passion, if it were not on the part of a woman who is not quite right in the head. But if it is true, as you assure me that it is, that Mirzala sometimes thinks of me, that she is disposed to love me a little…oh, my God, that cannot flatter my self-respect very much, since she knows no other man in all the world but me…"

"An unfortunate mind," Politée puts in, "always ingenious in turning away from belief in that which is."

"I'm sorry—let's move on. I assure you that, if you have told me the truth—and I have every confidence in you—I am so touched, so grateful for that charming child's sentiments, that, in order to convince her of them, I am ready to sacrifice my life...more than that, to change it completely, to adopt a life contrary to my education, my habits, my tastes, my temperament and my principles. In brief, I am ready to go to war."

"Is it possible?" cries Politée, rising to her feet excitedly. "Is this really the sage Philirène speaking—the man who solemnly accepted at Constantinople the fine title of *friend of peace*?"[47]

"Yes, it's him—but you know, my friend, that no principle is absolute, and that, to make any principle hold good, it is often necessary to bend it, modify it and turn it in its essential direction. Isn't it often by means of war, in consequence, that peace can be secured? I, therefore—peaceful by nature, and, to the extent that it is in me, by conviction—I, Philirène, who had devoted my entire life to the triumph of peace, will commence a terrible war against this enemy...these enemies...of the repose of humankind. They do not know with whom they will have to deal. It is not a warrior who will measure himself against them; it is a man who neither seeks the joys of power, nor those of glory, but who puts himself at the service of a idea, of civilization against barbarity, of order against chaos; it is a man who knows

---

[47] Bodin inserts a note: "It might be necessary to tell our female readers that this is the translation of the name Philirène." Nowadays, of course, it might be necessary to tell our male readers too, so I have already done so—although I used slightly stronger language, of which Bodin and his skeptical non-hero might not have approved.

how to animate other men with his mind, because disinterest has something that always makes itself felt, which never escapes the instinct of the masses. They have to their credit all the vile passions and ignoble appetites of their nature; I shall mobilize against them the noble sentiments, the true interests. They will deploy courage; I shall show them coolness—and I know, better than they can, how to deploy the immense lever of science."

"You know, Philirène, that's a superb speech—but there's no longer much of the lover in it, and I'm beginning to see nothing in it but philosophy."

"You're right," says Philirène, a little confused by the observation. "But, you see, we're never moved by a single, unmixed motive; everything in this world is mixed up to some degree. I'll speak to you with an open heart. Without love, I would not have taken my course so promptly; but now my course is set, I'm not sorry to leave philanthropy behind in favor of honor. You know full well, Politée, that I'm uncommonly frank; I allow myself to be see clearly, and perhaps that's why I've never been successful with women, who always want illusion and always need to be deceived."

"That's all too true, alas," says Politée, suppressing a sigh. Let's start on means now, and get down to business. What's your plan?"

"In the first place, I'm counting on all your resources in finance and materials of war, as well as my own, Indeed, Politée, this concerns you as much as me. It's as much a matter of avenging your honor as mine. We can no longer have any doubts about it—the famous chief of the polygamists and brigands, Aëtos, is *him*."

"I'm certain of that now. But I'm far from thinking about a vengeance that is unworthy of me, after having sufficiently experienced that of spite. What I must avenge is an insult issued in my domain, before my very eyes, to my sister, my friend, by infamous pirates. What I must desire is to liberate her, to grant her freedom in her affections."

"Good—as you wish, provided that the result is the same," says Philirène, darting a glance at the forsaken beauty that was veiled but keen.

"You can't resist the desire to disenchant others as you have yourself. Leave me, at least, the illusion of my indifference, if it is an illusion."

"Very well, I respect that. It shall be me who attacks Philomaque, your husband, and you shall only attack the kidnappers. But we're dealing with a powerful opponent. Did you know that while I was making pretty speeches to the isthmus Congress, depicting the situation of the world more kindly than I really saw it, according to invariable official custom, he had himself proclaimed *Emperor of the Skies*?"

"Yes, I've just heard. A new madness!"

"If it pleases you to think so—but it proves that his forces are considerably increased. If it's true, as they say, that all the hordes of Tartary, and all the qualified soldiers of the recent wars of Hindustan against China and the Mongols against Hindustan, are flocking to join him from all directions, as well as the tribes on the shores of the Caspian Sea; if it's true that he has a fleet on that sea and an extent of territory sufficient to assure his subsistence; if it's true that his airfleet's equipment has been considerable augmented by consignments from all over Europe, whether in kind or in money, and that he's fully prepared to come whenever he pleases to burn a few of the capitals of the civilized world; if the so-called Poetic Association has lent him, however clandestinely, the powerful aid of its finances and its moral influence; if, finally, he succeeds in contracting an alliance with that other lunatic, that virago who has taken it into her head to revive the Amazons of legend, and who has succeeded in gathering around her a multitude of hare-brained fanatics, extraordinarily bold and highly skilled in aerial maneuvers—well, in that case, I say that he's certainly not an enemy to be disdained."

"I'm far from thinking the opposite—so there's no point in going to sleep. I intend to employ all my influence in the Association of Civilization. I'll go to Jerusalem, where the financial committee meets."

"And I'll go to the military committee in Athens, to which I will explain my plans. We ought to rendezvous in Constantinople, where the immensity of resources of every sort will make it easier for us to coordinate our means of action. Our supplies and our munitions are assured in the fertile realm of Asia Minor and its rich capital, Ilium. To destroy the principal hornet's nest, which is in the Caucasus, we must adopt the heights of Trebizond and Mount Ararat as our base of operations, and transport our advance guard to Colchis, to the Classical land of flying dragons—the very place where the terrible Medea learned of Jason's infidelity." Politée bites her lip. "That's the plan for the airfleet—as for the terrestrial invasion that Philomaque is planning, perhaps for Khorasan, our only hope of repelling it is the military forces of the constitutional Sultan of Babylon. His interest in the matter is sufficiently strong for us to be able to count of him; the existence of his empire is at stake."

They continue to discuss their plan of campaign in this manner, and Politée gives proof in the conversation of very extensive statistical knowledge, which will make no small contribution to the accomplishment of their common project.

When they go their separate ways, Politée thinks about the man who has disdained and abandoned her, against whom she does not seek vengeance, as a vulgar woman would—no, her soul is too noble for that; but she does want to see him vanquished, incapable of creating further victims, and she wants most of all to show him that she has no personal resentment, that she is perfectly happy without him, that she has forgotten him....

Is all that really true? She believes it sincerely, at least—but when one has such a fervent desire to prove such things, it is often because they are not entirely true. Then the thought that her husband has proclaimed himself an emperor rapidly crosses her mind, and it is not without an impulse of resentment that she thinks it; superior woman as she may be, she is still a woman.

For his part, Philirène, while getting his projects under way, wonders what has become of his tender Mirzala, his flower of the rose-bush. It must be acknowledged that she is terribly exposed to danger in the hands of a man who has little respect for anything, and who has taken the turban in order to reestablish polygamy—the most essential, according to him, of the practices of Islam.

XIV. The Poetic Asociation

"Andando mas tos tiempos,
y creciendo mas la malicia," etc.
"The malice of men having increased over time,
knight-errantry was instituted to protect maidens,
widows and orphans..."
The goatherds listened to this long and futile
harangue, utterly flabbergasted, and without a word
of reply. Sancho ate chestnuts and visited his bottle.
The incomparable *Don Quixote*.

Whatever embittered individuals might say who persist in believing that humankind has merely been repeating the same cycle since the beginning of time, elevating itself from barbarity to civilization and then falling back from civilization into barbarity, not to mention the less numerous pessimists who go as far as thinking that everything, people and things alike, deteriorates from day to day—that races, for example, are less beautiful than they were in the days when they were closer to their primitive types, that rivers have been less beautiful since canalization has drained them somewhat, that mountains no longer raise summits as proud, and that pears and peaches are less tasty despite being larger—in spite, I say, of all these dismal theories, progress does exist and is continuing: that is as clear as daylight.

Is it not the case that there is an evident political and social amelioration?—that governments have all renounced their armies on land and sea; that taxation has almost been reduced to local subscriptions raised to cover administrative expenses, save, in great political aggregations, for a few communal funds to dispense life and ease to parties that are withering away completely and to defray the general and indispensable expenses of government? In consequence, great enterprises, whether of colonization or philanthropic war, have been sustained and directed by public spirit, and by the forces and collective resources of all those in the civilized world who have taken an interest in such colonization or are passionate for the triumph of some such principle. It is associations, rather than governments, that are responsible for distant expeditions, and it is subscription that underwrites fleets and armies.

The result of this has been that taxes are no longer exacted, except for expenses whose utility is directly felt by the taxpayer and whose results are visibly manifest. People no longer pay, involuntarily, the expenses of conquests to the advantage of European civilization, from which only their great-great-nephews profit. People no longer go into battle for interests that are quite foreign to them, or ideas to which they are perfectly indifferent. Armies are no longer composed of any but people who have a common end, and who march for its accomplishment with a common enthusiasm and a shared consciousness. The rich march at their own expense, the poor at the expense of their subscription, everyone in the expectation of a share of the benefits proportionate to the funds he has put in and his personal cooperation, if it is a matter of colonization or commercial speculation, everyone with the same expectation of glory and a dividend of recognition, if it is a matter of generous enterprise. It is thanks to these powerful means that European civilization has accomplished prodigies of colonization in the two hemispheres in the last two centuries, and that the work of the abolition of political and domestic slavery has been achieved, after so many wars sustained with admirable perseverance.

The means invented for a praiseworthy end have, however, often been placed at the service of directly opposed intentions. That is how opinions that are anti-progress and anti-civilization have taken advantage of association and subscription to fight against the impulse of European civilization, in order to put a stop to it and, if possible, to reverse it. Everyone knows the degree of importance attained by the so-called Universal Anti-Prosaic Association, to which are affiliated the various societies founded in the same spirit within all the nations in the world.

About 100 years ago, the English aristocracy, mortally wounded by the abolition of the hereditary peerage, combined its debris and formed what came to be called the Nucleus, the cornerstone of that vast association. That initiative was its prerogative in every respect, for no one could deny that it was the premier aristocracy in Europe—the one whose titles were the most authentic, the one that had played the most glorious political role.

The other aristocracies did not fail to follow its example and to group themselves around it, but the law of division of inheritance had rendered the conservation of large fortunes within families so impractical that, if the associations had not been able to recruit incessantly from what as then called the bourgeoisie, they would have ended up being reduced by the passage of time to a very small number of individuals. Nothing is easier to understand.

In the century of Louis XIV, an era when the benefits of the nobility were transmitted integrally to eldest sons, it was noticed that of the ten families *d'épée,* which had been the only feudal nobility, only three had maintained themselves for more than 200 years; the rest had died out naturally, either by the ruination of fortunes or for lack of direct descendants, their titles passing to the rich bourgeois individuals who bought their lands. Genealogical research carried out in that period on the peerage, by order of parliament, proved how few of the families that were among the most illustrious really extended back beyond the 16th century. As the person who bought an estate was given its title from the time of the Regency onwards, and as one could, at a later date, even without such a purchase, easily acquire titles by means of a few 100 gold coins, one could not say that there was a body of hereditary nobility in France. It became almost impossible to track these relationships; fortunes were more mobile and families died out more quickly than ever; all titles were lost within the bourgeoisie.

In England, however, where what is called *the peerage* was a political institution on which the entire nation kept its eyes, and whose archives were strictly maintained, no title could be usurped. It was, therefore, easy to make statistical observations of the duration of families in that country. Well, when an assessment of the English peerage was published shortly after the reform of the House of Commons, everyone was astonished to discover how small the number was of families that went back more than three centuries, and it was ascertained that the majority of those titles had been passed on to relatives by marriage or to outsiders on whose heads they had been bestowed by royal favor. As for the Lords whose peerages only dated back to the previous century, whose ancestors had generally been famous lawyers who had rendered conspicuous service to crown and country, it was obvious that they formed the great majority of the House of Lords.

This digression, which might have seemed puerile to our readers, was necessary to explain how it came about that in France, for example, the members of the Anti-Prosaic Association who had the greatest pretensions to antiquity of origin, had difficulty in tracing their families further back than the beginning of the 19th century. At any rate, those who believed themselves to be descended from the imperial nobility, about which the Faubourg Saint-Germain makes so many jokes, considered themselves as the first rank. After them came those who could connect their genealogy to one or other of the bourgeois notables who called themselves, I believe, the *juste-milieu*,[48] who founded the parliamentary regime in France, and on account of whom the party called "legitimist" was able to rest easy. Those plebeian ancestors of our proud anti-progressive aristocrats, who treated shopkeepers pitilessly and blackened the name of grocers, would have been astonished if they had been able to foresee what the offspring of such a superb posterity would become. I have no doubt that it would have teased their self-respect somewhat.

Apart from the vanity that was the foremost of the initial constitutive agents of the great association, other

---

[48] This phrase—whose literal meaning is "exact middle"—is used to describe a method of pragmatic procedure, which seeks to calculate an evenly-balanced compromise between opposed two extremes. It had a particular significance with respect to the Parliament in which Bodin served, whose philosophy was dominated by that principle, and his antipathy to its applications undoubtedly contributed to this sarcastic adaptation of its meaning.

elements combined to fortify it: religious beliefs which, mistakenly, believed themselves menaced by progress; industrial interests jeopardized by the abandonment of certain technologies; philosophical, political, literary and artistic convictions. It is evident that there are pure intentions and serious motives therein, as well as less respectable afterthoughts. As in all parties, there is an honest flock of men of good faith, and leaders who push them towards an interested goal—but let us speak sincerely, and admit that there is a certain grandeur in the enterprises of this association. One cannot contemplate without admiration the enormous expenses it has expended in Europe and Asia to save curious ruins of churches, mosques, pagodas, châteaux and abbeys, and to conserve entire ancient monuments of which industry was on the point of taking possession, in order to convert them to its own use or demolish them: precious relics that governments do not always have the means to save, and which negligence allows to perish.

It was this association that contrived the restoration of so many beautiful examples of Lombard, Gothic, Saracen and Hindu and many other architectures. It also expended large sums, though without success, for the maintenance of old national costumes in the countryside, and to save the dialects that had been the languages of famous peoples, like Gaelic and Basque, from the total disuse into which they had fallen.

Just as the museums of the naturalists display specimens of the various races of red or bronzed men which have disappeared from the face of the Earth, conserved in formaldehyde or alcohol, and their botanical gardens exhibit families of savages following the ways of life of forests or savannas, the association has acquired a multitude of physical and truly horrible curiosities, which are more interesting to art and poetry than to science. One can read in one of its financial committee's reports:

"The association now includes in its domains 59 subterranean caverns and 77 grottoes open to daylight; 36 rocks of bizarre form have been preserved from mining, and, thanks to you, 44 waterfalls, some of them nearly 100 feet in height, which would have been muzzled as captives of industry and ignobly set to operate mills manufacturing textiles, paper, iron bars or nails and needles, continue to vomit their roaring waters into the depths of precipices, without their white and noble foam being impertinently arrested by the stupid tumblers of a wheel."

The following passage was observed in another report made on the reassembly of Stonehenge: "The frightful subdivision of private land in England, which has probably gone much further in England since the new legislation than in any other European country, without even excepting France, is leading to the disappearance of all the sites that owe their picturesque appearance to uncultivated nature. Two centuries ago, the historic Sherwood Forest, abode of Robin of old Albion, had already been cleared and invaded by barley, hops and turnips. Before long, no one will be able to form an idea of those vast and dismal spaces covered dark and poetic heather, in which the imagination of the great Shakespeare was able to render the appearance of the witches in *Macbeth* so terrible. All of it is ploughed, sown and harvested every year by the inevitable and imperturbable power of steam. The committee has felt obliged to acquire 6000 acres, but its efforts to reintroduce a few hares thereto has not been successful, even thought it has spared no effort or expense; it will be absolutely necessary to buy more in southern Europe. As for the fox, we have some to the sad conclusion that this precious quadruped has disappeared from our island, providing striking proof of the decline of our ancient rural aristocracy; a female has been brought to us for which the equivalent of 3500 pounds sterling in old money was paid, but it has been impossible to find a mate for her."

In another report made to the English section of the organization, someone expresses himself thus: "We have devoted scrupulous attention to the inquiry requested of us into the state of coal mining in the British Isles. We can offer our compatriots of the association, in consequence of our research, the consoling perspective of a future exhaustion of that odious aliment of mechanical industry, that powerful agent of a dismal, uniform and monotonous civilization destructive of all poetic life. Nevertheless, we do not think that the lack of this combustible can make itself felt for a century. In the meantime, the beautiful races of horses bred for traction or the saddle, which are one of our national glories, will gradually disappear from our soil, and we have considered it our duty to have several of them stuffed in order to exhibit them in the association's museums. This is both as an epigram addressed to mechanization and a warning to the nation to think about the future."

XV. A Debate

The world is given over to strife.
Holy Writ.

Given what is known about the Universal Anti-Prosaic Association, it is easily understood that in vulgar places, in modern buildings deprived of memories, that its committees hold their meetings. It is in abbeys, cathedrals, palaces, ruined castles or large caverns. In England, for example, there are assemblies in the cavern near Lancaster called Dunald Mill Hole, and on the site of the magnificent cromlech called Long Meg and Her Daughters, a druidic monument in Northumberland formed by enormous blocks of granite arranged in a circle around a single block of greater dimension.[49]

On this occasion, a general meeting of the Central Committee, comprising delegates from all the European sections, summons them to the famous cavern in Derbyshire known as the Elden Hole or Poole's Hole. This mineralogical curiosity has been adapted with marvelous taste to the purpose attributed to it; all the picturesque beauty and bizarre effects that nature displays there have not only been conserved but heightened by accessories that make them even more striking. The entrance is no longer low, narrow and uncomfortable, without having entirely lost its former dark, mysterious and terrible

---

[49] Actually, the single stone called Long Meg—which qualifies as a cromlech—is not inside but outside the circle of her 67 "daughters," some 17 paces to the south.

character. The little river that flows through it has been diverted slightly in order not to be a hindrance, but it still pours into an abyss that one cannot consider without horror.

I almost regret that this cascade happens to be there, because we have previously seen something similar, which makes it repetitive, but there it is, and at the time of writing it is still roaring; it is absolutely impossible for me to get rid of it. Furthermore, the intention of the decorators has been, it is said, to leave an image of the gulf in which everything that has been honored on the Earth will be swallowed up. The rich natural tapestry of gleaming stalactites augmenting the walls is also still on show, and a bright red grille has been put around the pillar formed like a crystallized fountain, which has become historic [50] since the unfortunate Mary Queen of Scots, who was long detained in the town of Buxton, wept while she leaned upon it in order to surrender herself to her melancholy reveries.

The ground has been covered with a parquet floor on which luxurious carpets are spread; thousands of candles, their light reflected by the stalactites and artfully-placed mirrors, give the members of the audience the satisfaction of not being lit by vulgar gas. Their costumes ensure that they are no less remarkable and no less

---

[50] Bodin inserts a footnote in English: "Scotland's Queen's pillar." The more usual designation in English is "the Queen of Scots' Pillar." The formation in question, created by the fusion of a stalactite and a stalagmite, is in Poole's Hole near Buxton, but Bodin is mistaken in equating Poole's Hole with the Elden Hole, which is a couple of miles away; it is, however, the Elden Hole that contains the allegedly bottomless pit described in the text.

brilliant than their singular surroundings. Here are manifest again the rich and elegant clothes of the Middle Ages and the Renaissance, and ample Oriental vestments abandoned in the 19th century, all luxuriously resplendent with diamonds, precious stones and embroideries. The women—who, in accordance with ancient custom, are only admitted as spectators—display beautiful costumes, which still ornamented the courts of Europe 100 years ago and are still maintained in the greater part of Asia.

The membership of the Central Committee is, as one might suppose, formed of rather disparate elements, but careful distinctions of rank are maintained. Sovereign princes are found there in rather large quantity, not with the same titles as those who figure in the Universal Congress. They are not national delegates; either they sit on behalf of powerful subscribers from their countries or by virtue of enormous contributions made from their personal funds. They occupy the places of honor, as do illustrious military leaders long condemned to complete inaction. Below them sit the superiors of monastic orders, in the habits of their rule. After that come poets, celebrated artists, and even a few philosophers.

There is no need to emphasize here the great importance of this Central Committee, which is one of the great active powers of the world; the Central Committee of the Association of Civilization, its antagonist, which is meeting at this moment in Vienna, the capital of Austria, is the other. The former has some analogy, although on a much greater scale and save for one radical difference, with the famous Holy Alliance that opposed the spirit of political innovation at the beginning of the 19th century; the second has the same analogy with the Grand

Alliance of constitutional governments, which so effectively protected the progress of nations.

If, after having passed through the long lines of guards, on foot and on horseback, formed by several hundred domestic servants in embroidered coats, we penetrate into the mysterious circle of deliberations, we shall hear several fashionable orators. The request for help made by Aëtos, the Emperor of the Skies is, in fact, in the order of the day. The discussion could not be more animated.

A handsome young man with long blond hair, whose curls frolic over his broad and almost radiant forehead, rises to his feet. One can tell by his costume that he is a sovereign prince; it is said that he governs one of the most beautiful states in the German Union.

"My lords and gentlemen," he says, "all the questions submitted for my examination are, for me, subordinate to the great philosophical and religious question. Others may be guided as they see fit, but this is my pole: reason and faith constitute the magnet with whose aid I always seek my way. Although I am as convinced as any of my listeners of the deplorable results of the material progress of civilization, it is nevertheless impossible for me to associate myself with blind hatreds that envelope its intellectual and moral progress within the same anathema, or which, not recoiling from any means of combating industrialism and democratic exiguity, welcome without scruple all the allies that present themselves, be they despotism, brigandage or impiety."

(Violent murmurs on the right-hand side of the assembly.)

"The responsive murmurs from this part of the committee prove that I have struck home. Yes, gentlemen, the allies that you propose, those who are asking you for subsidy, are despots, brigands and blasphemers."

(Bravos from the left.)

"And what can you expect from this monstrous alliance? The triumph of the stupid hordes of Tartary, or those shameless women who, under the title of Amazons, have organized polyandry for themselves..."

(Whispers of curiosity from the ladies' gallery.)

"...or those Asiatic despots who wish to reestablish the slavery of both sexes with an ancient Islam captive to the text of the Koran? Personally, gentlemen, I want the earthly triumph of generous sentiments, not the triumph of injustice, and I am not one of those who mistake barbarity for poetry. What would the shades of those many knights who, for centuries on end, shed their blood for the defense of the faith, the oppressed and the more delicate sex, think if they saw men claiming to be animated by their spirit, some of whom have reason to claim to be their descendants, contracting an alliance with the enemies of the Christian faith, of human dignity, and the liberty and modesty of women! No, gentlemen, that is not where I go in search of poetry and noble emotions. A thousand times rather civilization, entire with its interests, its calculations, its mechanical monotony and its dreary uniformity, than raise up such enemies against it! For me, gentlemen, the true civilization is the complete development of the most sublime, the most philanthropic, the most universal and the most moral of truths, Christianity. Let us aid its development; let us oppose without respite the egotism and the brazen love of material enjoyments that has become its obstacle, and then we might achieve the triumph of the entirely religious and poetic civilization that Providence, I firmly believe, has reserved for this world of sorrows and trials in order that humankind might pass more smoothly into a better world."

This tirade, greeted by the murmurs of a part of the assembly that appears to be in the majority, is welcomed by the acclamations of the opposition, and by applause from the ladies' gallery. That part of the auditorium was, it is true, favorably predisposed towards the orator by his handsome appearance, his sonorous voice and the gestures full of nobility with which he expressed himself, but in coming out so strongly against polygamy he could not fail to win the feminine vote. It is for the same reason that a Spanish orator has been vigorously applauded for this passage: "At the time when Christian truth appeared to the Roman world, a voice said: 'the gods are departing;' later, the same was said of kings, when their absolute power fell; if the elite of Christian Europe allies itself today with the tyrants of the more beautiful half of the human species, with those who refuse to deliver to her faith the honor and security of their love, holding her ignobly captive under the guard of hideous jailers victim to atrocious suspicions, who do not deem her capable of experiencing and satisfying the pleasures of the senses, and, not content with oppressing her in this life, do not even accord her a soul [51] to console her with the hope of a life to come, then, gentlemen, one may say that love, that child of Christianity and feudalism, has departed."

The orator of the majority who has followed the philosophical Christian prince is no less than the Tsar of

---

[51] Bodin inserts a note: "It must nevertheless be admitted that there exists in the Koran a text according to which it is promised that wives faithful to their husbands will remain at the age of 16 for all eternity, and also that they will have other husbands than those they had on Earth."

southern Russia. He is very careful to address himself, like his predecessor, to the rationality of his audience. He has set out to excite their passions only by caressing them. He has painted the darkest possible picture of social conditions at the point to which civilization has presently led them; he has skillfully emphasized the continually increasing importance in the world of industrial wealth, scientists, physicists chemists and technologists; he has displayed in the most unfavorable aspect the prodigious subdivision of landed property, the equal mediocrity of non-industrial fortunes, the almost complete absorption of money—through the medium of savings banks—by the working class, and the fruits of the great development of primary education and maternal schools: the ideas of dignity and ability that such an excellent education has put into the heads of the poorest people, the shortage of farmer-workers, day-laborers and vine-growers in several parts of Europe, and the excessive cost of domestic servants or the impossibility even of finding them in certain countries. Finally, by means of adroit transitions, he has come to the matter of finding for the remedies for such a horrible situation; he can see none, for the moment, but the proposed alliance. Without approving of all the actions of the auxiliaries who present themselves in opposition to civilization, he paints a brilliant colors their energy, their courage, and their knowledge of an art which, in other times, was the highest source from which men could drawn glory: an art that has now wasted away, fallen into discredit and been forgotten, to the point at which, he says, no one dares appear in public in a uniform for fear of ridicule, and which one scarcely sees any more, except in theaters and in this august assembly—just as one only sees antique arms and armor in museums.

(Vigorous applause from the military benches.)

"Finally, my lords and gentlemen, shall it be said that the time is gone forever of heroes, of conquerors, of those glorious and powerful living centralities of human races, which the Earth, with common accord, saluted with the title of Great Men? Shall Napoleon have closed the list of those gigantic names which absorb all the glories of this world, and shall we see humankind marching from now on as a nameless multitude?

"Do you think, gentlemen, that it was not a beautiful spectacle to see these immense masses of men moving under the empire of a single will, at the signal of a single finger, sacrificing their liberty, their thought, the lives with such complete abnegation? Do you think that humankind was diminished, as our utilitarians and democrats claim, when it surrendered itself to that noble enthusiasm for its leaders, when it followed them with such absolute, blind—fanatical, if you wish—confidence? Ah, it's democratic equality and industrial egotism that is really diminishing it, by exciting a stupid and impotent pride therein!

"Do you imagine that every one of those 500,000 soldiers, followers of a conqueror, who overran the land with him, overturning everything in their passage, did not feel his own valor doubled by the idea that he shared in his leader's valor? Did not every one of them believe himself to be ten feet tall, and was that not the cause of the irresistible impetuosity of these torrents of men? And do you see similar examples of exaltation and devotion in the philanthropic armies which do battle for their interest, or with the more ridiculous pretension of doing so for the benefit of their enemy, in obeying, without impulsion or passion, some rickety and impotent leader who makes every effort to demonstrate to them by $a + b$

176

that he that he commands them as scientifically as is possible and for the greatest good of the greatest number."

(Laughter and applause from the majority.)

"You desire, gentlemen, to bring poetry back to the world!—and is that not the highest and most beautiful poetry that is available to you? That which was great and poetic within Islam: the power represented by the sword and the turban. That which was great and poetic in war: a leader who is the idol of his soldiers and endowed with everything that speaks to the imagination; a character of steel, a fiery genius, a hero whose entire person might stand as a model of the beautiful and the grandiose! To those who are not antipathetic to novelties or who display a poetic side, I will say that this man, whose name draws entire nations to his flag and yields immense territories to him, has greater forces at his disposal than have ever been assembled before in the atmosphere, and he has had himself proclaimed Emperor of the Skies.

"And this man makes proper and authentic war, rather than that bizarrely mechanical war of which our great industrial nations have recently provided examples: that warfare in which extensive armies of machines combat one another, without anyone ever seeing the faces of the men who operate them, overturning one another and destroying one another piece by piece, until one of them is reduced to scraps—after which, on either side, a dozen mechanics have been killed or wounded by the explosion of their instruments, so much precaution does the civilized man take to protect his precious life; ridiculously parodies of warfare, which one might take for a masquerade of grotesque demons mocking the human species."

(Laughter and applause from the military bench.)

177

"He makes true war: warfare in which hundreds of thousands of men are deployed in the immensity of the plain, covering the soil like ants and delivering serious battles, in which thousands of explosions sound simultaneously, sowing death with a racket that makes the Earth tremble and sets fire to the sky; in which, once it is all over, rapid cavalry units gallop through the scattered dead and dying in pursuit of those in flight to the sound of fanfares, triumphantly completing the victory."

(An enthusiastic stamping of feet.)

"When will his like be seen again on Earth? Is he not perhaps that last of the great captains? I fear so. And while we wait, we allow civilization calmly to pursue its course, covering everything with its slime, reducing to its own level all that remains of the grandeurs of the past, the heights of the former social estate, just as the superb heads of pines and trunks of ancient oaks are felled by its axe. Shall we, degenerate children of our fathers, stand here with arms folded, watching the accomplishment of the work of destruction as impotent and bewildered witnesses, protesting only in timid murmurs, presumably waiting with magnanimous courage to inscribe a poetic epitaph on society's tomb?"

This bombastic peroration has no lack of effect. The portrait of Aëtos, most of all, has seduced feminine imaginations, and the same galleries that applauded the crowned philosopher from Germany let loose frantic applause for the imperial orator. Such is the inconsistency of certain minds, and the tendency among the weak to surrender to the admiration of the strong who oppress them!

It is easy to anticipate the captivation of a large part of the assembly that will be the result of the debate. The majority is already known. The explicit language of the southern Tsar suggests that he has contracted a secret alliance with the enterprising Aëtos, whether out of fear of a troublesome neighbor or in the hope of a generous share in the spoils of Europe or Asia. It is in vain that the constitutional Tsar of Petersburg speaks on the moderate side. The influence of the former on the Central Committee is palpable; his northern colleague is eclipsed.

Other orators, one French, one Italian and one Swedish, attempt to continue the debate, but they cannot make themselves heard in the tumultuous and distraught assembly. An Englishman, whose social position is considerable, and who claims descent from the Duke of Wellington and the Bonaparte family, vainly launches into a pompous comparison between Aëtos and Napoleon. The only impact is contrived by a loud interruption made in the voice of the General of the Jesuits: *"And what if he were the Antichrist?"*

This statement, unexpected hurled from the midst of the Committee, produces a singular effect. At first, it strikes a kind of terror into souls, and for several minutes a general silence reigns in the cavern—but a few outbursts of laughter are hazarded, and the greater part of the audience soon associates itself with this manifestation of disdain. A voice from the extreme right dares to cry out: *"And what if he is?"*—but it is stifled, by murmurs of disapproval. Meanwhile, the General of the Jesuits is congratulated by his colleagues in the opposition for the courage of his Christian interjection.

The full import of this exclamation is tangible in the mouth of the man who is regarded as the champion of the old Catholicism, and who puts himself forward as the successor of the old Popes now that the Roman Church, in opening its bosom to the principal Christian sects, has found it necessary to modify itself. The conservative

Society of Jesus having rallied to it a rather large part of the rural population, in which the sacerdotal tradition is preserved with all its rites and dogmas, has become a spiritual power of the first order. Given that the appeal made by Aëtos is addressed not only to the bellicose passions of all uncivilized people, but also to the fanaticism of that literal Islam which remains faithful to the Koran and to that Roman Christianity which is a trifle neglectful of the letter and spirit of the gospel, it might have been feared that the Jesuits would only lend it the support of their influence over their docile religious adherents; at any rate, the opinion of that society, manifest by the voice of its supreme chief, is of great importance to the cause of civilization.

It does not prevent a massive vote in favor of Aëtos—but that audacity is not pushed to the point of granting him, as his fiercest partisans would have wished, effective assistance in men and materials of war. Even so, an almost equivalent result is attained by virtue of the large number of European volunteers who, stimulated by the Poetic Association, leave from all parts to join his regiments.

XVI. Catalepsy

The nervous system is the mystery of life,
and life is the mystery of the soul.
An amateur physiologist.

Personally, I say that the soul explains life,
and that life explains the nervous system.
Another amateur physiologist.

While the Central Committee of the Anti-Prosaic Association were taking this decision, the one that had met in Vienna appointed Philirène Generalissimo of the air, land and sea forces of the Universal Association of Civilization by acclamation. He refrained, for reasons of discretion and so not to exercise influence on the voters, from taking his seat on the committee, of which he was one of the most important members. He even waited for his election as Generalissimo, assured though it seemed, before taking his seat on the military committee at Athens. He remained in Carthage for secret discussions with Politée regarding the means of financing the expedition, and opening active communications via ambassadors and couriers with the principal capitalists of the three sectors of the Earth, who had the greatest interest in the success of his vast project.

He has witnessed, with a curious emotion, several of Politée's consultations with her Pythonesses, intended to shed light on the fate of his dear Mirzala. He has learned, with a satisfaction that has revived and fortified his love to a singular degree, that the charming sultana has thus far obstinately refused her handsome abductor admission to her presence. The skeptic's tepidity cannot resist that unequivocal proof of fidelity.

Revelations no less important to him, however, need to be imparted by an analogous voice.

The lack of sympathy that Madame Charlotte manifests towards Philirène has been evident for a long time. Independently of the political motives that inevitably make the aristocratic great lady unfavorable to the hero of modern civilization and the living symbol of the intellectual and industrial alliance, it is supposed that the obscurity surrounding his birth makes a considerable contribution to the scorn of the governess with royal blood. Indeed, Philirène is widely known to be a foundling, in whom the celebrated capitalist Agathodême [52] was sufficiently interested to have him brought up with great care and, later, to make him heir to his immense fortune. This circumstance, of which Madame Charlotte disapproves so strongly, is precisely what inspired Philirène to take a tender interest in the gentle Mirzala, seeing in her a sort of conformity with his own destiny, which the slight mystery hiding the circumstances of own her birth from her could only heighten further.

Madame Charlotte being one of the most devoted and most generous subscribers to the Poetic Association, her hero of preference is Philomaque, and she knows

---

[52] Agathodême decodes as "the good people"—presumably Bodin's collective conceptualization of capitalists. The elevation of capitalism as a moral ideal was unusual at the time; Ayn Rand, the chief 20th century advocate of that philosophical position, also wrote a "Romantic Manifesto" for literature, of which Bodin would probably not have approved, but she was a futuristic novelist too, of which he surely would.

perfectly well that he is the man who, under the name of Aëtos, has been appointed leader of the birds of prey; it is understandable, therefore, that the election of Philirène as Generalissimo of the forces that must fight him will not have done anything to make her look upon our pacifist hero with a more favorable eye. Not only was it noticeable that this news seemed to have increased Madame Charlotte's antipathy, but it was obvious that her health was seriously affected. She has not come out of her apartment for several days, and even Politée has not been admitted thereto.

Despite the great discretion of her physician, it has been known for some time that Madame Charlotte has experienced fits of catalepsy several times in her life, albeit at fairly long intervals. It is naturally supposed that this is the cause of her retreat. It is also known that the attacks of this bizarre malady are caused by extreme frustration, and it has been easy to observe various symptomatic precursors whose prognosis is always infallible.

There has been no mistake, but Madame Charlotte's physician is an excellent magnetizer; he is so profoundly initiated into the secrets of the nervous system that he easily cuts short the duration of these crises, which were more indefinitely protracted in times of medical ignorance. He would even have been able to prevent their recurrence entirely had he not acquired the certainty that they were a salutary necessity for the irritable constitution of the patient. They are a sort of periodic calming that restores the nerves, the deprivation of which can have harmful effects on one's reason. Moreover, he knows how to precipitate and assist the occasional invasion of these attacks, which, far from being in the least painful, provide the respectable lady with a useful means of passing into a magnetic trance—which no one has been able to provoke in her by any other means.

Given all this, Philirène is quite astonished when the hermetic savant Kalocrator,[53] doctor of the faculty of Epidaurus,[54] comes to inform him, mysteriously, that Madame Charlotte has a strong desire to speak to him, and invites him to come to her private chapel. Without having the time to form any hypothesis as to what might have drawn such unexpected attention to him, he follows the doctor, who introduces him to the chapel and then withdraws.

Madame Charlotte's chapel is a small one, built in the style improperly called Gothic, which left such beautiful models in Europe from the 13th to the 15th century. The stucco with which this little architectural jewel has been constructed is as hard as marble, and has been wrought with a fineness of detail and lightness in the fabric of its sculpted lacework to which the stone of the most famous cathedrals, such as Westminster, was not susceptible. This artificial marble, warmly nuanced with bitumen, variegated with bright patches of color and gleaming metallic and crystalline veins, is simultaneously severe and pleasant in tone, imposing itself upon the soul and caressing the sight. Thick stained-glass windows representing subjects of religious history and

---

[53] Bodin initially gives this name as Calocrator, but subsequently uses an initial K, which I have substituted here for the sake of uniformity; the latter is more faithful to its Greek derivation, although Kalokrator might be reckoned even more faithful. Its significance is "noble authority."

[54] Epidaurus, which existed only in ruins in our 20th century, although it has presumably been rebuilt in Bodin's, was the site of a famous temple of Aesculapius, to which the sick once flocked from all over ancient Greece to hear its oracles.

curtains of a fine and shiny enameled fabric that intercept the daylight further emphasize the effect of that curious interior, so appropriate to inspire pious meditation.

Madame Charlotte is sitting beside her *prie-Dieu*, on a long wide chair in the Moorish style, covered with squares of velvet fringed with gold. Philirène, having passed abruptly from the vivid light outside to the mysterious semi-darkness of the chapel, only perceives her attitude at first, without noticing that her eyes are closed. As he comes in, she rises swiftly to her feet, runs towards him, clasps him in her arms with a convulsive tenderness, punctuated by sobs, and immediately begins to swoon.

Philirène, almost as touched as surprised by such an inexplicable scene, takes her to the checkered chair and sets her gently upon it. While an abundance of tears clears a path through the invalid's eyelids, she says in a weary voice: "Ah, these tears are doing me good, since I have not been able to shed them for 30 years!"

I don't know why I have represented Philirène as an almost insensitive creature, incapable of great emotion. Perhaps he does not feel things as acutely as others, but he is so unfamiliar with sympathy, and so scarcely warrants comparison in the midst of nervous commotions to those vitreous insulators that allow physicians to touch with impunity bodies charged with the most terrible doses of electricity, that, without knowing why this woman is so powerfully affected, and without having the least idea what the two of them have in common, solely by the communicative virtue of the physical sensibility that I shall call "the conductor of tears," he becomes emotional himself; his eyes are moistened and he feels that he is ready to weep.

I am afraid that my style cannot really do justice to the scene I have to relate. I dread that I might destroy its effect if I do not postpone it to another chapter, in which I shall make every effort to take a nobler tone by adopting a more serious physiognomy.

People who have seen Mozart's *Don Giovanni* performed by one of the musical societies that put on the old Classical masterpieces in order that they should not fall into oblivion will have heard with a sort of terror, in the lively and pretty comic duet between Don Juan and his servant Leporello, certain trombone notes: a kind of other-worldly music that announces to you that this is no longer a joking matter, and that the statue of the commander is a character to be taken very seriously. This is precisely the situation in which I find myself—or, if you prefer, I am at the moment when that same statue has just interrupted the joyous refrains of Don Juan during his supper. The chandeliers go dark then; the trombones sound their lugubrious but the sonorous brass notes again; the double basses boom forth their deep chords— and one senses that a tragic scene is about to begin.

A good opportunity presents itself here to treat the question, which critics belabor perpetually, of the extent to which the comic might be mingled with the serious— to which it is permissible for eyebrows that have been frowning with sadness to be raised again towards the temples by some joyful joke, or a mouth that has been widened by a hearty laugh to be suddenly contracted by compassion—but I am wary of pronouncing an opinion on so irritating a question. I shall limit myself, for the moment, to observing that some people speak rather jokingly about very serious matters, just as many others speak with all the seriousness in the world about the most ridiculous things.

XVII. Revelation

Faulconb. *By this light, were I to get again,*
I would not wish a better father.
...Ay, my mother, With all my heart
I thank thee for my father!
Shakespeare.[55]

Bartholo. *This is your mother?*
Marceline. *Has not nature told you that*
a thousand times?
Figaro. *Never.*
Beaumarchais.[56]

After a few seconds' pause, during which her tears continue to fall abundantly, the tall and majestic woman next to whom Philirène finds himself seated wipes her inundated cheeks and releases a deep sigh.

"You don't understand any of this, Philirène," she says. "I see, or rather sense, your astonishment. Your prejudices are weakening, though; you're able to experience sympathy for me..."

"Why should I not, Madame?" he replies, softly. "You're suffering, and the nature that has not spared me sorrow has not refused me compassion for another."

---

[55] The lines are from *King John*, where they are normally attributed to "Philip the Bastard;" he is speaking to his mother, Lady Faulconbridge, by means of whose surname he is identified in this presumably-bowdlerized version.

[56] The lines are from *Le mariage de Figaro*.

"Ah, I sense that you're telling the truth. You're good. Why have I been condemned by my character and my opinions to show you such antipathy? It seems that the Devil wished it so; I shall not complain of it. But I implore you to forgive the arrogance of the woman that you have known in me until now!"

"It has not offended me, because I have always known its explanation. I understand your beliefs; I even respect them as a sublime portion of the truth, as the truth of the past."

"Oh!" says that singular woman excitedly, taking Philirène's hands and pressing them tenderly to her heart. "Let's set aside my ideas, which scarcely have any empire over me in that state that I'm in at present. I'm now detached from the passions of the world, to which I am so ardently attached; I look upon them almost with pity; I hear their noise without emotion, as the distant murmur of the waves reach those who sleep on the shore. No, I only hear one sole voice at present: the voice of nature, which speaks to me more loudly than all the voices of the Earth, which cries out to me—oh, you have not divined it, and why I am hesitant to say it?— which cries out to me that you are…that you are my son, my beloved son; my son, a part of my very self; my son, whom I carried so dolorously—alas!—and with a sorrow that was not in the least calmed by tenderness and hope; my son, whom I had the inhumanity not to press against my bosom, not to embrace upon my knees; my son, whom I have seemed not to know, who has not known me, and who, because of me, has not even had the privilege of knowing his father! Can you not hear me, dear Philirène? Can you not believe me? Oh, yes!—you believe me; how could I lie about such a thing?"

"I believe it," says Philirène, embracing her with filial tenderness. "You must be my mother, since it is you who says so."

"Ah, there's a kiss that opens my heart, so long desiccated by the passions of the world!"

She rests for a moment, and then resumes speaking in a calmer tone. "Listen, Philirène; I shall finally explain this enduring mystery. You do not know, I suppose, that I am Basilica Augusta [57] d'A***, descendant of Emperors and Kings of Europe. It is an advantage of which I am very proud when I see life from outside, but which I hold in scant regard at present, while my soul, folded in upon itself, is less entangled by earthly bonds and is in direct communication with other souls—elevated souls like yours, emanations close to the Divinity. Orphaned at an early age, I was placed and brought up in the convent of Sainte-Hélène in Constantinople, which, as you know, serves as a retreat for women of my rank who have no chance of contracting a marriage in conformity with ancient customs, the majority of whom decide to take the veil—but that was not my destiny.

"The celebrated Agathodême, the richest landowner on the island of Crete, had been a protégé of my mother; it was in our house that he began to make his fortune. His chemical studies of alimentary substances and his discovery of a means to extract starch from numerous vegetable species rendered services to humanity that could scarcely be underestimated, and which also made

---

[57] Bodin inserts a note here: "To represent these names as they are pronounced in Constantinople and Greece, it would be necessary to write *Vassiliki Sévasti*." The point he is making is that the Emperors from which Madame Charlotte is claiming descent are Byzantine.

him rich. At any rate, he was far from being ungrateful to us, and I do not know whether I ought to attribute the strong passion that he developed for me to his gratitude or to my beauty—of which I may speak today without being accused of vanity. Given the ideas with which I had been brought up, however, I was inevitably bound to reject that passion vigorously. Although the fortune and power of our family had been overturned, I could not for a moment contemplate accepting the name of an artisan of his power and fortune.

"The visiting-room of the convent of Sainte-Hélène, as is well-known, is not strictly closed to visits; it is even accessible to young men of high birth who are not fitted for religious austerity. One day, I saw Prince Nadir Khan there, better known under the European name of Alexander III, chief of the Uzbek Tartars; the sight of me made a sufficiently strong impression on him that, a short while after our first acquaintance, he asked for my hand in marriage. I admit that the extreme distinction of his manners had struck me too favorably for me to be able to refuse. Free in my actions, I followed him to Bukharia.[58] Shortly after our marriage, however, he perished in a disastrous campaign, in which he had set out to conquer the Punjab and Kashmir. I returned to Europe with the very few valuable jewels that he had left me, and a son. It is as well to give you his name immediately: that son is Philomaque."

"Merciful Heaven!" cries Philirène, with profound distress. "I expected as much! We are brothers, then! Yet

---

[58] In our 20th century, the former khanate of Bukharia was divided between Uzbekistan and Turkmenistan when the Soviet Union was formed.

another Thébaïde, or Braganciade: enemy brothers![59] I could do without that grief!"

"May God forbid that odious conflict, my son; what concerns me most of all is to prevent it."

"And how can that be done, Madame? But I should not interrupt you."

"We shall see; I shall continue. My fortune was much depleted. All I had left was what I had inherited from my mother, a Greek princess: half of the island of Ithaca—but that property, mortgaged to several creditors, would have been lost if the generous Agathodême had not secretly bought it in my name; it was only then that I discovered that I owed him that debt. He renewed his propositions, which would have been very seductive for any other woman. By virtue of his immense enterprise of the highway from Tyre to Heliopolis, Damascus and Palmyra, and the railway from Palmyra to the Euphrates, which opened up a new route connecting the Mediterranean and India, resuscitating those magnificent desiccated cadavers of desert cities as if by an electric cable, he was the industrial king of the superb Tadmor. He was, so to speak, offering me the throne of Zenobia.[60]

---

[59] *La Thébaïde, ou les frères ennemis* (1664) was the first of Racine's tragedies; it tells the story of the conflict between the two sons of the Theban King Oedipus, Eteocles and Polynices. Bragança or Braganza was the name of the ruling family of Portugal, whose scion headed the revolution that separated Portugal from Spain in 1640; the reference to that circumstance as if there were a tragedy based on it is metaphorical.

[60] Zenobia was the wife of Odenathus, the ruler of the kingdom of Palmyra, also known as Tadmor, in the 3rd century A.D. She shared his throne until he died in 271, then became regent for her son, but her armies were swiftly defeated by

"After taking a great deal of time to overcome my repugnance, I finally gave in, but on condition that our marriage would be hidden from the world. A Lebanese priest blessed us in secret.

"Whether it was because I could not vanquish, or at least hide, my arrogance, or because, as he came to know me better and saw me, as it were, at closer range, and felt his love growing cold—I speak with a sincerity that would be impossible at other times but costs me nothing now—Agathodême no longer mentioned any desire to make our marriage public. I felt wounded, and although he certainly had not refused the accomplishment of the condition that he had ardently desired himself, I was too proud ever to admit it. I chose another reason to tell him that I was leaving him. He did not spare his efforts to turn me away from that resolution, but it was irrevocable, even though I was pregnant and that circumstance should have re-tightened the bond between us. I withdrew to an obscure village in Attica, intending to leave there after my delivery to re-enter society. I gave birth to a son, whom I sent to Agathodême, as had been agreed between us, with a nurse who had not been told anything. That son is you."

"Oh, mother!" cries Philirène, unable to suppress the impulse of his joy, "How I thank Almighty God, to be the son of so great a man, a benefactor of humanity who has been given the name *Evergete*,[61] to which he is fully entitled!"

---

those of the Roman emperor Aurelian; her capital city fell the following year and she was taken to Rome as a prisoner.

[61] Evergete is derived from a Greek word meaning "benefactor;" the nickname was given to one of the Ptolemaic Kings of Egypt.

"And I," says Basilica, sadly, "am punished as I have fully deserved, in seeing you take so much pride in your father, and so little in your mother."

Philirène embraces her tenderly to soothe that poignant sentiment, but his initial impulse was understandable. Although Basilica counts great Kings and illustrious Emperors in her genealogy, which extends back to the 8th century, Philirène, who is aware of the uncertainty of historical hypotheses, knows as well as any schoolboy that after a mere ten generations—which is to say, two and a half centuries at the most, even admitting the transmission of blood from Lucretius to Lucretius, according to Boileau's expression—we have only the 84th part per 1000 of the blood of each of our ancestors, while it is evident to him that he can count on the great Agathodême Evergete for half of his existence. "My father, my dear father," he cries again, "Why did you refused me the favor of giving you that title, of revering your memory like a loving son!"

"If he had lived longer, perhaps he would have revealed the secret of your birth to you—but that secret belonged to me also, and he had promised me that I would remain its keeper. Austere in his behavior and respectful of opinion as he was, he preferred to write you into his will as the son of one of his friends, orphaned in the cradle. As for me, I was careful not to divulge the secret, although my conscience reproached me for leaving you ignorant of your parentage. A revolution favorable to my son recalled me to the lands of the Uzbeks, where I devoted myself entirely to giving him a military education worthy of his birth. The world knows the extent to which I attached my life to his. In devoting the few years that remain to me to his son, here, I am merely continuing that sacrifice. What other purpose could I find in this sad life? What other bond do I have in this world, I which the glories to which I have given my admiration, my faith and my worship are perishing day by day? Those ideas have so powerful a hold on me that the sentiments of nature are resuming their empire over me as I speak; I feel that I am insufficient detached from them.

"One of the great anxieties of my life was of seeing antipathy flare up between you and your brother. I left no stone unturned to prevent any proximity or connection between you—but was that possible, since the differences in your inclinations, your education, your positions, was bound to call you to play such opposed roles in the world, and to provide each of you with a flair that could not fail to make you enemies?"

"Oh, for myself, Madame, I swear to you that I do not hate him. I merely pity him—but my duty is to curb his criminal exploits."

"Well, dear Philirène," says Basilica forcefully, throwing herself on her knees to hold him in her embrace, "if the voice of a supplicant mother has any authority in your heart, take no action in that regard. I implore you, although I admit that I have scant right to do so. Don't think that I'm speaking now solely on Philomaque's behalf—no, it seems to me that, at this moment, you are equal in my affection. Perhaps I love you more than him, you who have had the generosity to let me in, now that I see with the pure life of the soul—I, who, in the blind life of the world have the injustice to accuse you of hypocrisy and ambition!" Kissing his hands, she repeated: "Philirène, I beg you, do not take up arms against your brother; do not confront me with the frightful spectacle of a sacrilegious war whose theater I bore within my womb, accursed by God!"

As she finishes this supplication, by which Philirène is so moved that he is ready to yield to it, at the risk of covering himself with shame before the world, Basilica falls to the ground, exhausted. Her son brings her round partially, but she signals to him that she needs to rest and gives him a farewell kiss. Kalocrator comes back in to tend to his royal patient.

There is no need to describe the agitation that this extraordinary scene leaves in Philirène. He takes himself off in order that none of it should show; indeed, he want to keep his secret and wait to find out whether Basilica will treat him like a son in her normal state. "In the final analysis," he says to himself, still feeling her unexpected caresses, "I, who have desired that happiness so strongly, have been pressed to the bosom of a mother— but if it had been up to me, she is certainly not the mother I would have chosen!"

Two more days pass without Madame Charlotte coming out of her apartment. The doctor says that she had recovered completely, after sleeping profoundly and uninterruptedly for 24 hours. She soon reappears, and resumes her duties with regard to her pupil. She sees Philirène with the same eyes as before, without giving the slightest evidence of what has passed between them.

Although Philirène has carried out physiological studies adequate for him not to be in the least astonished by this phenomenon, he cannot help being hurt by it, and says with a sigh: "Ah, I had good reason to wish for another mother!"

Indeed, he has little chance of recovering the one he has until the next attack of catalepsy.

It is not for the benefit of lovers of drama that I have lingered rather a long time over this situation, somewhat dramatic as it is. It is solely to give pleasure to the individuals who have made a start on physiological and psychological research into the mysteries of the nervous system and the double existence of human beings. Even so, the critics will reproach me for having put three scenes of somniloquism into this volume; two would have been sufficient. I shall try on another occasion to avoid a similar compositional fault—but I thought that some readers might be pleased to know what this chapter has taught them. Authorial presumption!

XVIII. The Barbarians

And when the thousand years are expired,
Satan shall be loosed out of his prison,
And shall go out to deceive the nations
which are in the four quarters of the Earth,
Gog and Magog, to gather them together to battle:
the number of whom is as the sand of the sea.
Apocalypse, ch XX, v. 7.[62]

Italiam! Italiam!
Barbarian cries.

Paris! Paris!
Cossack cries.[63]

The Tartarians are barbarians
to their enemies alone.
Comic Opera March.

Meanwhile, Philirène and Politée have left Carthage separately. They are traveling through parts of Europe, Asia and Africa rousing populations, raising troops, gathering together birds of prey, ships, armaments and chemical products, and coordinating the means of their

---

[62] Actually, verses 7 and 8.

[63] Cossack troops rode through the streets of Paris in triumph following Napoleon's defeat at Waterloo in 1815—an incident whose memory was still raw in 1834, to which Bodin might conceivably have been a witness.

gigantic expedition. Let us transport ourselves on the wings of imagination, which have served many others, and in the blink of an eye we shall be in the heart of Philomaque's estates—or the estates of Aëtos, to give him the name by which the world now knows him.

The great warrior having conducted his preliminary campaigns with the combined forces of the Manchus and Mongols—at the head of which, at the age of 23, he achieved the conquest of China—he is still idolized by the Tartar tribes, whose character, essentially bellicose and predatory, is entirely in harmony with the all-consuming martial activity of such a leader. Although their arms, under his leadership, have not been success-ful against Hindustan, defended by its imposing forces of well-disciplined Anglo-Indian "half-castes," they have not lost their blind confidence in him. The super-stition of those coarse folk has further augmented the prestige with which his person has been surrounded by such a precocious military reputation and such striking feats of arms. He is supposed to possess miraculous vir-tues; a host of bizarre prodigies are attributed to him; and had he wished to commit himself to playing the boring role of the Dalai Lama, he would undoubtedly have succeeded in being considered by his soldiers as a veritable incarnation of Buddha, as the living god—but such a fantasy could not enter the head of a man of the Earth, who has a great need to travel over it incessantly, and to leave traces of his passage there. He prefers to keep the immobile pontiff of the yellow religion, the leader of so many faithful millions, as a useful instru-ment in his hands, just as the Manchu leaders had once done in their Celestial Empire. He has contented himself, to please the pious Tartars of Tibet, with the title of Kutuchtu: a human divinity of the second rank, after the Dalai Lama.

In the same way, when it was briefly in his power to take the Imperial throne of China for himself and the title of Son of Heaven, he preferred to re-establish a scion of the ancient dynasty. Skillful in manipulating popular ideas, he has cultivated the impression that he is reserved for the highest destiny. Finally, among the no-madic tribes, who military affiliations are the most illus-trious, and which are most imposing in the imagination, it is the general and widespread belief that Philomaque is the descendant of Tchinguiz or Genghiz Khan, of Peter the Great of Russia, and of Nboloun—the name under which the immense renown of Napoleon is perpetuated among them. For the various Mongol tribes, therefore, be they Khalkas, Eleuths, Sungors or Kalmuks, as for the Manchus themselves, he is the Tzagan Khan, or White Khan *par excellence*, the Changun, or great general.

The reverse that he suffered in his campaign against Hindustan resulted in his eclipse from the world stage for several years, and it was then that the unfortu-nate Politée became one of the numerous victims of his idleness. When his affairs took a turn for the better, he did not hesitate to leave her to recommence his life as a warrior, and he made the series of conquests that have rendered him more powerful that Tamerlane among the Tartars.

At present, Aëtos' specifically terrestrial empire extends from southern Tibet through Bhutan, Nepal, the Punjab and Kashmir, Kandahar and greater Bukharia as far as the Aral Sea. To the north it is limited by the vast territories of the Siberian Confederation, whose Kirghiz tribes, which are opposed to him, have kept him from the shores of the Caspian Sea for a long time. The army of

400,000 men that he has assembled in the two Bukharias, 50 regiments of which are Manchu regulars who have been on the march for six months from the shores of the Sea of Japan and the Sea of Okhotsk, which bathes Kamchatka; it is evidently intended to invade the Turko-Persian Empire by way of Khorasan, and to march directly westwards from there to take possession of the two major communication links between India and Europe, that of Euphrates and the Persian Gulf and that of the Red Sea. Other armies under the orders of his dozen field marshals will presumably emerge from Kashmir and other points to march upon Hindustan.

Since the birds of prey, or aerial brigands of the Caucasus, the Taurus, the Lebanon, the mountains of Arabia, and even the Atlas Mountains, have recognized him as their suzerain, he has advance posts overlooking the richest possessions of European civilization, which give him the means of combining this invasion plan with feigned aerial attacks on Alexandria, Cairo and Jerusalem, or on Algiers and Carthage, or even on Ilium and Constantinople, which will strike sudden terror into the capitals of Europe and create a useful diversion for him.

Finally, to conciliate old passions, the fanatical hopes of the ancient Islam that still has a powerful effect on the minds of large populations, he has taken it into his head to abduct the Sultana Mirzala, the daughter of the Sultans of Stamboul and Babylon, the only offspring of the blood of Mohammed. His plan is to proclaim her Empress of the Skies at Mecca and he intends to employ the greater part of his atmospheric forces subsequently to take possession of the summits of Horeb and Sinai, with the aim of celebrating his own coronation there. But these points, so important by virtue of the religious memories that they will recruit to his cause, and by virtue of their military situation, are so strongly fortified by the Israelite government that such a scheme presents the greatest difficulties.

What a bizarrely animated scene one of the great Aëtos' terrestrial encampments offers to the eye! There are the Manchus, who have conquered China more than once, showing yet again their skill as administrators, finer politicians than audacious warriors. Then there are the Mongols, formerly their allies in the conquests and their tributaries after the victory, one time conquerors of Hindustan themselves, and still so proud of the memory of Tchinguiz, from whom their petty chiefs claim descent. You see them under their felt tents surrounded by numerous flocks; you see their camels and their little horses, inured to fatigue, like those of Cossacks. A large proportion are organized into regiments and equipped in the European manner, but others still use arquebuses supported by forked sticks, or even bows and arrows. One also observes helmet and chain-mail which might date back to the campaigns of Genghis Khan, handed down from father to son. Other antiquities no less peculiar are small cast-iron cannon mounted in pairs on camels; these living gun-carriages, so well-trained in maneuvering, which kneel when one fires, resemble fantastic creations by Callot.[64] A poor artillery, in truth, which creates more noise than damage! But they are still bellicose, these Mongols, entire armies of whom are employed in tiger hunts—those little wars in which, as in

---

[64] Jacques Callot (1592-1635) was an artist famous for his caricaturish sketches and engravings, whose grotesquely exaggerated habits of representation are nowadays familiarized as the stereotypical method of cartoonists, but which seemed strange and sinister to his contemporaries.

the times of the Manchu emperors of China, the Order of the Peacock Feather (Third Class) is still awarded to reward acts of bravery—and they are still paid in pieces of tea-brick, the ancient currency of Mongolia.

But the most handsome contingent of Aëtos' armies comes from his hereditary estates in Bukharia. The Uzbeks are still the bravest of all the Tartars, and have mobilized more than 100,000 combatants. Zealous Muslims of the rigid Sunni sect, enemies of the numerous sectarians of Ali [65] who remain in Persia, they have the stimulus of fanaticism, and their extreme sobriety is another advantage in battle. They are a handsome race, which displays the purity and nobility of Caucasian form; the women follow their husbands into battle and fight by their side.

Is it necessary to describe the other warrior hordes that make up the great Khan's army? Is it necessary to mention the corps of European volunteers who, by virtue of their discipline and their racial superiority, form that army's elite? Or the special corps that have multiplied the science of destruction; the herds of elephants, carriers of Greek fire; the terrible steam- and gas-batteries, more terrible than cannon; the monster-mortars drawn by 50 horses? That would be tiresome and might perhaps distress the reader. It is sufficient to show him the mass of ferocious human faces, as ugly as those of Attila's army must have been: those flat faces with snub noses, widely-separated eyes and enormous mouths, with yel-

---

[65] The Shia Muslims, whose heartland in our 20th century is now known as Iran, reject the first of the three caliphs and consider Ali, Mohammed's son-in-law, as his rightful successor; in consequence, they reject the body of tradition known as the Sunna, from which their rival sectarians take their name.

low and greasy skin and hair, as thin and dirty as all the rest: Kalmuks, Pashkirs, Kalkhas, children of those who once—provoked, it is true by an aggression caused by heroic fire—came to spoil and degrade the monuments of Paris, all brought from remotest regions of the steppes.

The oft-predicted time has arrived! Working men have forgotten how to handle weapons, and their trades are plied for you, whose arms are always strong. March on their towns, so brightly painted, on their rural regions, so well-groomed; there is enough there for you to enjoy for years: to enjoy drinking, eating, smoking and doing nothing; to enjoy wallowing in civilization's bed; to enjoy demolishing houses, felling trees; to enjoy destruction and burning things, and then bursting into laughter as you watch! March, run, gallop, lances forward; there are friends out there who are waiting for you, who are calling you, who will open their doors to you and that you will pillage and kill for their trouble!

What savage cries are piercing the skies? Howls of ferocious barbarian joy can be heard. There are the singers. Let us listen.

"Work, work, men of peace: the men of war are coming to pay your wages.

"Push, push your ploughshares, men of peace; the men of war are coming with swords.

"What good, what good are ploughs? We shall work the iron for our horses and lances.

"Work, work, etc.

"You beg your living from the soil arduously; it is from men that the brave demand their needs.

"Nothing is refused to him whose heart is firm and whose hand is hard, and whose eyelid does not blink in the face of death.

"Death! For the brave, it is paradise; a thousand time better death than the sad life bought, day after day, by toil.

"Work, work, men of peace; the men of war are coming to pay your wages."

Aëtos' maritime forces are the weakest element of his power. They consist of scarcely more than the pirate fleets of Malaya, Java, Australia, New Holland, New Zealand, and the islands of the Pacific—forces too widely disseminated and incapable of acting together with a common objective, but adequate to trouble commerce by frightening small ill-defended ports.

But the supreme leader, the will deicing so many agents of evil, the redoubtable Aëtos—where is he? He has a talent for not over-familiarizing gazes with his person, thus rendering himself almost mysterious. The care with which he conceals his actions and his journeys serves to further his plans by disguising them. One never knows where he is, and he falls unexpectedly from the clouds upon the place where his presence is necessary and unforeseen. As inaccessible as the ancient Asiatic despots, he appears thus in the minds of the servile peoples he commands, and he exercises an empire over their imaginations like that of the divinity which is respected most of all because it is never seen.

In the end, though, where is he at this moment?

Some say that he is at his principal air-base in the gorges of the Caucasus; others that he has gone to a meeting that he has arranged with the famous Queen of the Amazons in the valley of Kashmir. Some claim that he is still in Samarkand, his Occidental capital, where he is preparing to seduce the young sultana Mirzala, his beautiful prey: a fête fit for the *Thousand-and-One Nights* by virtue of his prestigious magnificence.

These are the first things that I shall tell the reader, if he is curious enough to ask me for a second volume and indulgent enough to inspire me with the courage to write it. Indeed, this volume is, to tell the truth, only an exposition, and I shall lower the curtain at the moment when the action is about to commence.

Post-Scriptum

Is this a *post-scriptum*, or is it not rather an *ante-scriptum*? The name is of little importance. What I mean is: why stop at this volume? Why abandon the reader half way through? Please listen to me for a moment.

The book is finished, and that is as well for all those—and I fear that their number might be large—who will have found it boring, or those who, without finding the least interest therein, without devoting enough of their attention to the characters to have the slightest curiosity as to the fates that are reserved for them, have only wanted to know what form might be given to a literary conception that is bizarre, to say the least, and have limited themselves to handling, turning over and testing the weight of that conception in order to assess its value. These are the critics, difficult people to satisfy—all the more so because they all differ in their fixed opinions or ways of feeling.

Some, who are in the majority, will not have found that this future corresponds to the one they have imagined; they will have judged it too similar, or not similar enough, to the present. Others will have desired more clarity, fewer things left unexplained and thrown at the reader with a *qui potest capere capiat*;[66] others, on the contrary, will regret not having encountered enough of the half-light of metaphysical poetry, the cloudy dusk of synthesis applied to the future history of humankind; or the lightning-streaked darkness, with the brief and figurative form of the verses of the *Apocalypse*.

---

[66] "Let him accept it who can."

Without answering all of these people for the moment, I shall simply say to the last-named that had I placed the future viewpoint on too distant a ground I would have strayed into what I call *the epic of the future*, which ought to be the work of another time, and certainly of another man. Overly daring conceptions, which would nevertheless have paled beside those of Monsieur Charles Fourier,[67] that utopian armed with analogy as a trenchant instrument, with the aid of which he has become the most marvelous as well as the most intrepid of imaginers of the future—such conceptions, I repeat, would have had the inconvenience of being too injurious to plausibility and interest, and of not allowing the great majority of readers to see that which pleases them most: characters with whom they feel they have something in common, with whom they sympathize, and, above all, whom they understand. I know perfectly well that there is a respectable minority of readers—on this side of the

---

[67] Charles Fourier (1772-1837) adopted a kind of utopian socialism that he attempted to systematize in a mock-Newtonian fashion, in which the adequate satisfaction of the 23 human passions would be satisfied by the organization of society into "phalansteries" of 1620 individuals whose shifting social roles would be carefully regulated. His works were notable not merely for the astonishing detail of their hypothetical constructions, but for their wryly flamboyant flights of fancy, whose extravagant wit Bodin surely appreciated, even though he must have disapproved of Fourier's Rousseauesque tendencies; the one most frequently remembered today is the suggestion that oceanic salt water might one day be technologically replaced by lemonade, although his cosmogonic account of copulating planets is far more grandiose. *Le nouveau monde industriel* (1829) had the advantage over his earlier works of being relatively sober and concise.

Rhine, of course—who only like what they cannot understand; I confess that I feel very little inclination to satisfy them, but I might try some day; I think that if I took as much trouble to be obscure as I habitually take to make myself clear, I might find the task less difficult than is generally believed.

As for the Biblical and Oriental style, that style in which one hurls forth images by the handful, more than a dozen Saint-Simonian[68] writers or orators have brought to that kind of pastiche a talent, a verve and a richness of imagination that no priest, however great a writer, has got remotely close to attaining—and which moreover, decorate conceptions much newer than the evangelical democracy of Millenarians and all the sects armed with a few of Christ's words with which to attack the social order. That style is suited to ardent faith, to religious exaltation. It should not be overly abused. Today, though, people use and abuse everything; poetic language and metaphor are mixed into everything, and

---

[68] Claude-Henri de Rouvroy, Comte de Saint-Simon (1760-1825), became a leading figure of the Restoration period, when he published extensively in periodicals. In the final year of his life he published two books, *Opinions littéraires, philosophiques et industrielles* and *Le nouveau Christianisme*, which enjoyed a spectacular posthumous vogue. The two books synthesized anti-egalitarian ideas regarding the future development of society with an eccentrically licentious Christian mysticism; their admirers founded a utopian community at Ménilmontant, whose contrived religion anticipated the advent of a female messiah. In 1832, the community was brought before a tribunal on charges of immorality, and the trial became one of the great sensations of the year. Remarkably, the great champion of positivism, Auguste Comte, had once served as Saint-Simon's secretary.

newspaper articles are perfumed with poetry. A fortunate time, when talent overflows its bounds, but which complains of its sterility, as all times do!

Finally, there are critics who will articulate more specialized grievances: they will accuse me of being too monarchic, too aristocratic, of leaving Christianity, property and marriage standing—or, if they are modified, not spelling out the modifications. To respond adequately to such reproaches, a whole volume would not be enough; I hope, therefore, that I might be granted a dispensation for the moment.

Those amiable and indulgent readers who ask no more than to be interested in characters, in the action, in settings, however—oh, those good readers!—if they have the slightest regret about not knowing how it will all come out, of not seeing the development of characters that it has only been possible to sketch, merely to prepare the theatre in which they will emerge; if those readers were to extend their courtesy to the point of inquiring into the antecedents of Philirène and Politée, the circumstances of the latter's marriage to Philomaque, and their separation, I should be so profoundly touched that I would do anything to be agreeable; I shall rummage through the Marquis Mummio de Foscanotte's heap of manuscripts again, and I shall draw a second volume therefrom in spite of my love of the *dolce farniente*.[69]

Are there any charming female readers who want to know whether the tender Mirzala will persist in her beautiful resistance to the enterprises of the audacious Aëtos? And that Aëtos, the hero that I promised them but whom they only glimpsed through the clouds of second sight, are they really curious to see him at closer

---

[69] "Sweet idleness."

range? I thank them 1000 times. All that will be reserved for the second part—that and many other things. Those birds of prey, whose mores are well worth the trouble of observation, should they not be visited? And those air-women who imagined total submission to the benefit of the male sex as a slavery analogous to that to which their sex was submitted by the despots of Asia, what is to be said about them? Will not Philomaque, like another Theseus, seek to seduce the queen of these new Amazons? Will he pass himself off as the Antichrist? And will some great atmospheric battle be delivered against him? Will civilization triumph over the barbarians? And little Jules, what will become of him? In another time, poetic flattery claimed that a little Iule [70] was the stock of the Caesars; will there still be Caesars? Oh, as to that, you ask too much; more, perhaps, than I can ever find out from my manuscripts. At the end of the day, though, these questions that I imagine hearing are immensely flattering, and I shall do my best to rely to them on another occasion.

Finally, to those who might have the generosity to desire in the narration the seriousness of sincere authors who believe in what they are saying, I promise to be as serious as one can be when one plays the prophet and the augur.

If, by misfortune, I am not able to fulfill these promises, then it will be necessary to inscribe at the end of this volume the usual final sentence of newspaper ar-

---

[70] Iule, or Iulus, is the new name that Virgil's Aeneas gives to his son Ascanius in order to symbolize his alleged association with the family of Julius Caesar. It is Ascanius (or, in fact, Cupid disguised as Ascanius), rather than his father, with whom Dido initially falls in love in the *Aeneid*.

ticles on European politics and events in the Orient: *The future will tell, etc.*

Notes

On The Preface

A fragment of the preface was published, etc.

This was in the *Gazette littéraire* of February 17, 1831.

I have thought for a long time that, in this century so fertile in bold literary ventures, historical systematizations and religious and social creations, some sort of register of hypotheses ought to be established for the conservation of ideas. I was very interested in that notion, having wanted to fix dates for and stake claims to a few ideas, half-ideas or quarter-ideas of my own—for I believe that I have as many as the next man. While awaiting that useful institution, however, newspapers and reviews supply the need to a certain extent.

It was in this spirit that I attempted, in the year of grace 1822, to be the French Walter Scott; then, after having published scraps here and there, calmly went to sleep on it, without claiming any patent of invention but merely an import license. Fortunately, others exploited that mine with more success than I would have had.

About 1828, I thought I had a new half-idea and set out to apply the methods of Water Scott to Antiquity; I wanted to display the Greeks and Romans, not booted in tragedy [71] but speaking and acting as one may suppose

---

[71] This item of popular critical wordplay—*chaussée du cothurne*—does not translate well, as it revolves around a double-meaning of the word *cothurne* (buskin/tragedy), but the basis of the expression is a contrast that likens tragedy to an overshoe and comedy to a sock.

that they spoke and acted in life. Before going to sleep completely on that half-idea, I fortunately took it into my head to publish a few fragments of Roman drama in literary reviews and magazines towards the end of 1830. It was just in time, for something similar appeared soon afterwards with precisely the same subject. If, by chance, it was not me who had given birth to the idea, at least I retain the mild satisfaction of being able to exhibit that I had it, entirely and independently (save for Ben Jonson).

In the same era, around 1829, I was witness to experiments in magnetism: I undertook some of them myself in order to dispel my doubts, which came exceedingly close to incredulity. I was convinced. I thought I had a quarter of an idea, which was to introduce magnetism into the arts and literature, as a poetic and dramatic element; but I learned that Germany was ahead of me, and I son read a very interesting novella by Monsieur Zschokke,[72] in which the somnambulistic state plays a leading role. Even so, I hastened to divulge my quarter-idea by way of the press, but the time to apply it had not yet come, so much prejudice against magnetism being widespread in France. I contented myself with risking, at a later date, by way of a trial, a little magnetic and romantic scene, which was published in several collections. Now that the incredulity of worldly people has entirely yielded to the striking nature and quantity of

---

[72] Heinrich Zschokke (1771-1848) was a prolific writer whose collected works fill 40 volumes. He believed himself to be gifted with Mesmer's power of "animal magnetism" and wrote extensively about it. There are secondary references to a story of his known in English as "Hortensia," which might be the one to which Bodin is referring, but I have not been able to identify the original.

proofs, I see with great pleasure that literature is taking possession of this marvelous wellspring of emotions and interest.

But the novel of the future, that idea—half- or quarter-, if you wish—which has been running through my head for a dozen years or so, tormented me much more! I published a fragment of the preface without having written a line of the book, for fear of being anticipated; I was very anxious to put enough on record to fix a date but not to reveal my plan. And on that too I went to sleep... but the sleep was a veritable nightmare: I could not read the slightest sentence that touched upon my idea, however remote the approach might be, without trembling at the thought that someone might trap the poor idea and put it to profitable use before me. The mere mention of the word *future* made me shiver. That state of mind was intolerable; if it had continued I would be dead and my book sunk. Subject to continual frights and an extraordinary sloth, I fought a violent struggle... the sloth has been vanquished (so much the worse for the public, some might say) and the book has been written in 20 days. Time has not put the matter to rest.

I do not believe that anyone can make his literary confession more candidly: it is a little footnote on the tribulations of an idler who, if he is doing nothing, is at least not like the gardener's dog, and is pleased to do justice to those who will act in his stead. Even so, he does not wish to fall completely into oblivion. This is also an explanation and an excuse, which I ought to make for the incomplete publication of this work, which evidently lacks a second part.

I beg pardon for having spoken at such lengths about matters of considerable indifference to the reader.

On Magnetism

It is perhaps not inappropriate to offer a few explanations of magnetism to readers who have not studies.
This is what I published on the subject in 1829; it then
required a sort of courage, for the pleasantries of Hoffmann [73] (in the *Journal des Débats*) had more authority
of judgment; in addition, a few days after that publication, I had the privilege of reading in a newspaper that I
had not written it seriously—or, if I had, then my reason
was in dire peril:

"The extraordinary phenomena produced, particularly on organic matter and of a mental nature, by the
influence known as *animal magnetism* can no longer be
called into question by those who do not wish to take the
trouble to verify them. It is therefore time to have their
existence declared, although one still cannot do so without exposing oneself to ridicule. But the truth is well
worth the trouble of risking such a petty danger on its
behalf, since it was deemed worthy in other times of the
sacrifice of one's life. Today it seems ridiculous; in ten
years the ridicule will cease, for facts are more tenacious
than that.

"Public experiments, repeated several times before
a number of scientists and physicians, ought to have rendered incontestable for enlightened individuals the reality of the agent called *magnetic* and the singular state
improperly called *somnambulism* by the magnetizers. An
immense quantity of similar experiments reproduced on
a daily basis almost throughout Europe display the development of a sixth sense or instinct elevated to the

---

[73] Presumably the French critic and dramatist François-Benoît
Hoffmann (1760-1828).

highest degree. They demonstrate in certain cases the power of the human will, extended to a point that would once have seemed miraculous, and can easily seem incredible today when it has not been observed.

"Here, therefore, is a new science, or rather an ancient one renewed; born in a milieu of mockery, often compromised by charlatanism, it no longer has anything to combat but prejudice. Subject to examination, it will perhaps reveal to us a universal agent, glimpsed since remote antiquity but too often misconstrued, and serving, whether in the hands of hierophants or conjurors or manifested by chance, to encourage belief in supernatural powers: angels or demons, intermediaries between the Divinity and nature. More enlightened now that everything has been related to immutable laws of physics, we should at least excuse our forefathers for having admitted many superstitions that are partially based on real phenomena; we should only blame them for having believed that the Devil had something to do with them, and for having arrested by torture the spirit of observation that might have been exercised upon the facts sooner, explaining them scientifically.

"But it is perhaps as well that the historical skepticism of the 18th century created a *tabula rasa* for all facts inexplicable by means of the laws of physics then known, because the principle of the immutability of the laws of nature has been established in the mind. Some say that it undermines the basis of religion, others think that it is necessary first to seek the truth.

"Perhaps too, far from destroying religions, this science will only serve to purify them, in fortifying their truly historic foundations and reattaching them all to an order of facts that, so to speak, *poetizes* the human species. It will delve into the ante-Diluvian past of Asia and

Africa for traces of a sort of instinctive revelation, to which it is necessary to return in order to understand the history of ancient societies. Finally, the magnetic agent, or whatever one cares to call it, will be discovered to be a modification or a generalization of electricity, galvanism, motion, light or life, apparently having the purpose of guiding humankind to sublime notions, physiological or psychological; and, entrusted to prudence and to philanthropy, it will doubtless summoned to soothe or cure diseases that were thought incurable, to retighten social bonds and to contribute to moral amelioration. Since it exists, it can only exist for a good purpose. Human being can abuse anything, but utilitarian usage always prevails over abuse.

"The magnetic medicine that, without supplanting conventional medicine, is at least called upon to direct and improve it, will not be one of the least benefits reserved by Providence for our posterity. The as-yet-inexplicable cures that it effects nowadays on a small number of people will be multiplied immeasurably, and new experiments must be expected. The state of complete insensibility that magnetism can sometimes obtain will allow a sick person to contemplate without fear, and undergo without pain, surgical operations that have until now alarmed desperation itself. Finally, and this will be its principal destination *in order to avoid grave inconveniences*, magnetism will become the medicine of the family and of friendship."

Again, this is what I wrote in 1832, at the head of my little magnetic novel:

"It is not at all convenient to be known in society as someone interested with magnetism. Many of your best friends will then consider you with a sort of compassionate anxiety, like that inspired in us by people who are not quite right in the head. I find that entirely natural; for several years now I have been treated thus by others, and today, for the same reason, I am almost ashamed to be identified as a follower of Mesmer, Puységur and the good Monsieur Deleuze.[74]

---

[74] The Austrian physician Franz Anton Mesmer (1734-1815) was the originator of the theory that the human body is possessed of a therapeutically-manipulable "magnetic fluid;" he began to popularize his ideas in France in the 1770s, so successfully that the government set up an investigative committee whose members included Antoine Lavoisier and Benjamin Franklin (then in Paris on a diplomatic mission), which reported in 1784 that it could find no evidence of any such fluid; in response to its criticisms, Mesmer revised his theory and his therapy, abandoning magnets for the technique of entrancement, nowadays called hypnotism. Armand-Marie-Jacques de Chastenet, Marquis de Puységur (1751-1825), was the most notable of Mesmer's disciples and the one who developed his therapies into the form in which Bodin became familiar with them; it was his *Recherches, expériences et observations physiologiques sur l'homme dans l'état de somnambulisme naturel et dans le somnambulisme provoqué par l'acte magnétique* (1811) that resulted in the centralization of the term "somnambulism" alongside "animal magnetism," eventually displacing it, even though the latter was perpetuated by his contemporary Joseph-Philippe-François Deleuze (1753-1835). It is interesting that Bodin makes no mention of the third major contributor to the contemporary debate, the physician Alexandre Bertrand (1789-1831), who ran a series of articles on the subject in the *Globe*, one of the periodicals to which Bodin contributed, and published a treatise on somnambulism in 1820; Bertrand was, in Bodin's terms, a "spiritualist" who conceived the somnambulistic state as one of *extase* [ecstasy], while Bodin was, at heart, a "physiologist"—although Fabio Mummio, the fictitious source of the future narrative, appears to have taken a keen interest in "ectastics."

"Are not the disadvantages of a reputation of this sort immediately obvious? In politics, it inevitably categorizes you along with the feeble-minded; in philosophy, along with the empty-headed; in literature, along with the foolish. Thus, for example, if I ever find enough confidence in myself to gather from my papers enough to fill one or two octavo volumes, and after that take it into my head to put myself forward, like many another to join the ranks of the Académie Française, do you think that such a footnote to my career would be a very good recommendation in the eyes of *Messieurs les Trenteneuf*? Imagine, then, an appointment as a *député* at stake and a candidate strongly suspected of magnetism; how would the electors welcome him with such an antecedent—or, if you wish—a precedent? I can already see all the jokes coming: he wants to magnetize the Chamber, put Europe to sleep; in the end, a rain of darts that kills a candidate in the principal town of an *arrondissement*.[75]

"What a very strange thing that is! In a time when magnetism had not yet been publicly observed, when charlatanism was responsible in great measure for its exploitation and mystery added to its marvels, it was

---

After 1830 the *Globe* became a significant organ of Saint-Simonian mysticism—of which Bodin disapproved—while Bertrand became a key inspiration for some of Bodin's more prestigious literary rivals; Charles Nodier adapted Bertrand's ideas in an article on "De quelques phénomènes de sommeil" (1831) and Honoré de Balzac drew on them in his novella "Louis Lambert" (1832).

[75] Before being elected as a *député* in his father's old (primarily rural) constituency, Bodin stood for election in the city of Saumur and lost; his opponent might well have poked fun at his belief in magnetism, with a more telling effect on the electors than was achieved in a different setting.

fashionable to get mixed up with it, and anyone, without risking his reputation, could believe in it entirely at his ease. People believed in that and in many other things. I remember one fine old fellow, a former captain of dragoons, who, on his return from the emigration, had conserved, like a sort of baggage of the *ancient régime*, magnetism, the magic wand and a number of anecdotes regarding Monsieur le Comte de Cagliostro, all intermingled with quotes from Voltaire and a quantity of old woman's remedies borrowed from the *Journal de Verdun*. The worthy old fellow had only had the greatest good fortune through being given his prescriptions and having his simples administrated, and he believed in their efficacy as firmly as he was convinced that, but for Monsieur Necker,[76] the French Revolution would never have taken place! Apologies for the digression.

"I was saying, then, that before the Revolution there was nothing inconvenient about believing in magnetism—which, however, had not been demonstrated in the least; so how does it come about that today—when a large number of experiments have been solemnly carried out in the presence of the most celebrated faculties in Europe, and numerous cures have been publicly effected in a Parisian hospital in front of all the physicians, students and curiosity-seekers who wanted to witness them; when an *ad hoc* commission has concluded that the phenomena of animal magnetism and somnambulism exist; when one meets people everywhere who have seen, or

---

[76] Jacques Necker was the finance minister who attempted to bring about sweeping economic reforms in 1777, and again 1788, but did not succeed in ameliorating the circumstances of the lower classes sufficiently to prevent the Revolution of 1789. He was also the father of Madame de Staël.

who have been cured, or whose friends have been cured, or who admit to having experienced some other effect of that singular physical agent—that any ridicule at all is attached to the study of magnetism or belief in it?

"That, however, is now the situation. It is one of the bizarre inconsistencies of human nature. Some believe because they have seen it or experienced it, others do not believe because they have not had the proof; and everyone stops at that. Those who have not been convinced prefer not to believe in it than to go to see it, and find it equally comfortable to mock those who have judge that the thing is worth the trouble of being verified. Let us try to figure out the reason for that.

"When a discovery is made in the physical sciences, which is sufficiently observed by the witnesses of the scientific world, no one takes the trouble to call it into question; everyone would sooner take the word of capable specialists, who have something akin to the power of attorney of the civilized world to admit new verities and give them currency. When I heard talk for the first time of the extraordinary action of galvanism on the nervous system, even after death, I was undoubtedly quite amazed, but, as the fact was not contested by anyone, I did not hesitate to give it credence. If it had been contested, I would have thought that it certainly warranted further inquiry to make sure of it, and I would have done my utmost to find out exactly what to make of it. That is what I have done with magnetism; that, it seems to me, is what everyone ought to do, or I certainly don't know any more what is worthy of curiosity, especially in a time when so many people strive in search of poetry.

"But there's something, you see, that is damaging to magnetism; it is that it reveals to us a side of the physical world with which we are entirely unfamiliar, it is that science, according to its habit, has irrevocably fixed the laws of the known world; it is that science is bound to regard as impossible anything that seems to deviate from those laws, and that the vulgar, less scrupulous than science, readily admit the marvelous. That manner of reasoning is, indeed, quite plausible: that which is apparently marvelous is judged impossible, so one decides that it is not worth taking the trouble to investigate it. But how many other facts, now admitted, once passed for marvels because they seemed to conflict with received ideas and to violate the natural order? Did not the phenomena of electricity, galvanism, mineral magnetism, etc., appear marvelous at first, and are they not perfectly explicable today? Well, those of animal magnetism must enter into the domain of physics, although unexplained, and they must also have their law, which will perhaps be discovered one day, and will explain them.

"Oh, my apologies—there I go, treating the scientific question, when I promised myself that I would do no such thing. I only want to place myself at the moral, poetical, philosophical—picturesque if you wish—point of view. I have no wish to give you a clinical witness statement signed by three doctors, nor a theory of magnetism, nor a debate for and against: all that would be irrelevant.

"However, it is necessary that I take my precautions with respect to the serious reader. Please, therefore, allow me to add a few more words to this preamble. I assure you, then, that I believe in magnetism, and even in somnambulism, which it would be better to call by another name.[77] I believe in it, because I have examined a

---

[77] Bodin inserts a footnote, presumably drawn from the original article: "Magnetic somnambulism is the development of a

number of somnambulists, at first with the most unfavorable prejudices, and afterwards with the most impartial attention. I will tell you again that the nervous apparatus is particularly responsive to magnetic action, and that, in consequence, the less nervous sensibility there is, the less effect magnetism has. One understands from that why women are more easily magnetized than men.

"I believe too that charlatanism has often taken possession of this discovery, undoubtedly renewed many times over, and that enthusiasm has exaggerated it; but tell me—what discovery in medicine has not had its enthusiasts, its rogues and its dupes?

"The physical and moral panacea, the means of arriving at the absolute, at the universal truth—there are people who see that, and many other things, in magnetism. There are also those who are neither dogmatists nor illuminati, but who observe the facts with the aid of experiments and reasoning, in order to limit themselves to studying the most possible of magnetic facts with all the prudence of doubt and also to guard against formulating a theory that other facts might soon overturn. There is

---

sixth sense, the sense sometimes revealed in presentiments, sympathies and many other phenomena of ordinary life; it is, if you wish, natural instinct stimulated to such a degree that it perceive things that our senses refuse us in a waking state. We do not know why or how the faculty developed in this way; somnambulists cannot give us an account of the nature of their perception, their vision. The people who take the trouble to observe the fact, however, cannot deny it. I have seen many instances of it in the home of Doctor Chapelain, that ardent magnetic experimenter who has sacrificed his entire career to the progress of the science, and who, having taken that route, effects astonishing cures." Pierre-Jean Chapelain was also the mesmerist practitioner that Honoré de Balzac consulted.

always a tendency to think that the epoch of synthesis has arrived, but how many of the planet's systems have vanished along with its generations, monuments and empires? In the next 2000 years more of them will be constructed, which will subsequently be supplanted. For myself, I like systems well enough, but only as methods—and that is sufficient."

Finally, incredulity in the matter of magnetism has come to be tolerated and is no longer ridiculed; that is a big step forward. And science marches on; and the observations multiply and are gathered together; and in England—where, less than four years ago, no one would have deigned to examine the question—physicians of the greatest merit put their names to special publications on the existence and the power of magnetism.

On Literary Essays on the Future

I have said that, until now, futurist literature has only been attempted in the forms of utopias and apocalypses. Indeed, I have no knowledge of any novelistic narrative transported into the midst of a future social or political situation. I have found indication on the following works in the *Bibliographie Universelle*:

Memoirs of the 20th Century; being the original letters of state under George the Sixth, relative to the most important events in England and Europe, etc. between the middle of the 18th century and the end of the 20th and the world, received and revealed in the year 1718. London, 1733; octavo, which was to have been followed by five further volumes. This work—which was suppressed and is very rare, according to the bibliography—is by the Irish philanthropist Madden.[78]

Memoirs of Europe at the end of the 18th Century, published in 1710, 2 vols; octavo, by Mrs. Manley. I do not know if this is correct.[79]

There exists in England a well-known work entitled *The Century of Inventions*.[80]

These are only utopias without action, like *L'an 2440* and *The Voyage of Kang-Hi* by Monsieur de Levis,[81] of which I read an analysis in 1810 or thereabouts in the *Journal de l'Empire*, which made an impression on me as a schoolboy that I can still recall.

---

[78] Bodin gives this book's title and subtitle in French, as the *Bibliographie Universelle* does, although it was never translated; the transcription is incorrect in one detail—1718 should read 1728. The author was Samuel Madden. The book was not suppressed by any legal authority; Madden is thought to have destroyed most of the printed copies himself.

[79] Mary de la Riviere Manley (1663-1724) lost her reputation after being tricked into a bigamous marriage and wrote several sets of satirical memoirs, including a vengeful account of *New Atalantis* (1709), in which various prominent individuals are blithely slandered. As Bodin has deduced, this title is misquoted; it actually refers to the 8th century, not the 18th; the satire poses as the memoirs of Charlemagne's secretary.

[80] *The Century of Inventions* (1655) by Edward Somerset, Marquis of Worcester (1601-1667), is not really futuristic, although it does deal with hypothetical as well as actual inventions, and is notable for its description of the principle of the steam engine.

[81] Pierre-Marc-Gaston, Duc de Levis (1755-1830), published *Les voyages de Kang-Hi, ou Nouvelles letters chinoises* in 1810; it includes extracts from newspapers from the year 1910.

As for apocalypses and ends of the world, several have been published in France and England. There exists, I believe, more than one poem entitled *The Last Man*; the best-known is that of the celebrated Thomas Campbell.[82]

I remember having heard mention for the first time, about ten years ago, of a French poem of which the subject is also *Le dernier homme*, by Grainville—a poem known to a small number of interested parties, which I have never seen: *Habent sua fata!* [83] It was Charles Nodier who brought it to my attention, with a partiality and

---

[82] Thomas Campbell's poem "The Last Man" (1823) was soon supplemented by an identically-titled parody by Thomas Hood, published in 1826—the same year in which Mary Shelley published a long futuristic novel with that title, of whose existence Bodin appears to be ignorant—although he would probably have considered it an "apocalypse" rather than a "novel," and would certainly have thought it lacking in melodramatic action; even so, it provides one of the several significant contradictions to his claim to being the first person to come up with the idea of writing a novel set in the future.

[83] *Habent sua fata libelli* [Books have their destiny] is an aphorism credited to Terence. The text to which Bodin is referring is *Le dernier homme* by Jean-Baptiste Cousin de Grainville, a prose work first published in 1805; although it is a religious fantasy in the sense that it represents a sketchy fulfilment of the prophesies of *Revelation*, it also devotes some attention to the technological and social progress that had overtaken the world, and then passed into near-oblivion, before the crisis that eventually puts an end to the world. Grainville had, however, originally conceived it as an epic poem rather than a prose work, and its substance was recast in that form, with certain variations, by Auguste-François Creuzé de Lesser in 1831—another work that obviously escaped Bodin's attention.

an enthusiasm for which I know to be thoroughly typical of him.[84] There is a tendency for honest literary men to protest against the cessation of fame, or, rather, the whimsicality of fashion. Although it is said that good books never fall into oblivion, there are so many stupid works whose reputation is perpetuated that one can deny the former point by virtue of the contrary argument! Since I have cited Charles Nodier, I shall say here that if the *Roman de l'avenir* had to have been written by someone other than me, he would certainly have been the man to do it. The idea was entirely suited to the richness of imagination and the versatility of his pen. I regret, for literature's sake that it has not been the case. I do not say that I also regret it for my sake, because no one would believe me.[85]

---

[84] Nodier wrote a glowing introduction to a new edition of *Le dernier homme* issued in 1811, but Bodin does not appear to have seen that edition and presumably obtained Nodier's recommendation in person at about the time he wrote *Eveline*, when he might conceivably have attended the famous "cénacle" that Nodier hosted, at least for a short while.

[85] No one would, indeed, especially bearing in mind that Nodier had published a satirical futuristic short story—or a fragment of a futuristic novel—entitled "Hurlubleu, Grand Mantifafa d'Hurlubière, ou La perfectibilité" in the August 1833 issue of the *Revue de Paris*. It is possible that Bodin wrote *Le roman de l'avenir* before that date, but it is also possible that it was the appearance of Nodier's piece (which has a conservative ideological slant very different from his own) that stimulated Bodin to stop "sleeping on" his idea and get down to work, and caused him to be so insistent that he had got the prospectus for his own work into print in 1831. Nodier's short story will be included in an anthology of proto science fiction stories entitled *The Germans on Venus* forthcoming from Black Coat Press.

As for Germany, I have absolutely no knowledge of what might have been attempted in this genre. I have read a remarkable piece by Ph. Chasles [86] on Jean-Paul Richter, an original genius worth of such a translator as Chasles; I do not believe that I saw there that he has made the future the object of one of his conceptions.

If I publish a second part, I shall certainly be able to add to it, in the notes, a summary of Mercier's work. Those who have not read it will perhaps find it convenient to have a summary in a few pages of the man's ideas, which are often as good as they are bizarre; he had a fine mind, although he was a diffuse and declamatory writer. One finds in his book most of the opinions of economists, and the whole range of hatreds, enthusiasms and pitiless judgments of the past, of the philosophical and sentimental school of the 18th century, and, along with that, an interminable criticism of the present, accompanied by long oratory flourishes, appended to each future improvement. But how can one avoid the imprint of one's era, however much originality one may claim? It is still the case that, in the long medley of Mercier's predictions, much can be found that has been realized, and which is almost ancient history today. The comparison of his future with our present is particularly amusing in that respect.

I remember making a foray of my own into that genre a long time ago, but without much mental effort, because my prophecies were already beginning to come true. That was in 1822; the Greek insurrection had burst forth and, with regard to a curious panorama of the Turkish Athens, I published the following article on

---

[86] Philarète Chasles (1798-1873) went on to become a noted critic and bibliographer.

"Athens in 1840" in the *Miroir*, which I requested permission to reprint by virtue of an authorial weakness for rediscovering old trivia:

"Thanks to the illusion of the panorama, we are enabled to see Athens. But which Athens? It is no longer that of Pericles! It is the Athens that time, war, barbarism and the Turks have made. The painter has rendered his canvas eloquent. He has made despotism even more detestable.

"I shall not try to bring back all those noble ruins in the imagination, by transporting myself to the days when so many great men circulated beneath the elegant porticoes of which I can hardly see the traces: that fiction, often reproduced, gives birth to too many painful comparisons. I prefer to deliver more consoling images. I shall forsake the comparison of the past with the present for that of the present with the future. I shall strive to forget Athens flourishing under the laws of Solon in order to think only of the Athens promised to us by the 19th century.

"It is not in the vast enclosure of the Pnyx that the laws and affairs of state are discussed. Societies no longer govern themselves in the open air. Where are the men who might be making themselves heard from the platform on which Demosthenes thundered? Today political assemblies are delegations, and the orators operate under mandate. Citizens no longer have slaves to work for them, and the workshops of industry have emptied the public plaza. The turbulent factions of a blind and impassioned democracy, madly creating popular idols who will soon become tyrants, will perhaps succeeded by the venality of a debased representation or elections falsified by violence. But what institutions do not have their abuses? If the republican police of the ancients had more energy and grandeur, the regime found in the forests—as Montesquieu puts it—offers more security and guarantees to the individual; that is the government of modern society.

"The Parthenon, that glorious monument to the genius of Phidias, is restored. It is there that the Congress of Athens holds its sessions. What palace is more worthy of a body of legislators than the temple of Minerva? The Propylaea, which Venetian bombs destroyed, has been rebuilt. An immense crowd fills these superb vestibules and moves towards the Parthenon; the Athenian civic guard is under arms; I can hear cannon-fire in the Acropolis. What festival is being celebrated? It is the anniversary of the liberation of Greece, and also the opening of a legislative session. The procession heads, in the first instance, towards a tall column built to commemorate men who served the cause of Greek independence. Their names are inscribed thereon; I draw nearer and recognize some French names among them, and I feel my heart tremble. Higher up is a large inscription of which I can only read the word alliance. Does it refer to an alliance of peoples? I suppose that it is probably the famous alliance of kings at the beginning of the century; but the distance of the inscription prevents me from finding out how it is judged by posterity.

"The Turkish prison, that old tower, remnant of a Venetian fort, has been demolished. The column of the liberation has been erected on its site. In front of the dark grottoes that once served as the dungeons of the Aeropagus are delightful gardens, comfortable and peaceful retreats. Close to the place where Socrates and Phocion drank hemlock live virtuous men exiled from heir own countries for their political opinions or religious beliefs.

Galileo or Sydney,[87] were they living, would find a refuge there. The modern Athenians desire that, until the moment when tolerance and liberty are established throughout the world, these gardens will provide shelter to those pursued by despotism and fanaticism. O Socrates, most illustrious of the victims of intolerance, you must find your death worthy expiated!

"The ports of Phalerum, Munychia and Piraeus have recovered their antique splendor. A forest of masts is assembled there. Vast and expert constructions offer a welcome security to the vessels of 20 nations. The commerce of Asia and the Mediterranean finds warehouses here open to all its produce, and indigenous commerce is protected by the bellicose navy of Hydra, whose first efforts were so glorious, and which forced the Dardenelles and bombarded Constantinople. It is at Hydra that the tall ships of the Athenian navy are stationed.

"Plane-trees are growing again in the gardens of the Academy. It is there that the members of the Athenian literary elite gather. Everyone there makes every effort not to speak of commonplace things in affected language; they only occupy themselves with serious and useful matters. Everyone there professes eternal principles of morality and religion extracted from the works of Plato, Cicero, Rousseau and Franklin. Ptolemy's Gymnasium is a subsidiary branch of the Academy. Greek letters are taught there, and also the literature of modern Europe.

---

[87] Algernon Sydney (1622-1683) fought in the Parliamentary army during the English Civil War and later served in Parliament; he fled the country after the Restoration but returned to England in 1677, before being arrested on a trumped-up charge, convicted of treason and beheaded.

"There, where the Areopagus held its sessions, I see Athens' hall of justice; an enlightened jury has replaced the Anitus. Instead of the laws of Draco—written, according to one of the ancients, in blood—the Athenians have a code based on the principles of Bentham and Beccaria.[88] Nothing prevents the advocates of Thessaly and Macedonia from coming to Athens to defend their friends.

"I see a school of mutual instruction where the Turkish school once was, in which poor children received more lashes of the whip than instruction from ignorant dervishes. A printing works occupies the site of the Mosque of the Bazaar. Finally, I discover the famous pedestal that was the podium from which the orators of Athens governed by speech. A balustrade surrounds this venerable monument, to which so many glorious memories are attached, this point of support from which the lever of eloquence moved so many thousands of men bearing arms for the fatherland. A portico has been built above those stones, so majestic in their rustic simplicity, on the front of which one reads these words: *Athenians, you are represented.*"

Saint Malachy and The End of the World

I have said somewhere that the action occurs toward the end of the 20th century. People who are familiar with the curious prophecy of St. Malachy,[89] an Irish monk

---

[88] Cesare Bonesano Beccaria (1738-1794) wrote a famous treatise *Dei delitti e delle pene* [On Crimes and Punishments] (1764; revised 1781).

[89] Mael Maedoc, alias Saint Malachy (1094-1148), was a pioneer of Gregorian Reform in Ireland; the apocryphal Prophecies of Saint Malachy were compiled and published by Dom

undoubtedly endowed with a second sight longer than that of his compatriots, who died at Clairvaux in the arms of his friend, St. Bernard, will know that I have taken the liberty of giving some respite to this poor world—which, according to his erudite prophecy, will not last until then. Indeed, according to St. Malachy, there will be no more than a dozen Popes between now and the end of the world. Now, estimating the mean duration of a pontificate at ten years, which is probably too long, if one considers the care the Cardinals take to place the crown on the most decrepit heads in order to improve their own chances of acquiring it, we have no more than 120 years before us.[90]

The singular correspondences that have come to pass between this prophecy and reality are well known. A two- or three-word motto is attributed to every Pope since the 12th century, and several have been applicable without overstretching the meaning. Thus, the motto *Aquila rapax* [Rapacious Eagle], bestowed upon Pius VII, has been explained by the confiscation of the papal estates by the Imperial Eagle. The continuators of the

---

Arnold de Wyon in 1595, reflective of a European resurgence of mystical apocalyptic fervour that gave birth to such legends as the story of Faust and the Rosicrucian Brotherhood and rejuvenated others, including the myth of the Wandering Jew. The phrases referring to all the popes up to Clement VIII were, therefore, retrospective rather than anticipatory.

[90] In fact, there were not as many Popes as Bodin estimated before the end of the 20th century, and Benedict XVI, elected in 2005, is only the 11th of the 12 supposedly remaining when he wrote this note. According to this schedule, therefore, the world will end during the reign of the next Pope—which is, I suppose, as good a note as any on which to sign off this translation.

commentary would undoubtedly not have lacked explanations for the succeeding mottoes: *Canis et coluber* [Dog and Adder] for Leo XII, *Vir religiosus* [Religious Man] for Pius VIII, and *De balneis Etruriae* [Bath of Etruria] for Gregory XIV. For the benefit of aficionados, I shall reproduce the end of the prophecy, which is to say the 12 Popes that remain to be appointed:

Crux de cruce. [Cross of Crosses]

Lumen in coelo. [Light in the Sky]

Ignis ardens. [Burning Fire]

Religio de populata. [Religion Laid Waste]

Fides intrepida. [Intrepid Faith]

Pastor angelicus. [Angelic Shepherd]

Pastor et nauta. [Pastor and Marine]

Flos florum. [Flower of Flowers]

De medietate lunae. [Of Half of the Moon]

De labore solis. [Of the Eclipse of the Sun]

Gloria olivae. [Glory of the Olive]

In persecutione extrema sacrae romanae ecclesiae sedebit PETRUS ROMANUS qui pascet oves in multis tribulationibus, quibus transactis, civitas septicollis diruteur et judex tremendous judicabit populum. [In extreme persecution, the seat of the Holy Roman Church will be occupied by Peter the Roman, who will feed the sheep through many tribulations, at the term of which the city of the seven hills will be destroyed and the formidable judge will judge his people.] [91]

THE END

---

[91] The corresponding Popes are: Pius IX, Leo XIII, Pius X, Benedict XV, Pius XI, Pius XII, John XXIII, Paul VI, John Paul I, John Paul II and Benedict XVI.

Afterword

The Novel of the Future and the Future of the Novel

All novels "of the future" are, in reality, novels of the time in which they are written, so the very notion of a "novel of the future" is somewhat paradoxical. Bodin's narrative voice makes this obvious; although he states in the introduction that "it is necessary, for the sake of clarity and flow, to recount all these future things as present or past, as if the novel itself had been written and published 200 years hence, and as if it were addressed to the public that will exist at that time," there is an obvious flaw in the execution of that plan. Although the narrative voice uses formulations like "everyone knows" when filling in elements of back story, which are tacitly addressed to 20th century readers, his continual references to readers—especially female readers—who might find his chapters boring are obviously referring to the readers of 1834. The artifice of using the present tense to tell the story instead of the conventional past tense is, therefore, a trifle confused.

The principal sense in which future-set novels belong so obviously to their own present is, of course, that nothing dates quite as fast as the images of the future imaginable at a particular point in time. Although Bodin's preface complains that other literary attempts to depict the future have done no more than paint utopian hopes and apocalyptic anxieties, it is unclear that his novelistic aspirations have made much difference to that limitation. The late 20th century that he imagines is, in large measure, the fulfillment of the various programs that he tried to advance in his parliamentary career and the culmination of his particular ideals of social and technological progress, and it is subject to dramatic tension precisely because it is haunted by the nightmare that afflicted those hopes: the violent resurgence of everything that moral progress might render obsolete.

To argue, however, that Bodin's novel of the future is not really a novel of the future because the future did not turn out the way he painted it, would be manifestly unfair. The future is implicitly unpredictable, not simply because it is always shaped to a greater or lesser degree by discoveries not yet made—whose accurate anticipation would, in effect, be their making—but, more importantly, because of the paradox of prophecy.

Our anticipations of the future affect our behavior; we act in the present in the hope of preventing or ameliorating the evil outcomes that we can foresee, and the hope of increasing the probability of the favorable outcomes that we can glimpse. Prophecy is not so much the art of predicting the future as of preventing it; issuing warnings of doom is sometimes the only way to avoid doom, and usually tends in that direction, although the argument is (alas) not symmetrical: creating designs for utopia is always more likely to stir up angry controversy than make peaceful progress towards universal happiness any easier. Bodin's novel *is* a novel of the future in the sense that its narrative backcloth offers a vision of a future that was not merely conceivable, but plausible in 1834, some features of which did come about, while others might have, had new discoveries not emerged. It is, however, also very much a novel of the present, especially in every sense that makes it a novel.

When the former village schoolmaster in Bodin's lovingly-described Loire valley is called upon to comment on the literature of the early 19th century from the lofty plane of the 20th, he says that "I neither praise nor blame that unhealthy, neurotic and almost epileptic literature; I seek only to explain it. It is obvious that those people were making prodigious efforts to retain the poetry of the intermediary times that seemed to be under threat from the positivism of civilization. In order to save it, they were attempting to outdo it, to magnify it beyond all measure...or, to put it another way, in a milieu of relaxation in religious belief and a thirst for material pleasures, they gave in to the corruption of the time and prostituted poetry in order to save it again."

In this respect, the schoolmaster—with whose opinion Philirène agrees—is presumably speaking for Bodin; but Bodin is well enough aware of the fact that he cannot avoid the same corrupting processes of prostitution, no matter how much he might protest against them. This corruption cuts much deeper than the trivial fact that he had earlier written a novel that had deliberately pandered to the tastes of the contemporary audience, or his awareness that, in formulating a plot of sorts for the imagined novel that *Le roman de l'avenir* stopped well short of becoming, he is meekly reproducing the same "unhealthy, neurotic and almost epileptic symptoms." He jokes openly about substituting a magnetic researcher for an ancient alchemist as an apologetic source for his tale, and about some of the other melodramatic clichés he deploys, but the fact remains that, in order for his work to qualify as a novel at all in the reckoning of the readers and critics of 1834, he has no alternative but to use some such devices.

As Eupistos and Philirène observe, in response to Eudoxie's questions about whether early 19th century people really behaved and spoke in the ways that characters in post-Rousseauesque Romantic fiction did, there was nothing naturalistic about early 19th century literature; it did not depict the world as it actually was. Precisely for that reason, however, its mythology was difficult to break down, and—perhaps more importantly, in the context of the possibility of writing "the novel of the future"—so infinitely adaptable that it was by no means confined to mimetic historical settings. Indeed, just as the mythic past provided a more comfortable backcloth to Romantic excess than the mundane historical past, so imaginary futures had the potential to provide a more appropriate setting than any accurate description of the world as it really was or had been.

One of the many things that Bodin's "novel of the future" does not even attempt to describe is the novels of the future—not so much as a title, let alone a critical analysis. Philirène's endorsement of the schoolmaster's apology for Romantic literature includes that judgment that it was "the means that the way was prepared for our great poets of the 20th century" but all that the narrative voice permits him to say about those successors is that they "justify the title of VATES" because they are "our poets of the future." It is not entirely clear how we are supposed to interpret this, but it is very tempting for the modern connoisseur of science fiction to construe it as a prophecy of the future importance of futuristic fiction. Within the cheerfully sarcastic context of Bodin's "novel of the future," however, the notional author of the introduced tale really is a visionary oracle, so what Bodin is actually suggesting is that the great poets (and novelists) of the 20th century might accomplish their work by means of somniloquism—much as Bodin had appeared, or pretended, to compose "*La langueur*" while under the influence of second sight. That, too, might be regarded as prophetic in the sense that it is something surrealist writers and artists have tried to do—but the triumph of somniloquism as a domestic medical and oracular technique is, alas, one element of Bodin's futuristic anticipations that has not been justified.

Philirène does not make the explicit suggestion that the novels of the 20th century might be more naturalistic than those of the early 19th, and nor does the narrative voice, but there is a tacit rhetoric contained in the narrative voice's continual complaint that his readers (in 1834) might find his descriptive and expositional passages too boring, which implies that there might, and certainly should, one day come a time when readers might have different interests and might make different demands. One of the hopes reflected in the book's utopian aspect is surely the hope that the readers of the future might not be bored by those aspects of *Le roman de l'avenir* that contemporary readers would probably find tiresome, and might, indeed, be delighted by their assumed intellectual seriousness—but that is yet another hope all-too-obviously complemented by its antithetical nightmare: the anxiety that even the readers of the end of the 20th might still be far more interested in whether Philirène will defeat Philomaque, forgive his mother, liberate Mirzala and/or find true happiness with his actual soulmate than they ever could be in the organization of the Universal Congress, the intellectual interests of little Jules or the possibility of universal peace.

In that nightmare anxiety, as in so many others, Bodin surely was justified; modern poetry and fiction is as deeply steeped in sentimentality, violence and glamour a fiction ever was—and that applies to novels "of the future" just as much as novels set in the present, the historical past, the mythical past and various other mythical milieux. Whatever apologetic claims might be made for modern futuristic fiction, the claim that it is 1834's "novel of the future" is not one of them.

Somniloquism and Consciousness

Although Bodin's anticipation of a revolution in medicine brought about by the acceptance of "magnetism" was over-ambitious, it was not entirely mistaken. Medicine has, indeed, been revolutionized, even though the part played by relics of Mesmerism in that evolution has been relatively tiny and highly controversial, and some of the developments Bodin expected in the uses somniloquism have been mirrored, or at least echoed, by psychoanalysis and other schools of psychiatric therapy. The depictions of somniloquism that Bodin inserts into his novel are not as remote from actual 20th century applications of hypnotism as they might have been, and might be even more similar if Sigmund Freud had not abandoned hypnotism as a fundamental technique of psychoanalysis. Although two of the three depictions of induced somnambulism contained in the novel involve the treatment of a physically-manifest illness, those two are far more interesting psychologically than they are in terms of soothing feverish symptoms, and the third is also more interesting in terms of psychological self-revelation than it is a conduit of useful information.

Bodin's narrative voice apologizes for including three scenes of somniloquism into his story, judging that it is one too many and promising to limit himself more severely in future. In fact, though, it is absolutely necessary that there should be three such scenes, because the reader would be unable to find the second anything but absurd had the groundwork not been laid by the first, and would still retain deep suspicions of its ridiculousness had the third not been added as confirmation. This is one literary instance in which the rhetorical rule of three—sometimes vulgarized as "what I tell you three times is true"—holds good. Even after three exemplars, no modern reader is likely to find Bodin's depictions of somniloquism remotely plausible, but the triple repetition does serve to establish and confirms an interesting pattern that cries out for analysis and explanation.

The first scene of somniloquism, featuring Poonah, informs the reader that Poonah loves Philomaque, and has confessed as much to Politée while entranced. More significantly, however, it informs the reader that "Poonah-the-somniloquist" has begged Politée not to reveal to "Poonah-awake" that the secret is out, because the latter could not bear knowing that Politée knows it, even though the former knows it perfectly well. (Politée is, of course, glad to comply.)

The second scene of somniloquism, featuring Eudoxie, informs the reader that "Eudoxie-the-somniloquist" not only loves Philirène but knows, beyond the shadow of a doubt, that she, not Mirzala, is his true soulmate. Again, Eudoxie-the-somniloquist begs her entrancer not to tell her waking self that she has any interest in Philirène—and "Eudoxie-awake" is, in fact, quite indifferent to him, having far more natural sympathy with Eupistos.

The third scene of somniloquism, involving Madame Charlotte, confirms the parallel between the first two; "Charlotte-the-somniloquist" loves Philirène, whereas "Charlotte-awake" hates him, and Charlotte-the-somniloquist can tell him the awful secret that Charlotte-awake would never dream of disclosing—and presumably, although it is not explicitly stated in this instance, could not bear to know that it had been divulged by her *alter ego.*

The psychological assumptions bound up in this pattern are very remarkable, especially in the context of 1834. It had been observed previously that the "public selves" people present to the world are sometimes in discord with their "private selves," but the notion that the conflict could be so sharp was highly unusual. Bodin takes it for granted, it seems, that our "false" selves lie so well that they many of them alienate themselves completely from our "true" selves, by virtue of being unable to tolerate the kind of self-awareness that our true selves not only have but cannot disown—which is presumably one reason why "second sight" is a fugitive talent, routinely blotted out by consciousness. In Bodin's view, the waking self—the conscious self—is a creature hiding in plain view; an artifact that has cut itself off from its source. He does not use the French terms that were later drafted into use as translations of the German Freudian terms that are rendered into English as "repression" and "the unconscious," but that is perhaps as well, given that his model of the mind (or, at least, of the female mind) is considerable more radical than Freud's, seemingly leaving little or no possibility for a therapeutic abreaction and consequent reunion of the fragmented personality.

The most striking corollary of this remarkable image of the mind is where it puts, or leaves, "true love." Poonah's sexual love for Philomaque, Eudoxie's spiritual love for Philirène and Charlotte's maternal love for Philirène are all properties of their somniloquistic selves; not merely do their waking selves know nothing about them, but their waking selves are determined to avoid knowing anything about them, because they could not

tolerate them—or, at least, could not tolerate their revelation. Not one of the three women is a subscriber to the
cult of *sensibilité*, as poor Eveline was—quite the reverse: all three of them have buried and banished their
honest sentiments, to the point where it requires medical
treatment to expose them. Two of them, a least, are ill,
and although the French equivalent of "hysteria" is another word that Bodin does not use, the modern reader is
bound to suspect that their illnesses are psychosomatic,
their crises precipitated by the awful pressure of hiding
from themselves. Are Politée and Mirzala any better?
Are Philirène and Philomaque? Was Félix Bodin, in his
own estimation? Eveline was, in the reckoning of the
contemporary literary audience—but she died of it.

There is, of course, another side to this coin. If this
is Bodin's image of human nature—not merely in the
present but in the farthest future that he can imagine—
the real question is not so much "where does it leave
love?" but "where does it leave progress, democracy and
civilization?" Such matters are the business of the conscious, waking self; *civilization* is, in its educational
sense, the essence of the training process to which that
outward self is subject, while democracy and progress
are two of the finest fruits to which the fundamental process is supposed to give birth. In a world of unified
selves, such as is tacitly assumed in all utopian fiction,
the process of *civilization* world work on the inner self
as well as the outer one, so democracy and progress
would have deep roots—but that is not the kind of future
world that Bodin depicts. In his future, the discrepancy
between the inner and outer selves of his characters is
extreme and awkward, and the tension between the
spontaneous passions—the *sensibilité*—of the inner self
and the urbane behavior of the outer self is acute and

tortuous. In this sense, at least, Bodin's novel of the future really is a novel rather than a utopia, and that is its misfortune a well as its glory.

The abyssal divide between the inner and outer selves of the female seers featured in the novel is not explicitly replicated in the individual representations of its male characters, but it graphically mirrored in the overall social organization of the novel, where the Poetic Association holds its meetings in deep underground caverns while its great adversary, the Association for Civilization, holds its congresses and committee meetings in Benthamia, Vienna and Athens. While Philirène's carefully-tailored address to the Universal Congress paints a sane and rosy picture in which even he has no faith, the sly orators of the Underworld make their appeal to the diseased passions that have been incompletely repressed. In that kind of world, can sanity, civilization and progress possibly prevail?

Paradoxical as it may seem, it is precisely—and solely—because Bodin's novel is not only a novel a quintessentially Romantic novel that we can be fairly sure that the dire and violent threat of Aëtos the Antichrist will eventually be thwarted; the sole literary purpose of villains is to come to an ignominious end—eventually. Within the cracks in the novelistic surface, however, it is hardly surprising that Philirène is as querulously skeptical about progress as he is about love, no matter how powerfully committed to it his conscious self might be. Bodin's model of human being is evidently not incapable of progressive thought and action, but it is certainly not perfectible; it is, instead—no matter what books its exemplars might read—essentially unhealthy, neurotic and almost epileptic.

It is no wonder, given this, that Philirène is so pale and sickly, while Philomaque seems, even in his conspicuous absence, so red-blooded and robust. We know from Eudoxie's inspired testimony that Philirène is far from being able to confront his true self, but at least he is trying; we can easily infer, however, without ever having confronted him, let alone got inside his head, that Philomaque/Aëtos is not subject to any such queasy qualms, He, at least, is a unitary individual, far beyond the pale of semi-sanity and quite free from its debilitating symptoms of inner tension. Philirène, as he dutifully informs us, has science on is side in the impending battle of Armageddon, and we all know that the race is not always to the swift nor the battle to the strong—but we all know, too, that only idiots bet on the hesitant and the weak.

Bodin's narrative voice takes the trouble to raise a number of questions when he cuts his narrative short, but they are mostly rhetorical (will Aëtos try to seduce the Queen of the Amazons?—of course he will), and the over-riding question of who will win the impending battle of Armageddon is rhetorical too. Because the novel is a novel, Philirène will win, because Philirène is the good guy and the good guy always wins—that, as Miss Prism wisely observed, is what fiction *means*. The god-like power of authorship is granted by adoring readers on condition that it is exercised with god-like responsibility; if a novel of the future really is to qualify as a novel, then good must triumph in the end, and it must triumph in earthly terms rather than by means of some transcendental Apocalyse. If *Le roman de l'avenir* had an ending, that is the way it should, and presumably would, end.

In fact, though, *Le roman de l'avenir* does not have an ending; it stops short—and it does not really matter, at the end of the day whether it stops short because the author was lazy, or in a hurry, or because he thought that stopping short of the ending was somehow more aesthetically satisfying. The fact is that it does stop short, leaving readers free to wonder whether, in fact, Aëtos, his birds of prey and his barbarian hordes might wipe the floor with Philirène and the entire peace-loving, civilized and democratic world, science and capitalism notwithstanding. Such a catastrophic victory of evil would have been unthinkable in the novels of the early 19th century, is still pretty much unthinkable in the novels of our early 21st century, and will probably remain pretty much unthinkable in the novels of our future—but within Bodin's idiosyncratic theory of psychology, setting literary issues aside, a catastrophe of that sort is neither inconceivable nor unlikely. He is, after all, writing about a world in which people do not know, or want to know, their true selves, even though contemporary therapeutic methods make it possible for them to do so: a partially-sighted world in which, however paradoxically, the willfully blind man is an entirely plausible king.

Bodin, of course, does not want Aëtos to win; he is a peace-loving Philirène through and through, and the pale and sickly Philirène is his avatar. His openly-expressed anxiety than his female readers might consider Aëtos to be a more attractive and convincing hero than Philirène is presumably resentful, derived from his own lack of success in love, as is his implication that Philirène might never get together with his true soulmate, because even she cannot tolerate, while conscious, the knowledge that she *is* his soulmate, and will probably languish and die before taking the idea aboard. Bodin does not believe that the ordinary people of the world, in either the real 19th or the hypothetical 20th century, want the Antichrist to triumph and the culminating phase of social and technological progress to be nipped in the bud—but he does seem to believe that the real 19th century equivalents of the hypothetical members of Poetic Association are misguided enough to want it, and perhaps powerful enough to achieve it. Perhaps, even if he had lived long enough and found the time, he would have been unable to bring the story of Philirène and Philomaque to a conclusion, because he was too conflicted within himself to construct, let alone believe in, the Romantic conclusion that convention demanded and he fervently desired.

Progress and Providence

Bodin's anxieties regarding the anti-progressive tendencies of early 19th century literature and painting are, as seen from the viewpoint of our 20th century, rather odd. As a historian, he knew perfectly well that the arts had always been regarded in the past as significant agents and illustrations of civilization; like everyone else, he saw Classical architecture and sculpture as the very essence and embodiment of the commencement civilization, knew perfectly well that the style of architecture mislabeled Gothic was the stuff of cathedrals whose enterprise was defiantly opposed to the very real threat of barbarism, and recognized artistic endeavors as the very heart of the Renaissance, while science and technology had been mere by-products. He thought, however, that something had recently gone wrong with the relationship between art and civilization: that the two had fallen out of step.

Bodin thought that, while contemporary civilization was continuing to progress, moving forward technologically and morally, contemporary literature—whether

Classical or Romantic—had become excessively fixated on the past, and not even, for the most part, on the actual historical past, but on the imaginary mythical past that the art and literature of the past had transmitted, maintained and continued to fabricate. He did not know exactly when or how the upset had taken place, although he thought that Rousseau had played a key role in reflecting it, if not instigating it, but he was prepared to entertain the thesis that it was a necessary phase in the evolution of art and society. In his preface to *Le roman de l'avenir* he suggests that there has been a significant separation in human thought of the "poetic" from the "positive" (a term which, in the Comtean sense, is almost synonymous with "scientific"):

"The progress that must be anticipated is that the different systems will increasingly adapt themselves to their own order of things. The positivist systems will gradually prevail with regard to material organization and the state of society; the poetic systems will be in possession of religion and the arts."

Bodin goes on to say that he does not think that this separation can ever become absolute, but he does not hold out much hope for an easy resolution to the antagonism implicit in the split. He is, is essence, sketching out a prospectus for the "two cultures" debate that C. P. Snow introduced into our 20th century, with the important exception that Bodin takes it for granted that political culture will migrate to the positivist side of the debate, while C. P. Snow was obliged to lament that it had not, and that the culture of science had therefore been excessively isolated.

This anticipated split is another reflection, within Bodin's fragmentary novel of the future, in the sharp division of the human mind envisioned in his depictions of somniloquism. In Bodin's vision of the future, the positivist political and technological culture represented by Philirène, Politée and Madame Charlotte's waking self has separated itself so completely from the poetic culture represented by Mirzala, her abductor and Eudoxie's somniloquist self that it is actually in denial, unwilling and unable to entertain and confront it. That vision is presented in a determinedly non-serious fashion, as a "hoax"—but Bodin defines a hoax as something farcically serious as well as seriously farcical; even the joke is fundamentally in conflict with itself.

The apparent recent commitment of the arts to the anti-progressive elements in society is not a situation of which Bodin, the poet-turned-politician, can approve, and he certainly seems keen to find a way out of the seeming impasse. He proceeds rapidly from the passage quoted above to repeat an aphorism from one of his earlier works, which is not entirely consistent with the first judgment: "Civilization tends to distance us from everything in the past that is poetic; but it also has its own poetry and sense of the marvelous."

There is a sense in which *Le roman de l'avenir* is a halting attempt to develop that "poetry of civilization" and its associated "sense of the marvelous," but it does so very weakly indeed; its principal recourse is the idea of that future dirigible aerostats will gives humankind a new freedom, but the only imagery he has to describe them is that of avian flight, which he deploys in an awkwardly vague manner. If this particular novel of the future could not take the prospectus any further, though, the genre that it was intended to found certainly could, and did. Futuristic fiction after *Le roman de l'avenir* was almost entirely written in the absence of any knowledge of that particular precedent, and without its specific inspiration, but the growth and expansion of such fiction testifies to the fact that Bodin's was an idea whose time was bound to come. His was not the only seed planted in his own era, and none of the others fared any better than his in terms of popularity or specific influence, but their shoots were, at the very least, prophetic in anticipating a much richer crop and harvest to come.

Hypnosis and psychotherapy never became the central medical applications that Bodin thought possible and desirable, nor did they confirm the clairvoyant and prophetic power of second sight, in spite of the dogged insistence of a few confirmed believers, but they did lend some tentative support to his notion of the divided self. In the same way, C. P. Snow's observations have lent support to Bodin's notion of a divided culture, and the development of modern science fiction has lent some support to his notion of the future scope and utility of the novel of the future. He is entitled to credit for all those anticipations, but scoring a futuristic novelist's quasi-prophetic hits has never been the best way to assess his achievement. It is arguable that the greatest achievement of *Le roman de l'avenir* is its identification and emphasis of an issue that is still largely unnoticed and still unresolved: the question of whether the "novelistic" aspects of novels of the future are really compatible with their "futuristic" aspects.

It certainly seems to be the case that the fictional aspects of modern science fiction still tend to be novelistic and "poetic" in the same way that Romantic literature was novelistic and poetic, rather than in terms of any new "poetry of civilization," while its scientific aspects are still "positive" in the same way that the progressive politics of the early 19th century attempted to be positive. If so, then modern science fiction is a genre whose every individual example is fundamentally divided, no matter how much it pretends (dishonestly, for the most part) to be pandering to a new sense of the marvelous rather than the old one. Given that, there is not the least residual mystery about the fact that admittedly, and necessarily, unsuccessful attempts to write "hard" science fiction have been so spectacularly outperformed in the literary marketplace by stubbornly Romantic varieties of anti-science or mock-science fiction, and by proudly Romantic varieties of quasi-Medieval fantasy.

If Bodin's calculatedly farcical representations are to be taken seriously—and they are surely entitled to that courtesy—then this is not merely a problem for *littérateurs* ambitious to write novels of the future, but also for the path of future progress. It is a problem because it really does place writers, including futuristic writers, firmly in the dark subterranean camp of the Poetic Association, essentially antipathetic to progress and, emotionally at least, openly or surreptitiously committed to the cause of Aëtos the Antichrist. It is a problem because it implies that progress itself has been, and perhaps always will be, corrupted and prostituted by exactly the same appetites and indulgences that corrupted and prostituted the Romantic literature of the early 19th century. It is a problem because it implies that that technological progress, instead of being the collaborator and supporter of moral progress, has been, and perhaps always will be, perverted to the ends of an obsolete form of poetic desire: desires and appetites to which it is intrinsically antipathetic, and which it cannot, therefore, ever fulfill.

Bodin's novel of the future, despite its own explicit prospectus, not only failed to find a new poetry to complement its new sense of the marvelous, but did not even know where to start searching; *our* poets of the future, unlike the fictitious ones mentioned *en passant* by Philirène, have not only done little or no better but seem blithely unaware of the existence of the problem (almost as if they could not bear to admit that contradiction to themselves). We ought, therefore, at least to consider the possibility that Bodin's image of the future, by virtue of being so determinedly novelistic, really did capture something that no utopian fiction ever has: an awareness that the long-standing harmonious relationship between civilization and literature really did break down in the 18th century, turning to intrinsic antipathy—a situation to which we have become so accustomed that it no longer seems as strange and noteworthy to us as it did to him. If nothing else, that might help to explain why so many of the world's actual late 20th century inhabitants lived in utopia but purported to hate every minute of it, eventually determining that the only way out was to precipitate an apocalyptic ecocatastrophe Apocalypse in the 21st century.

Perhaps, however, such a judgment is overly pessimistic. Had he lived and his audience been wise enough demanded it, Bodin really might have solved the problem that he had unwittingly exposed, or at least might have brought it into clearer focus. Perhaps Kalicratos, or his equivalent, might not only have found a way to heal poor Eudoxie's inner conflict, and to contrive a plausible climactic allegorical alliance between her and a victorious Philirène, but might have found a way to do the same favor for the entire world, by means of some kind of narrative Providence that would seem far more convincing than any hollow *deus ex machina* redolent with the poetry of the past. Perhaps, in consequence, Madame Charlotte, healed by that marvelous and newly poetic means, might have found a plausible program of education that would have enable young Jules to make his mother immensely proud, if not by discovering the ever-elusive Fourier method of turning the salt water of the oceans into lemonade, then by discovering a host of other things just as functionally useful, just as properly poetic and just as rationally marvelous.

And perhaps, even if Félix Bodin could never have achieved those literary *coups* had he lived to be 100, any more than any 20th century writer of novels of the future actually contrived to do, someone else still might. We can, at least, be sure that Bodin would have wanted that to be the ultimate outcome of his pioneering endeavor— and so should we.

WITHDRAWN
FROM STOCK
QMUL LIBRARY

9 781934 543443